P9-DYY-633

THE BLACK COATS

Colleen Oakes

HARPERTEEN
An Imprint of HarperCollinsPublishers

HarperTeen is an imprint of HarperCollins Publishers.

The Black Coats
Copyright © 2019 by Colleen Oakes
All rights reserved. Printed in the United States of America.
No part of this book may be used or reproduced in any manner whatsoever
without written permission except in the case of brief quotations embodied
in critical articles and reviews. For information address HarperCollins
Children's Books, a division of HarperCollins Publishers, 195 Broadway,
New York, NY 10007.
www.epicreads.com

Library of Congress Control Number: 2018952014
ISBN 978-0-06-267962-8 (trade bdg.)

Typography by Jenna Stempel-Lobell
18 19 20 21 22 PC/LSCH 10 9 8 7 6 5 4 3 2 1
❖
First Edition

For Katie,
who rises

Revenge, at first though sweet,
Bitter ere long back on itself recoils.
—John Milton, *Paradise Lost*

THE
BLACK
COATS

PROLOGUE

Grapeland, Texas. 1972.

Robin Peterson always knew when there were football games. Her parents' brick house stood across from the school, where only a field of wildflowers separated her front yard from the lights and the noise of Grapeland High. On Friday nights, she could hear the chants of the cheerleaders from her bedroom window.

"Are you ready?"

No.

"I said, are you ready?"

Still no.

Robin would play her music loudly to drown out the noise, but that accompanying sound track of Texas life always filtered through—the stomps of the crowd vibrating down from the stands, the smell of burnt hot dogs wrinkling her nose. She stared defensively back toward the school as the melodic strains of "Man in Black" by Johnny Cash spun on the record player.

1

As soon as she graduated, Robin would be gone. She would leave the jocks and the cheerleaders in a swirl of dust as she wove her way across the country, song by song, until she reached the West Coast.

Tonight, though, she didn't mind all the noise that carried across the field because Robin was going to meet a boy after the game. His name was Trevor Hitch, and he happened to be the cutest boy she'd ever seen. His confident green eyes had sucked her in like a black hole when he asked to borrow her geometry notes yesterday. She had stammered, "Yes, yes, of course," and he had arranged for them to meet after the game, in the field behind the stadium. That same dry patch of land that eventually ended up in her front yard.

He had no idea where she lived, had no idea she could just walk out of her house and be there. *Maybe*, Robin dared to hope, *that could change.* Trevor was the kind of boy who was a mystery to her: popular, lighthearted—a boy who could slyly wink and get away with it. Perhaps they would become friends. *Perhaps he will be my first kiss.*

The roar of the crowd peaked and finally receded. The team had lost again. The bright, blazing stadium lights went out a few minutes later, plunging the lot into darkness. Robin took a deep breath and shrugged on her father's black wool peacoat—completely unfashionable, but hip in a rock-and-roll way—and after debating it for a few seconds, decided to run a brush through her hair and put on a spot of Pure Magic Lip Gloss. *Just a little bit.* She mouthed words to herself in the mirror.

"Oh, hey, Trevor! Here are the notes. Deep Purple? Hell yes, I love them."

She paused a second before lifting the needle from her record player, letting Cash's pure sound wash over her, feeling each lyric cut deeper than the next.

Robin glanced at the clock and left her bedroom, tucking her notes inside the coat pocket. Her parents were watching Johnny Carson as she walked past them to the front door. Her dad, his owl-frame glasses reflecting the light, reached for her hand. "Where are you off to, kid?"

She gave his hand a squeeze. "Just meeting some friends after the game."

Her dad nodded and turned back to the screen, slapping his leg happily at something Johnny was doing. Her mother chuckled along.

Robin shut the door behind her and looked out across the field to the stadium. The last handful of students were loudly making their way toward the parking lot, no doubt on their way to a barn party.

It was almost a half hour later when she finally saw Trevor's silhouette making its way across the wild grass. As he approached her, she could see that he was freshly showered and could smell a hint of Ivory soap. *Maybe he wanted to look nice for me.* Robin's heart quietly thudded with hope as she approached him.

"Hey! I have the notes." Just being near him made her dizzy.

"Great." He regarded her coolly.

She cleared her throat. "Mr. Henson is tough. I remember that from last year."

"Yeah. He is." He glanced around them. "Did you bring anyone else with you?"

Robin tilted her head. "No, don't worry. It's not a big deal; it's just notes—"

His fist came so fast that at first she didn't even know what had hit her, but then it came down again on her face and nose. *Trevor?* Robin tried to cry out as she tasted blood in her mouth. She was on the ground then, and Trevor was on top of her, pinning her hands down, his breaths heavy. It started happening before she even understood what was happening.

Robin knew she should be trying to fight him off, but the shock was too strong, the shame cutting too deep. She couldn't get her body to move. Over her own screams, she heard disjointed Cash lyrics playing in her head.

An inhuman cry escaped from her throat as she looked across the field, seeing the flickering of the television through the windows of her house. Her parents were right there, so close and yet . . . Robin closed her eyes as Trevor brought his fist down against her temple, this one sending her spinning mercifully into darkness. The field tilted as her head bounced against the dirt, her thoughts folding one on top of the other.

My first time wasn't supposed to be this way.

She wasn't sure how long she was there or when he left, but Robin woke up in the same spot, goldenrods pressed against her face, their sickly sweet stems sticking to her bloody lips. She couldn't open her right eye, and her left wrist was swelling. Stumbling and sobbing, Robin wrapped her father's coat around her and instead of walking to her house, limped toward her best friend Julie's house, a yellow Victorian two blocks down. Only one thought repeated itself in her jumbled mind as she made her way there, step by unsteady step: *I can't tell my father. Not now, not ever. He will never look at me the same again.*

Later, Robin wouldn't remember walking there, or pushing the door open to find Julie Westing sprawled out on the couch, reading. Her friend would take her upstairs and hold her up in the shower. She would wash the blood out of her hair and ice her wounds, her hands shaking with rage. She would call Robin's parents to say that she fell down the stairs and that she was going to stay with her for a few days. Her best friend would hold Robin through that long, dark night, reassuring her that she was safe now and that they would have their revenge.

And three weeks later, Julie would stand by as Robin pulled on her father's black coat and, with shaking hands, picked up a baseball bat.

ONE

Austin, Texas. Present day.

Thea Soloman was up to her elbows in clay when someone secretly placed the envelope next to her bag. It was a busy pottery workshop, with almost wall-to-wall bodies in the small art room at Roosevelt High. Thea was at her favorite pottery wheel, the one in the corner, away from everyone. As the clay wove its way up through her long brown fingers—so cold and slimy and lovely—Thea had the distinct feeling that this wheel was made for her. It didn't ask anything of her. It didn't want her to talk about *Natalie*; it didn't want her to smile. Thea just wanted to pick her glazes in peace (today a cheery yellow semigloss, for the sunshine she couldn't muster), and then feel the simmering kiln kiss her skin with its hungry heat. A tight curl of brown hair fell over her eyes, and Thea blew it upward. She felt safe here in the back corner, and so she was a bit unnerved when, upon returning from washing her hands, there was a black envelope lying next to her bag.

"What?" Thea picked up the card, looking to see if anyone was watching her. No one was; the teacher was laughing loudly at something human-Barbie-doll Mirabelle Watts had said, and a bunch of boys were giggling in the corner as one carved a penis out of clay. Thea sat down on her stool, turning the envelope over in her hand. The front of it was bare, and on the back there were two letters, visible only when she turned it in the light, a hard script of black gloss on the black envelope: *BC*.

Thea frowned. Was this a prom invitation? The last thing she wanted was to go to prom. Also, no one wanted to take her, so that worked out great for everybody. She slipped her fingers under the flap and winced when the paper sliced cleanly into her fingertip. She brought her finger to her lips and sucked away the small dot of blood. She pushed open the envelope, the inside flap revealing a gorgeous yellow-gold backdrop covered with a myriad of black images in an Edwardian pattern: black-winged butterflies, a gold scale, splatters of ink that bled into thorny roses and sharp daggers. In the middle was a silhouette of a woman, her chin raised high. It was so beautiful that Thea ran her fingers over the pattern, feeling the soft texture of the black over the gold paper. She pulled on the card inside. Black cardstock slid out, bound with a black lace that covered up embossed gold lettering.

Thea again looked around to see if anyone was watching and then carefully unwrapped the black lace binding. Her breath caught in her throat as she read.

Angel of the Waters.
Ten minutes.
Don't be late, and don't share
this note with anyone.

Thea's head jerked back. *What is this? Is someone trying to trap me?* That couldn't be right—her high school was far too boring for something like that, and yet . . . worse things happened. Worse things *had* happened. But unlike her life for the last six months, this was something interesting, something mysterious. *Angel of the Waters.* Thea thought for a moment. The Bucket. Of course. She paused, her mind cartwheeling. What did she have to lose? Her clay vase was now puttering in a sad circle, neglected and deformed. Thea leaped to her feet and threw her book bag over her shoulder while grabbing the envelope with her other hand. Mrs. Brown followed her out into the hallway. "Thea? Are you all right, dear?"

Thea turned away from her and hid her face, playing the only card she had. "Sorry. I just need to see the counselor."

Mrs. Brown nodded. "Of course, dear. Go right ahead."

Once Mrs. Brown returned to her classroom, Thea took off, sprinting down the gray hallway that ran underneath her enormous high school. *Poor Mrs. Brown.* Poor friends, poor parents, always waiting for Thea to crack, always concerned. Maybe she finally had. Thea ran up the cement stairs, pulling her other arm through the strap of her backpack, taking the stairs two at a time. *Ten minutes. How long did I sit there, admiring the envelope like a total idiot, while this invisible clock ticked? Five minutes?* She ran past classrooms in a blur, her curly hair tangling in her backpack as she flew by the offices. She picked up speed as she neared the doors of the school, bursting past the metal detectors and out into blustering Texas wind, warm even in February.

The Angel of the Waters statue sat in front of their school. About twenty feet around and about ten feet deep, it had once been beautiful, or so she had heard. Now a bronze cherub with her hands outstretched towered over a circular fountain filled with green water. Across her draped robes, someone had spray-painted "Fuck this school," and her eyes had two black X's across them. The fountain itself had stopped working long ago, and now it simply churned filthy green water back and forth. There was a reason the students of Roosevelt High School had christened it "the Bucket." Thea examined the fountain, unnerved by the angel's blinded eyes. Thea walked slowly around the fountain, inspecting every possible surface for . . . anything. A note? A phone? There was a lone boy sitting beside the fountain, watching Thea with piqued interest.

Thea could find nothing. "Crap. Crap." She ran around the fountain once more, checking underneath the cement lip. Still nothing. Saying a silent prayer, she heaved herself onto the fountain, peering up at the angel, who watched her with black, dead eyes. When she looked *into* the fountain, she felt her heart drop into her stomach.

There it was, underneath the water: a black envelope, resting at the deepest point of the fountain under a heavy rock. A Red Bull can floated past it on the surface. With a grimace, Thea flung off her backpack and kicked her shoes to the ground. She took a deep breath as she remembered diving into their neighborhood pool as a kid, the shriek of Natalie's voice echoing in Thea's ears: *Don't forget to hold your breath, silly!* This was very silly indeed. Was she crazy? Maybe. *But being crazy is better than being numb.*

Thea stepped off the lip and sank deep into the fountain, gasping at the sudden cold. She let herself sink downward until her feet hit the bottom. Moving quickly, she grabbed the rock and shoved it roughly aside; the envelope then floated up from below. Thea caught it and pushed off the bottom of the fountain, her head breaking the surface with a gasp of air. The boy she had seen earlier was now standing in front of her, looking concerned. He had taken off his jacket, revealing the soccer jersey underneath, and had jumped up onto the ledge. He reached for her hand, but Thea was already climbing out on her own.

"Hey! Are you okay?" he asked.

Thea allowed herself to be momentarily touched by his kindness. It had been a long time since anyone had cared. "Yes, yes. I'm sorry. I dropped my, um, class schedule." She tucked the black envelope under her arm as the boy made a face.

"Uh, maybe just get another one from the office next

time? That water is nasty." He gave a shiver. "I'm serious. Take, like, ten showers when you get home, okay? I'm pretty sure that could give you hepatitis."

Thea nodded with a vague smile, water dripping everywhere.

His face fell momentarily, eyes widening under two strong brows.

"You weren't, like . . . trying to end your life or something, were you?"

Six months ago, I may have considered it, her voice answered silently in her head. She forced a fake smile. "No. And if I was going to drown, it would not be in the Bucket."

She pushed her soaked hair out of her face as she jumped down from the ledge. His eyes met hers, and she was surprised at how green they were, almost an olive color. She had seen him around, but they didn't have any classes together. She would have remembered that smile.

"Hey. I'm Drew Porter." He reached out his hand, but Thea shook her head.

"Trust me, you don't want to do that. I saw a condom down there."

"Yeah. I believe that." He withdrew his hand. She loved the way her heart was pounding in her chest, that feeling of being alive. *Is this what it feels like again? Normal life?* With a sudden twinge of realization, Thea reached back for her phone . . . tucked in her pocket. It was dead.

Drew's eyes lit up at her drowned phone. "Oh man!" he laughed. "I'm sorry, that just sucks."

"Damn." Thea frowned, but she knew she didn't have time to worry about her phone now. And as much as she wouldn't mind talking to this boy—the first in a long time—she badly needed to read what was inside the envelope. "Thanks for, you know, for almost not saving my life."

Drew watched her with interest as she grabbed her backpack. "Anytime. And your name?"

She was jogging away from him now, wanting to put as much space as possible between them before she opened the envelope. "Thea!" she called without looking back. "Thea Soloman."

Drew chuckled. "Well, I guess it's nice to meet you."

Thea ducked behind the gymnasium and crouched over the envelope. The paper was soggy, but she could still read the writing:

418 Black Lotus Drive
One hour until your destiny expires.

Thea stared at the message before taking off at a jog toward the parking lot. Soaking wet, she flung open the door to her rusty maroon Honda Civic and was in the car in a matter of seconds. Hands fluttering, she felt above her visor for the old Austin map her father made her keep in the car. If he could see her now . . . Thea shook her head. God, she would never hear the end of it.

After two minutes of turning the map and staring longingly at her very dead phone, Thea floored the accelerator and shot out of the parking lot, leaving a cyclone of dirt behind her. She gunned down the road, heading west, out from the city and into the wealthier suburbs. Thea opened all the windows in a pathetic attempt to dry her hair and shirt, which were freezing against her small chest. She raised her eyebrows at herself in the mirror. She looked like a drowned rat—her normally full, natural hair was plastered across her forehead. Her hazel eyes had black rings underneath them from her running mascara. Thea's light brown skin lacked the glow that it once had. Her mother's sharp nose sat firm above her large rose lips, lips that Natalie had always coveted. In the mirror, the sky behind her was growing gray.

Natalie. Thea willed her eyes back onto the road after they lingered on the glove compartment for a moment too long, where she knew a bottle of Xanax sat. "You don't need them," she said aloud to herself, a conversation she had at least daily. "You don't need them. Follow the envelope." She almost laughed out loud, thinking of what Natalie would have to say about this whole thing, about Thea following a random envelope to God knows where.

Where the hell am I? The map had taken Thea onto a long, wooded stretch of road. Bur oaks and cedar elms hovered over the area, their crooked arms stretched protectively through the space. Shadows passed over Thea's face as she slowed the car. The houses there were hidden from view by private driveways—their true size tucked away, a privilege of the very wealthy. She kept going, seeing no sign of Black Locust Drive, and pulled the car over when she came to a dead end. Thea got out of the car. The road had ended at a large cypress tree, absolutely massive, its thick trunk swallowing what remained of the road. Thea unfolded the map again, trailing her finger over the twisting path that had led her there. On the map, there it was, Black Locust Drive, and yet she was standing here and there was no house, no road.

The wind picked up and the tree gave a shudder. Its ancient arms—some wider than her body—creaked in the breeze. The roots carved out a hole in the earth around the tree and created a yawning void about five feet deep. An unfriendly finger of dread was creeping its way up her spine, and Thea had the distinct feeling of being watched. She spun around, shoving the envelope and the map into her back pocket, her jeans soaked and stiff. In the tree, a black shape fluttered and caught her eye; Thea squinted to get a better look. A magpie was nestled high in the tree, its sharp beak eating some dead thing.

Thea's heart leaped. Just over a few branches from the bird, a black envelope hung from a piece of burlap twine, curling in the wind.

TWO

Dwarfed by the massive tree, Thea put her hands on her hips, knowing that she looked just like her father at the moment.

"Well, shit."

She looked into the muddy crevasse, shuddering as a water moccasin slithered across the shallow water. *This is crazy.* Except, there was no turning back now. There was an answer in that envelope, or maybe in the next one, and besides, she hadn't been this awake in months. She had forgotten what it felt like to be excited; her heart was pounding, and the gray fog in her brain was lifting. It felt good. It felt scary.

It felt different from grief.

With a wry smile, Thea remembered that she was kind of awesome at this. Last year she had been the Roosevelt High track record holder in both the 200- and 400-meter dash. That was *before*, of course. Thea backed up about ten feet. She paused, remembering how it felt to soar over hurdles, the momentum pitching her forward. Then Thea broke into a mad run, flying toward the tree.

When her feet hit the lip of the ditch, she hurled herself into the air. Her momentum carried her over the ditch and up to the trunk of the tree. With a sigh of relief, Thea paused for a breath, brushing off her hands on her damp jeans. *Okay,* she thought. *I got to the tree, now how the hell to get up the tree?* Jumping was useless, seeing as how the branches were at least eight feet above her.

And then it began to rain, as bouffant gray clouds churned into themselves. Thea felt a sprinkle of water brush her cheeks. "Are you serious?" she shouted at the sky. *Why does so much of this adventure have to be wet?* Thunder crackled above, and the wind circled angrily around her. She watched as the tree swayed, its vines blown loose from their safe havens. Thea blinked. *The vines.*

She ran around the trunk, not wanting to lose the momentum of the wind. The branches at the back had the most vines, thick, loopy ropes that choked the huge trunk. She leaped three times before her hand closed around one.

Rain poured down on her face as she looked up.

"You can do this." Her voice wasn't as confident as she would have hoped. She planted one foot on the tree and, step by slippery step, began making her way up. The rain was almost blinding at this point, but she kept moving until the lowest branch was close enough to reach. Thea cautiously reached one arm around the slick wood before pulling her legs up. The envelope was maybe only ten feet above her now. Moving as quickly as she dared, she made her way from branch to branch, her hands clutching so hard that they hurt.

She reached for a branch, almost there . . . and then the branch she was standing on broke beneath her feet. Thea lost her footing and caught herself on the branch below her with a loud crack. She gasped as the wind was knocked out of her lungs, and she struggled to hang on. Finally, she inhaled, gulping greedily as she caught her breath—and her balance. The envelope was just above her now. Thea moved up another branch and snatched it with her fingertips. She yanked open the envelope, this time not pausing to admire the rich paper.

Take the slide, then quickly
make your way to the black gate.
Mademoiselle Corday waits for you.

Thea steadied herself on the branch beneath her feet, looking at the landscape below. Maybe a quarter of a mile from where the road ended, she could see a thick swath of trees swaying in the violent wind. Her breath caught in her chest. Beside the trees, a black iron weathervane shaped like a butterfly spun in the breeze.

"Oh my God," Thea muttered. This was real. There was a house in those trees.

And she needed to get inside.

She reached down for the branch below her and stopped with a jerk. *Slide.* Impossible to see when looking up at the tree, but now perfectly laid out when viewed from above, the trunk of the tree gradually declined into a smooth ramp that would spit her out at the edge of the ditch. This was madness. She should be just getting out of history class right now, hating her existence. Instead, she was going to slide. Thea let go of the branch. After a second of free-falling, she felt the trunk slam hard against her back. The rain sped her descent, and in a few exhilarating seconds the tree dumped her out onto the wet ground.

She began laughing at the absurdity of it all: the envelope, the fountain, this freaking tree. She laughed until her stomach ached, probably going mad but loving every minute of it. She hadn't laughed like that in so long. "Thank you," she whispered. She sprinted fearlessly toward the thicket of trees, deafening cracks of thunder shaking her teeth as she raced toward whatever mystery called her forward.

Once she passed the trees, the iron gate gradually rose above her as she neared it. The swirls of pointed metal, topped by a black butterfly, stood firm against the wind. Thea was surprised when the gate swung open at her touch. She took a deep breath as she made her way through the gate and underneath a portico dotted with yellow rosebuds.

Eventually, Thea stepped out into a clearing, her feet landing on smooth gravel.

"Whoa," she murmured. She was in front of one of the largest houses she had ever seen. A formidable fortress that loomed over the fields and trees, the enormous black house towered above her—vicious, beautiful. Slanted gables dotted with gold rose above her head, each one hosting ornamental gargoyles that leered menacingly down at her. The house and its land seemed to sprawl out in all directions and looked like it was constantly being built upon; a sort of madness in its very design. From where Thea stood, she counted at least four floors above her. Just behind it, she saw a hint of a gold-tipped dome.

She pushed her wet hair out of her eyes and slowly walked toward the gigantic door. A bronze plaque greeted her: *Welcome to Mademoiselle Corday.*

Beneath the words was the same symbol that adorned the weathervane and the envelopes: a black butterfly.

Thea blew out a long breath. She closed her eyes. This was the last moment she could walk away. This was either going to be life-changing or life-ending. She looked up at the sky, the storm churning the clouds into a foamy green gray. Somewhere deep inside she knew that her decision had already been made for her, had been made the minute the envelope slid across her bag in pottery class. Had been made that day, on the track.

Thea, something happened to Natalie.

That was the moment when nothing would ever be the same again. That moment had made the choice for her. Now there was only moving forward. The past was without a heartbeat.

Thea reached out to lift the knocker and paused, remembering the note: *Mademoiselle Corday is waiting.* Instead of knocking, she pushed against the wooden door and watched it swing open. The woods behind her filled with the sound of rain as she stepped inside. The door slammed, the loud bang echoing through the silent house. It was pleasantly warm, but Thea shivered nonetheless, overcome by the feeling—no, the certainty—that she was being watched.

The grand foyer was empty save for an antique table that held a black envelope and a pile of clothing. Thea stepped forward, leaving puddles on the floor with each step, and unfolded the note.

Change into these clothes.
Take the stairs to the right and
get through the black door.
Turn back or forever be changed.

On the table were a folded pair of leggings, a simple long-sleeved shirt, and a pair of ballet slippers. All were black.

"Please, God, don't let me be on the internet right

now," Thea mumbled as she stripped off her soaked flannel and peeled the dirt-soaked, waterlogged jeans from her legs. Thea pulled on the leggings and slipped her feet into the black ballet slippers before folding up her dirty clothes and placing them in a plastic bag on the floor. Her soaked, heavy hair was becoming a burden, so she twisted it up into a high bun. Behind the table a long staircase gracefully climbed upward, dividing halfway and turning into separate spiraling staircases. Thea went right, taking two stairs at a time. She circled above the main floor once, again, and then once more before they led to an open door. This time, she didn't hesitate. She walked through, ready for whatever complex obstacle lay on the other side.

Except that there was a boy on the other side.

Thea leaped back with a yelp as her heart pounded with fear. Had he brought her here? He stared down at her, unnerving in his intensity.

He stood about six feet tall, lean but muscular, maybe only a year or two older than she was. He wore loose white linen pants that dusted the tops of his veined, hard feet. His black hair was cropped close in a military fashion and stood in direct contrast to obscenely wild dark eyes. His skin was light brown, and he looked to be of Indian descent.

A nameless alarm began rising in her, a pulse that beat up through her ears. The boy stared at her, not speaking. Finally, Thea raised her voice. "Hello?"

The boy gestured to the door behind him. "Get through the door," he said simply. Then he stepped back.

Thea nodded. "Right. Get through the door." Taking a far step to the side, Thea moved toward the door, hoping that he was simply a kind of doorman, an ornamental finish to whatever this elaborate show was. He did not move from his position in front of the door, and the space between them didn't allow Thea to squeeze through.

"I'm sorry, I may need you to move." The boy stared forward, hands folded in front of his waist, body rigid and as still as a stone in a stream. He said nothing as Thea stepped cautiously in front of him. "Yeah, so . . . I'm just going to scoot through here. . . ." She tried to duck under his arm politely, but her shoulder bumped up against the cave of his ribs.

Suddenly and without warning, he threw her across the room. She felt her feet leave the ground as she slammed into the wall behind her like a rag doll. The pain was white-hot, throbbing. Thea clenched her teeth to keep from crying out as she clutched her arm protectively against her ribs. The man stepped back in front of the door without a word, his arms crossed calmly in front of him.

Thea lifted her head, staring at him with barely concealed rage. "What is wrong with you?" she spat. He didn't answer. She slowly climbed to her feet. "Let me through the door. Please!"

The boy, who seemed more and more like a phantom with each passing moment, stood quietly. *Get through the door. So it's going to be* this *way. Okay.* Thea sprinted toward him and slammed her shoulders against his stomach, hoping to push him back through the door with her. Instead, using her own momentum, he picked her up and spun around, roughly throwing her down on the mahogany floor. Thea looked up as he stepped back once again. He wasn't advancing on her, not willingly hurting her—he was just protecting the entrance. And she had to get through that damned door.

Thea was exhausted. Her limbs trembled as she stood, hatred raging through her at his strength, his calm demeanor, the way her attacks seemed to have no effect on him at all. It wasn't fair that she couldn't even push him back, that all her strength wasn't enough. In the end, she wasn't strong enough to beat him. *Just as Natalie hadn't been strong enough.*

Thea opened her eyes, rage swimming in front of them. *Natalie.* She let the sound of her cousin's name ring through her head like the beat of a persistent drum, one that pushed out of her wounded heart. *One more time,* Thea told herself. *I have in myself one more try.* She closed her eyes. *You're not strong, but you are fast,* she told herself. *Now go!*

Thea sprinted toward the boy. He put his hands out in front of him in a defensive crouch, but at the last moment, she faked to the right. He lunged to match her movement, but he wasn't expecting her to then throw herself violently left, back toward his body. They collided in a violent tangle. Using her momentum, she flung herself toward the ornate doorknob, shaped like a beehive. Her fingers closed around it just as his arms wrapped around her waist. The door pushed open, and Thea let go of the knob and fell to the floor in front of it. She flinched and waited to be dragged backward, but nothing came. The arms around her waist loosened. Thea rolled over, the door open in front of her head. The boy in white linen got up, dusted off his pants, and stalked out the door she had come in from.

Thea slowly, painfully, climbed to her feet. Her back ached, her mouth was still numb and salty, and her breaths were so sharp they cut into her ribs. Still, she limped through the door, hoping that whatever was on the other side was worth leaving a part of herself behind.

THREE

Upon stepping inside, Thea found herself in a circular room with a gold-domed ceiling. Strung across the circular walls were thick pieces of black ribbon. Attached to each ribbon, hundreds of black-and-white pictures were held by a single clothespin. Thea walked forward, her eyes tracing over the faces before her: women from their early teens well into later age. She limped forward another step, wiping her bloody mouth on the back of her hand.

In the center of the room stood an easel next to a single brown leather wingback chair. A black-and-white photograph was clipped to the top of the easel, and even before she reached it, Thea knew that face: She recognized the long black hair that had always made her jealous, the curls that bordered on the edge of messy. The freckles dashed across her brown skin, the radiant grin. Thea reached out and touched the picture of Natalie's face, her personality perfectly captured in this moment. "I miss you," she mouthed. She reached out and unclipped the picture, pressing it against her heart. Whatever this was, whoever had brought her here—this picture belonged to Thea, not to them.

From somewhere in the room came a voice. "We can give you what you want."

Thea spun around, annoyance flitting across her face. They were playing with her grief, and she was done with it. "What is this? Enough with the games!"

The voice trilled with laughter. "This is not a game, Thea. This was an initiation." At the distinctive click of high heels, Thea turned slowly. A stunning woman in her early thirties stood before her. Her hair was dark brown laced with shades of auburn and pulled back from her face in a tight bun. Her face was hard, with steeled brown eyes and jutting cheekbones, her lips painted a scandalous red. She wore a black dress under a tailored black coat. She stepped closer to Thea, who instinctively took a step backward and clutched Natalie's photograph to her breast.

"Hello, Thea. I'm Nixon." She paused, letting her fingers trace Thea's shoulder. "I know you're curious why you're here. Your cousin Natalie Fisher was murdered, is that correct?"

Thea nodded, unable to speak, as the word *murdered* ripped her apart.

"And there wasn't enough evidence to arrest her murderer, is that also correct?"

"Yes." It was too much, thinking about the thing that she never allowed to cross her mind.

"What if I told you that there was a way to get justice for Natalie? A way to make him pay for his unspeakable crime?"

Thea raised an eyebrow. "Are you talking about the police?"

"I'm talking about justice. Sometimes the two aren't the same," Nixon answered.

Thea met her gaze. "I'm listening."

"You are currently standing in the atrium inside Mademoiselle Corday, a very old Victorian house that happens to be owned by a quiet organization. Do you know anything about Mademoiselle Corday?"

Thea shook her head.

"Not in your history classes? Nothing?" The woman let out an irritated sigh. "Roosevelt High School, churning out tomorrow's leaders today. Anyway, history knows her as Charlotte Corday. She murdered Jean-Paul Marat, who was part of a bloody arm of the French Revolution. She stabbed him to death in his bathroom, and in 1793 she was executed by guillotine. It earned her the nickname *l'ange de l'assassinat*, which means the Angel of Assassination."

Thea stepped backward. "You're assassins."

Nixon smiled condescendingly, as if that was the most ridiculous thing she had ever heard. "Assassins—oh God, no. You won't be killing anyone anytime soon. What we do is administer justice, true justice, through our organization: the Black Coats."

The Black Coats. Thea blinked, remembering the *BC* on the envelope that had made its way to her in pottery class. "The Black Coats. You're a—"

"We're in the business of righting the wrongs done to women." Nixon began circling her like a wolf. "Thea, aren't you tired of being afraid in your everyday life, of not walking home alone after dark, of locking your doors, of making sure that your shorts aren't too short lest you attract some unwanted attention? The Black Coats believe we are called to tip the scales, to restore justice. It is one small step toward restoring the world to a kinder, gentler place for our sisters. A place that doesn't take the murder of a cousin lying down."

Thea wiped a stray tear on her sleeve as Nixon continued, the hard rap of her heels echoing through the room. "There are many good men in this world, and for them we are grateful. But that doesn't mean that we, as women, are meant to quietly accept the unending stream of violence against us. We are called to rise against it, and the Black Coats of Austin will answer the call, to give justice where justice has been denied. You have been invited to be part of that organization."

Thea narrowed her eyes. "Why would you want me? I have no special skills that may be of use to you. I'm not . . . you know . . ." She paused, searching for the right word. "A ninja."

Nixon laughed, an unnatural bark. "Neither are we. Some of us are very skilled in martial arts, myself included. But it's not a requirement. As a Black Coat, you will learn about martial arts, among many other things, but this isn't MI6. This is an organization of women who have lives outside the organization as well. The Black Coats term is limited, so women may move on with their lives afterward, finish college, and fulfill their professional dreams." She smiled. "Many of our alumni, inspired by their time here, grow up to be judges, prosecutors, detectives, and law enforcers. It is the ultimate justice to succeed in the real world and fight violence from within the system."

She rested her hands on Thea's shoulders, turning her gently to look at the photographs. "See these faces? For most of the women whose faces you see in this room, justice never came. That is, until we delivered it." She spun her back around, and Thea found herself staring into Nixon's intense brown eyes. "Thea, you were picked for the Black Coats because you have something to offer us. You are fast, you are intelligent, but, most important"—she nodded to the picture Thea was holding—"you have reason."

Thea bit her cheek. "So all of it, the fountain, the tree, the boy . . ."

Nixon tapped her fingers together. "They were all a test. The fountain served two purposes: to see if you were willing to be reckless, and to make sure you weren't wearing a wire. The tree was to test your problem-solving skills and your willingness to do something dangerous. And the boy, Sahil, well, that purpose should be obvious. We needed to see if you would be willing to hurt a man to get the outcome you desired. And you were."

A brief wave of shame passed through Thea.

Nixon clicked away from Thea and sat down in the chair, crossing her legs elegantly. "I've saved the best part for last. After you join the Black Coats and serve the appropriate amount of time, you will be entitled to your inheritance."

Thea looked down at Nixon, by far the most terrifying person she had ever met. "My *inheritance?*"

Nixon nodded to the picture in Thea's hands. "Justice. For Natalie. The man who took Natalie's life will feel the full wrath of the Black Coats, if you so desire. He will pay the price for what he did to your cousin. That's your inheritance, our generous repayment for the use of your services. What was his name—the man accused of murdering your cousin? Cabby?"

Rage poured into Thea's brain, the need for justice making a potent cocktail. *Justice for Natalie. My God.* "Yes," she whispered. "Yes. I'm in."

Nixon nodded. "That's what we figured you would say. However, we don't want anyone making rash decisions. We will send you home with the contract, and if you find that you still want to join the Black Coats, you will come back here tomorrow after school to begin your training and to meet your team. If you don't show, your potential contract will be burned and you will not get a second offer to join."

Thea clenched her fingers. "I understand."

Nixon handed Thea a black manila envelope. "Inside is your contract. Make sure to read it carefully. Show it to no one. Which brings me to my least favorite part of the initiation ceremony." Nixon sighed. "If you tell anyone about the Black Coats—your parents, your friends, your local police officer—we will release the numerous videotapes we have of you entering our residence without being invited, also known as breaking and entering, and attacking a young man who lives here without provocation. We will have no choice but to submit that to the police, along with the proof of your fingerprints everywhere, and the fact that you are dressed like a burglar."

"But . . . I was invited here! I was following directions," Thea gasped.

Nixon gave her a sympathetic smile. "They won't believe you. We have many lovely women on the police force here in Austin who are Black Coats alumni, so I'm sure they'll help us out as well."

Thea frowned. "I won't tell anyone." *I don't even have friends,* she thought.

Nixon shrugged. "It's necessary to protect ourselves. It's nothing personal."

There was a loud slam from behind them, followed by a frustrated shout. Nixon brushed back a single strand of hair from her face, tucking it neatly behind her ear. "That will be our next recruit trying to get through the door. Frankly, I'm not sure she's going to make it; Sahil is pretty strong, and the last recruit caught him off guard." She winked at Thea and smiled, showing off her perfect white teeth lined up in a neat row.

Nixon walked over to what appeared to be a solid wall and then, with a push of her hand, swung open a hidden door. "If you go out through here and take a right at the split, this will also take you to the main foyer. You'll pass a table with some light refreshments: some biscuits, pimiento cheese crackers, and sweet tea. Please help yourself if you are hungry. Your clothes will be in a bag near the door." Then she politely waved her hand. "You're dismissed."

Thea walked away from her, clutching the envelope in her hand so tightly she could feel her fingers going numb. The doorway led into a long, winding hallway of cherry-wood panels and cozy hanging lights. She passed several shut doors, each one marked with a number and a plaque with a strange symbol: a bird, a banner, a crown. One sat cracked open at the end of the hall, a small sliver of light spilling out onto the floor. From inside Thea could hear the cadence of older female voices.

"The water grows shallower each year. I'm just not sure it's a safe place anymore. They are building that gaudy new home not far from there, and it's a pebble's throw away from the Breviary—"

"Hush. Someone is coming." A loud voice, croaking with age, silenced them. "We will not speak of this until we have new information. It is not the time to worry now, not with new girls to vet."

Thea walked quickly past the door, finding her way back to the entrance. A tiny chalkboard sign hanging on a hook from the front door read, "Thank you for visiting us!" The plastic bag hanging from it was knotted with a bow of burlap twine and a small clutch of wildflowers. She pushed her way out the door and into the humid fog that was now filling the valley, swallowing the house and its secrets.

Thea drove out the way she came, carefully placing the picture of Natalie on the dashboard where her dear friend's eyes could watch her every turn. Bursting, awkward laughs tumbled from Thea's lips as she relived what had just happened to her. As she drove, she glanced periodically over to the black envelope resting on the passenger seat, touching it every few minutes to make sure that this wasn't all a dream.

FOUR

Thea was bursting with excitement as she pulled the Civic up in front of her white clapboard house. As she parked, a flash of a man climbing a ladder across the street caught her eye. She couldn't wait to open the black envelope and yet—what the hell was happening over there?

She tucked the envelope into her backpack and strolled across the yard, an uncomfortable lump making its way up her throat as she stopped cold on the lawn. They were painting *Natalie's house*. Her dad had told her last week that it had been sold and that the new owners would be moving in soon, but this . . . this was unacceptable. Natalie's house had once been a bright, happy yellow, the brightest on the block, and now two men dressed in coveralls were splashing a bright crimson red across the exterior. *Red.*

Fury rose up through Thea and she clenched her fists. *"Are you kidding me?"* she snapped, unable to control herself.

She felt a hand rest on her shoulder, and Thea leaned back against her mother. "I hate it," she stated. "Why does it have to be red?"

Her mother, a stunning black woman sometimes mistaken for a famous soap star, shook her head and sighed, her eyes betraying a new weariness. "I saw them come this morning, and I knew it was going to hurt."

They both stood in silence, watching the painters roll the lines of paint fluidly across the siding. Her mother squeezed her shoulder.

"How about we move?" whispered Thea, not the first time she had suggested it.

"We're working on it." She gave Thea a gentle pat and then turned her around. "Love, I got a call from your school today. They said that you left during fourth period and were absent for all your classes after that. What happened?"

Thea dropped her head, trying to think fast. "I, umm . . . I got upset in class and just wanted to go to my car."

Her mother's words were cautiously gentle, echoing the social-worker tone she used at work. "It's okay to excuse yourself if you need some time to process your emotions. However, after you are done, you need to go back to class." As she continued, Thea closed her eyes, listening to the same conversation her parents had with her week after week. They were trying to be supportive, but there was a wall, and she couldn't figure out how to get over it, to where her parents were, to where the rest of life was. Everything seemed numb, like she was looking at the world through a fogged-up window.

Then she remembered the black envelope in her backpack. That was something worth waking up for. A purpose, a mission, a secret. *Revenge*. Her fingers tingled.

"I'm going inside. I can't look at it anymore." Thea gave her mom a squeeze. "I promise I'll go back to class if I leave again. I just couldn't . . . not today." The lies came easily. As her mom watched the painters, Thea could see tears gathering in her eyes. She couldn't see her mom cry, not again. She had seen her parents cry more than any child ever should. "I'll be up in my room."

Her mom had a faraway look in her eyes as she stared across the street. "Sounds great."

Thea was already jogging toward the house, her backpack bouncing on her shoulders. Once inside, she whistled and Alma, their ancient Irish setter, padded over to greet her. Thea crouched down and gave her a kiss on her doggy nose. "Something exciting happened today," she whispered while she scratched behind Alma's ears and played with her floppy cheeks. "Come on!" Alma slowly followed Thea into her bedroom.

Thea plugged in the blue star lights that hung over her bed and tore into her backpack, pulling the envelope out of the bag. Taking a deep breath, she pulled out a multipage document, printed in lovely calligraphy.

On behalf of Robin Peterson and Julie Westing, luminaries and founding members of the Black Coats, we cordially invite you, Thea Soloman, to join the Black Coats of Austin.

As a part of our small team of new recruits, you will train, learn, and serve the Black Coats. If you fail to adhere to any of these core rules, an appropriate punishment will be administered swiftly, followed by an exile from the group.

A BLACK COAT'S RULES OF
ETIQUETTE AND SERVICE

A Black Coat is never to speak of the Black Coats outside of Mademoiselle Corday or at an official Black Coats function.

Assignments (called Balancings) for the Black Coats are given out by the luminaries only and are taken very seriously. Deviating from Balancings will result in immediate exile from the group.

Black Coats work only within their assigned teams. These three teams are Emperor, Swallowtail, and your team, Banner. Each team is led by a senior Black Coat (called presidents). President Nixon, whom you have already met, is the leader of your team.

Thea took a deep breath. "Team Banner, led by the

scariest woman alive. Okay." Still, she liked the way it sounded. With a grin, she tucked her legs up under her body and kept reading, heart pounding with excitement.

After you begin serving the Black Coats, you will become eligible for your inheritance, one Balancing for the person of your choosing. The luminaries decide at what point you will be given your inheritance.

At the end of your tenure, your service to the Black Coats will be terminated, and you will join our distinguished list of alumni and serve us in a professional capacity.

Mademoiselle Corday runs off the backs of new recruits like yourself. You will be expected to fulfill your duties to the house without complaint and in a timely manner.

You will proceed with your normal life during school hours and will come to us directly after school and all day on Saturdays. We will mail a form to your parents from the school detailing your new community service for the Historical Society for Restoration of Victorian Houses. This is your alibi for all Black Coat-related activities.

She flipped the page over, her hands moving slowly to avoid crinkling the delicate paper.

WELCOME TO THE BLACK COATS,
THEA SOLOMAN.
SIGNATURE:_____ DATE:_____
Soulevez-vous, femmes de la vengeance

Thea exhaled a long breath and leaned back against her bounty of throw pillows. Like an arrow, this organization had targeted her greatest desire: justice for Natalie. There was no amount of counseling that could give her this. She would be a part of something righteous.

Thea looked around her bare room. Her walls used to be lined with ribbons, newspaper articles, and handwritten letters from her track coach. It had been the thing she and Natalie had shared; track had been their life. After Natalie died, Thea had pulled down the clippings and the ribbons, and in a bout of hysteria, tried to burn them in the fireplace. Now there weren't any matches in the house, her bedroom wasn't as cozy as it once was, and Thea wasn't a part of anything, anywhere.

But now there was *this*, a chance to wake up, a chance to belong in an entirely different way, a place where she wouldn't be known as the sad girl anymore, where she could become someone new. Thea's smile grew. And then she would have her revenge, the cherry on top of this strange cake. Cabby Baptist would pay for what he did. Thea picked up a pen from her desk. Her hand trembled a little as she scrolled her name across the contract: *Thea Soloman.*

She read over the contract a few more times before folding it carefully back into the envelope and tucking it into her backpack. There was no way she was forgetting that tomorrow. She lay back against Alma's soft body, curling into her russet fur. "It's happening," she breathed. "It's real." That afternoon, when she had been numbly throwing clay, seemed a lifetime ago.

Bill Soloman's cheerful voice interrupted her thoughts. "Thea! A dad cannot live on air alone! It's your night for dinner!"

"Okay! I'm coming!" Thea shook off this new excitement and headed downstairs, the possibilities of her future overruled by the hope of finding black beans.

"Mrrmmph, that was delicious." After dinner her father leaned back in his chair, patting his belly as the overhead lights reflected off his balding white head. Even without hair, he was still handsome, at least Thea always thought so. He had snagged her mother, after all. "I liked the peppers in the quesadillas, Thea. Let's always put those in. Ladies, shall we retire to the viewing room? Tonight is the *Survivor* premiere."

Thea cleared her throat awkwardly. "One thing first—I want you both to stay for this." Both of her parents froze, clearly anticipating the worst. She spread her hands flat on the table, a strange guilt creeping up her chest. "Don't get too excited, but I've decided to join a new group at school."

Her dad's face lit up immediately, and her mother's eyes filled with tears. Thea sighed. "Oh my gosh, this is what I was talking about. Please don't freak."

"Oh, Thea!" Suddenly, her mom was wrapping her arms around her, smelling like lemon and coconut oil. "This is exciting, baby! We can't help but be happy for you." Her mother's voice was tinged with more than joy—a palpable relief was pouring forth through both of her parents. *Our daughter is participating in life. She's not suicidal. Maybe she'll be okay.*

Thea squirmed out of her mom's grasp. "Can you please, for just a minute, act like normal parents?"

Her dad straightened up as her mom returned to her seat. He said, "Yes. Absolutely."

Thea took a deep breath. "I've joined a club called the Historical Society for the Restoration of Victorian Houses."

Her dad looked ready to fly to the moon. "Victorian houses? Restoring them? Do they need any volunteers?"

Thea's heart rate raised significantly. Bill Soloman loved tinkering with old things. He was, after all, an engineer. "No. They have pretty strict rules about parents helping. Students only," she explained truthfully.

Her dad leaned back in his seat, obviously disappointed. "That makes sense, I guess—can't have adults doing all the work."

Thea looked over at her mother, who looked disappointed. "Mom?"

Her mother's voice creaked out from somewhere deep emotionally. "You aren't . . . doing track anymore?"

Thea looked down at the table to avoid her mother's distressed gaze. "No, Mom. I don't think I'm ready for that, not yet. Maybe in college."

Her mother stared at her, her face struggling to control its emotion, as her dad leaped up from his chair. "Menah! Be supportive! I know you love watching Thea run, but I think this is exciting! A chance to meet new people, to learn new things."

You have no idea, thought Thea, *how true that's going to be.* Thea noticed her mom was still staring at her. "I know you're disappointed. I can tell."

Menah gave her head a shake. "No. I'm not. Honey, I could never be disappointed in you. I just don't want you to throw away your future," she challenged.

Annoyance pricked inside of Thea. "I know it's not what you want me to do, but I'm not going to run track just because you want it to be like old times."

Her mom stood and went over to the sink, violently shoving her plate in. "Do you know what you're giving up? You are so talented, Thea—"

Thea cut her off. "I know, we all know—but every single time my sneaker touches that track, all I can remember is running with Natalie. It's too painful!" Her voice broke. "I know running has helped you grieve, but I need to do something else. Something that can make things better.

45

And this, this will help. Restoring these houses. It will help me forget."

"Thea." Her mom's voice faded away as steam rose from the sink. She closed her eyes. "Just don't forget what you can do."

Thea sighed as she stood. "I'm more than a runner, Mom. Maybe you've forgotten that."

She stomped out of the kitchen as her father's voice boomed out, "Girls, calm down!"

Thea pounded up the stairs and shut her door, leaning against it with a sigh. She had no right to be mad at her mother, especially when she was lying to them, but her mother's obvious disappointment made her crazy. Thea would never be the person that she was before Natalie died, but perhaps she could become someone better. Someone powerful.

A Black Coat.

FIVE

Thea's morning classes dragged on forever, one long period ticking into the next. Her legs bounced under her desk with restlessness. Mademoiselle Corday was waiting for her, and that made each minute in school seem like agony. Finally, the first half of the day was done and she was able to escape to her depressing yet comforting lunch corner, a small table in a secluded back section of the library surrounded by old math textbooks.

The discreet corner wasn't luxurious; the threadbare carpet was torn up under her feet, a half-painted wall sat behind the table, and overhead fluorescent lights flickered sadly. Thea slowly unpacked her lunch from her mother, and to her surprise she found a folded note. She opened it with a little smile; her mother hadn't left her notes in her lunch in a long time. Her smile faded when she read the words in her mother's loopy handwriting. *I love watching you* run. *Please reconsider.* Underneath that was the drawing of a happy face. Thea crumpled up the note and dropped it on the floor.

"I hear you can be fined for littering, but littering in a library . . ." The boy named Drew Porter tsked disapprovingly, and Thea jumped.

She sat up in her chair. "Sorry, you scared me!"

Drew smiled. "There's a special place in hell for people who destroy libraries."

Thea grinned in spite of herself as she picked up the note. "I wasn't planning on leaving it there, you know."

Drew looked down at her, playfulness lighting up his features. "That's good, because I don't want to have to turn you in to the authorities." He raised an eyebrow and nodded at Ms. Bork, who was humming while she stocked the young-adult book section. As he turned back to watch the librarian, Thea took a moment to really look at him. Dark brown hair in a neat cut framed his face, and his lean body showcased his Roosevelt soccer jersey perfectly, raised triceps filling out the triangles of black and gold. On his chest sat a giant cartoon hornet.

Thea felt a pang in her heart at the sight of it. The back of her closet was filled with a dozen tracksuits, each emblazoned with that stupid grinning insect. "Pretty strong words coming from a man with a giant bee on his chest."

Drew gestured to the hornet. "I call him Little Honey, and he's pretty good at what he does."

"And what's that?"

"Reading old sci-fi books. Driving on empty roads." He was still holding his tray in his hands. "Are you going to invite me to sit down?"

She shifted. "Uh, sure. Are you positive you want to sit here? Isn't your team missing you?"

Drew sat with a yawn. "Probably. But one can only talk about *Call of Duty* for so long. Besides, why would I want to sit in the beautifully remodeled cafeteria filled with natural light when I can sit back here with you, gazing at the wonder of"—he looked at some of the shelves surrounding them—"*Numerical Analysis in Boundary Value Programs.*" He burst out laughing, an infectious grin transforming his face. "Really? This is where you eat lunch?"

Thea couldn't help but chuckle as well—Drew's laugh was contagious. "I sit here so I don't have to answer any dumb questions, like, for example, 'Why are you sitting here?'"

Drew spread out his food.

"Do you just make yourself comfortable wherever?" Thea inquired.

He took an enormous bite of his cheeseburger. "I try to. What about you, Thea Soloman?"

Thea shrugged. "I'm not really comfortable anywhere."

Drew raised an eyebrow. "Then I think we're a perfect match." Thea blushed. He hastily continued, "I didn't mean it that way. Sorry. It's just, you make me nervous."

Thea almost spit out her apple. "I make you nervous? I don't even know you, and you just came and found me at my . . ."

"Soul-curdling lunching spot? I mean, can you blame me for wanting to get to know a girl I first saw jumping into the Bucket with all her clothes on to retrieve a lost schedule? I mean, who wouldn't want to know more about that person?" He sat back in his chair, looking serious for the first time since she'd met him. "I thought I knew everything there was to know about this stupid school. I just moved here at the beginning of the semester—my senior year; thanks, Dad—and was only looking forward to graduation. But then I saw you climb out of that fountain and something changed in me. I don't know what it was, but the thought of having the same exhausting conversations with the same people I always eat with was suddenly so depressing. I don't want to hear any more about how Gabe Anders thinks varsity soccer should be seniors only or who Mirabelle Watts made out with this weekend. I just can't. You know?"

Thea did know all too well about how conversation that used to flow smoothly could become a minefield between two parties, with her pretending to seem interested and them trying their hardest not to mention Natalie.

Drew finished the rest of his cheeseburger.

"You ate that whole thing already?" Thea was incredulous.

He licked his lips. "I'm almost always starving."

Lunch flew by as they slowly learned about each other in small, careful questions; Drew was the youngest of three brothers. He lived with his dad, a public defender. Thea told him a little about herself, but she didn't mention Natalie, though she was sure that he knew about her. Everyone in this school did. For almost thirty minutes, Thea forgot to feel alone. Everything about Drew pulled her in: the way he looped his arm across the back of his chair, the way he stabbed his french fries with a fork, the way she could tell he was smart just by how he spoke. He was a current that she enjoyed being pulled into.

With a cautious smirk, Thea shoved the last bite of her sandwich into her mouth. "So how is it that we haven't run into each other all year?"

Drew shrugged as he stood. "I think that's what happens in a huge high school like this. There are so many kids that you never get to meet anyone outside your immediate circle. I kind of resent that." Drew heaved his enormous backpack onto his shoulders. "Anyway, what are you doing right after school today? We don't have practice on game nights. Want to grab a coffee, take a walk?"

"I'm sorry, I can't. I have a commitment." Thea frowned.

A shadow of disappointment crossed his face. "A boyfriend type of commitment, or like a date-with-old-math-books kind of commitment?"

The flutter of excitement that ran up her spine was

followed by a twinge of guilt that she would have to lie to him. She'd just met him, for God's sake. "Not a boyfriend kind of thing, but a commitment nonetheless. I'm sorry. Maybe some other time, like a weekend night?"

Drew's face visibly brightened. "Yeah, we could do that. It's a date."

She stared at him for a long moment, her mind whirling. "I have to warn you, I might not be the most fun girl you've ever taken on a date."

"Oh, I know you won't be." He gestured to her now-empty table. "I mean, you eat here."

Thea frowned again as he shifted his feet. "Then why . . . ?"

Drew met her eyes, a blush running over his freckled cheeks. "Thea, I've taken lots of fun girls on dates." *I do not love this sentence already.* "But I'm kind of over fun. Fun has a sheen on it that wears off in the daylight, you know? I'm looking for interesting. I don't want my one year at Roosevelt to be exactly like all the years at my old school. And now that I've met you, that prospect is even more unfathomable."

Thea hoisted up her own backpack as she stood, confused at the feelings coursing through her—attraction, excitement, but also annoyance that this handsome boy had wandered into her life just as something bigger had started. *Where were you six months ago, when I could barely get out of bed?* But he was here now, lacing up his sneakers,

Thea trying not to notice his carved calves. "Need help to class?" he asked as he offered her his arm.

Thea declined. "Actually, I'm quite capable of walking there myself, but I'll take the company."

Drew's grin lit up every dark corner of the library. "I accept your compromise." Together they walked the halls, drawing the curious eyes of their classmates. Thea kept one eye on him and another on the clock.

SIX

As soon as the bell rang, Thea shot out of the building and tossed her backpack into the car before gunning down the highway. She was thankful that this time she would be going through the main entrance, not jumping trenches filled with snakes or climbing cypress trees. She drove through the front gates marked by two pillars topped with green moss. From the front, Mademoiselle Corday loomed even larger: a witchy shadow that stood starkly against the barren trees that surrounded it.

Moving as fast as she could, she climbed into the back seat and changed into the black leggings and shirt that she had worn the day before. She leaped out of the car, her heart pounding—with fear or excitement, she wasn't sure—as she ran up to the door. Four names were painted in gold above the door:

Thea took a deep breath and reached for the knocker—a heavy iron ring that looked to be about a hundred years old. The door swung open, and Thea found herself staring at Nixon's terrifyingly perfect face. Today she wore the same uniform as Thea: black leggings and a black shirt, though her shirt had a tiny black embroidered butterfly on the pocket.

Thea shifted. "Hi, I um—"

"You were almost late," snapped Nixon. "Don't let it happen again."

"Yes, I'm sorry, I left as soon as school got out—"

"In the future you will have to move faster to get here on time. Do you have the envelope?"

Thea nodded and pulled it from her backpack, then handed it to Nixon. "Yes."

"Good. Well, since we've already had our introduction, there's really nothing more to do than welcome you to the Black Coats." The president's bright red lips curled. "Follow me." Nixon closed the door behind her, and Thea had the distinct sensation of being swallowed by Mademoiselle Corday, of fading into her grand secrets.

Thea followed behind as Nixon wove through a narrow hallway, passing an elaborate modern kitchen on the right and a large, frilly sunroom on the left.

"New recruits such as yourself are confined to your

classroom, your private bathroom, and the Haunt. You may visit other areas only if you are assigned them for chores." She made a sharp right under a small wooden archway adorned with a mirrored dresser. On the dresser hung a white lace garland that read, "Team Banner."

Thea looked at it with surprise. "You would think that Martha Stewart lived in this house," she muttered.

Nixon raised a perfectly sculpted eyebrow at her. "That's the general idea. And if you forget to call me ma'am again, we are going to have some real problems."

Thea swallowed. "Sorry, ma'am."

Nixon placed a hand on the ivory door handle, carved to look like a rose. "Welcome to Team Banner."

Thea didn't know what she was expecting, but an actual classroom wasn't it. The room was a warm, cozy, window-less space. A small brick fireplace was tucked in the back of the room, and at the front sat a narrow walnut desk. Old-fashioned elementary school desks were lined up, and four were now occupied by girls her own age, with their eyes all trained on Thea. Nixon gestured to the empty desk, and Thea sat, her face flushing with embarrassment. She had driven as fast as she dared. *How did they get here so fast?*

Nixon stood at the front of the room, hands resting on slim hips, dark brown eyes staring down her new recruits. "Ladies, welcome to Team Banner. These women who sit around you will become more than your friends—they will become your sisters. Now, I'm assuming you all read your contracts thoroughly." She looked at the girls, some of whom nodded. "When I ask you a question, you will respond with, 'Yes, ma'am!'"

"Yes, ma'am!" the girls echoed.

"Good." Nixon walked over to the door and returned with the black garment bag that had been hanging there ominously. With a hard yank, she pulled off the bag and held the hanger up for everyone to see. "Who knows what this is?" A mousy brunette with a pale face, upturned nose, and a smattering of freckles raised her hand. "Yes, Louise?"

"A black coat, ma'am."

"That's right. A black coat, something you will need before being approved for Balancings. And let me be clear: a black coat is something you earn." Nixon twirled the hanger in front of her. "During the day, when I am not here at Mademoiselle Corday, I am whatever I am in my normal life: a student, a lawyer, a wife . . . whatever." Nixon shrugged into her coat. It fell over her perfect figure like a glove, cinching at all the right places, flaring at the sides. Thea could see even from a distance that it was meticulously tailored.

"However, when I put this coat on, I am none of those things. The black coat, Mademoiselle Corday, Team Banner—these things transform who we are. When we step through those doors, we become Black Coats, and our purpose is to administer justice. I know that high school can be all-consuming, but when you come to Mademoiselle

Corday, you will shed yourself at the door like a snake sheds its skin. When you put on this coat, you are serving the women who deserve justice. They deserve your all; don't you agree?"

"Yes, ma'am," breathed Thea, riveted by her speech.

"Good." Nixon shrugged off the coat and draped it over her chair. "Now, I have much to teach you, but today is going to be your basic introduction and first training session. When you have your first Balancing will depend on when I, your president, think you are ready." A collective silence fell over the room at this intimidating thought. "Scary, isn't it? The idea of the Balancings? Well, I promise by the time we get there, you will be chomping at the bit."

Nixon raised her hands. "Now, you were handpicked by a dozen Black Coat alumni, who sifted and sorted through hundreds of potential recruits. You have been called to a glorious purpose, as your contract stated: *Soulevez-vous, femmes de la vengeance.*" Nixon smiled, her crimson lips twisting into an unnerving grin. "The French translated means 'Rise, women of vengeance,' and rise you will. If you work hard, and you don't complain or give in to distractions"—Thea's mind flickered to Drew and she almost flinched—"you will become worthy of this." Nixon ran her fingers along the collar of her coat.

She cleared her throat. "Now, let's begin with quick introductions. I want you to state your first name only and what your skills are." She gestured to a tall blond girl at the back, who stood without being asked.

Thea almost gasped when she saw her stand, and was filled with a wave of horror. *It couldn't be.* The girl introduced herself, but Thea didn't need to hear. She already knew exactly who she was. The girl's name was Mirabelle Watts, and she was one of the most popular girls at Thea's school . . . and an all-around bitch to everyone. Mirabelle's kind drifted through the school on a cloud of untouchable supremacy. Up close she was stunning, with bright blond hair and cornflower-blue eyes, the perfect embodiment of a Texas rose.

Mirabelle put her hand on her hip with an exaggerated frown, her voice dripping with a Southern drawl that wasn't common for this part of town. "My name is Mirabelle, and I was picked for the Black Coats because of *this.*" She gestured to her face.

Nixon rolled her eyes. "It's true, Mirabelle is going to be what we call 'the face' on our team. However, she is also very, very strong. We could find a pretty girl anywhere." Mirabelle sat with a grin, her ponytail bouncing behind her. Underneath the desk, Thea pressed her fingernails into her palm. This had felt like an escape from Roosevelt, and now one of the girls Thea went out of her way to avoid was sitting two chairs behind her. She gritted her teeth. *Damn.*

Thea was next, and she felt bumbling and gangly next to perfect Maribelle. "My name is Thea, and, um, I was picked for the Black Coats because I'm fast." She cleared her throat. "I'm a runner. A sprinter." This was her best guess at why they picked her.

Nixon pointed at her. "Thea exhibited great adaptability and leadership potential, and yes, she's quite fast."

There were three more girls on their team. Casey, a girl of Middle Eastern descent with long black hair and heavily made-up eyes, shared that her strengths were driving and computer hacking. Louise, the plain brunette, just happened to have a black belt—quite the surprise. Finally, Nixon turned to the last girl in the group, a curvier girl with frizzy toffee-colored hair, a cute nose, and thick black glasses. Thea could tell just by looking at her that she wasn't comfortable in her own skin. She fumbled out of the desk looking absolutely mortified, a blush creeping up her cheeks. Nixon did not look amused. Then she adjusted her thick-rimmed glasses and squeaked out, "I'm Bea Hopwood, and I—"

Nixon groaned. "No last names, Bea. And let's save the introduction to your impressive talents for another time."

"Oh." Bea pressed up her glasses, her face falling. "Okay."

She sat down, and the desk gave a tiny creak. Mirabelle raised her eyebrows laughingly at Casey, who ignored her. Moving faster than Thea thought was possible, Nixon crossed the room and flicked Mirabelle's lips; she blinked in shock but said nothing. Nixon calmly wiped the pink lip gloss off her finger before turning back to the group. "You will not bully here, Barbie." Mirabelle looked completely taken aback, and Thea raised her hand to her mouth to cover her smile.

Nixon stalked to the front of the room again. "Moving on. How did each of you get through the door during your initiation? Past Sahil?"

Their answers were varied: Mirabelle went first with a nasty grin, trying to conceal the embarrassment flushing across her cheeks. "I tackled him and dragged him in behind me."

Casey barely looked up. "I punched him between the legs and then tripped him forward."

Louise: "We fought hard, but eventually I was able to reach the handle."

Thea added her own voice to the mix. "I basically ran through him."

Nixon watched them each silently, perched on the back of a chair like some sort of glamorous gargoyle. "I'm glad you are all so proud of yourselves. However, the shortest time among the four of you was six minutes. Six long minutes to pass through a door guarded by a single unarmed male who was of smaller physical stature than some of you." She nodded at Bea, who was staring at the floor and anxiously kneading her hands together. "Bea passed through the door in one hundred and sixty-two seconds, without anyone ever laying a finger on her."

The others sat back in surprise, except Mirabelle, who glanced skeptically in Bea's direction. Nixon tapped her chin thoughtfully. "Your team was carefully selected, with thought given to every weakness and strength. Right now you are utterly useless, but you won't remain that way. Any in-team issues will be stopped short with immediate expulsion of all parties, is that understood?" Her eyes flitted to Mirabelle.

"Yes, ma'am," replied Team Banner.

Their introduction continued. "I'm your president. There are two other teams of Black Coats: Team Emperor and Team Swallowtail. They are led by Presidents Kennedy and McKinley, respectively. You will have very little interaction with these other teams." Nixon began passing out pieces of paper. "We are a new team, and you can expect there to be some animosity at that decision. As for all the papers, please know that we don't use computers inside the Black Coats. Everything is handwritten or typed and then burned. Computers and the internet make it easy to leave a trail."

Nixon opened a simple manila folder and slid a piece of pretty cream paper across Thea's desk. "Here is a sample Balancing sheet. Your team will receive one of these when a Balancing is ordered by the luminaries. It can be once a month or three times a week, depending on the need. Thea, can you read for us?"

Thea's voice caught in her throat as she read.

TEAM BANNER, CODE MORNING
TARGET NAME: *John Doe*
DATE OF BALANCING: *June 24, 9:00 p.m.*
OFFENSE: *John Doe has been found guilty of constant*

sexual harassment of his female employees at White Dog Coffee Shop. Charges were pressed, but John Doe was let go on a technicality.

BALANCING: *Threatening, blackmail, intimidation.*

Thea's heart pumped with exhilaration.

Nixon paced as she continued her lecture. "These sheets are printed specifically to help you understand the delicate system of Balancings. The punishment must fit the crime, and we must fill the void where law enforcement has failed. Thus: threatening, blackmail, and intimidation as listed."

Louise's hand popped up.

"Yes?"

Louise lowered her eyes in submission to Nixon. "Do you ever have women targets, ma'am?"

Nixon stopped moving and turned to face the girls. "Occasionally, we will have a woman target. There are, unfortunately, women who hurt women out there and they are owed justice just like any man. It's rare, but it has happened. Men commit eighty percent of violent offenses in this country. The odds are in your favor that it won't be a situation you will have to face. Does that answer your question?"

"Yes, ma'am," exclaimed Louise.

"As you can see, the levels are represented by escalating times of the day." Nixon resumed her pacing at the front of the room. "A Code Morning means no violence will be used. It represents a nonviolent offense—online bullying, sexual harassment, stalking, and blackmail. We will not lay a hand on our targets. We may have to touch them for one reason or another, but we do not harm them. Their solutions are simple, yet enough to ruin a life and change the behavior. It's best to think of them as old-fashioned public shaming. Though violence is never used on this level, threatening it might be. The vast majority of your Balancings will be Code Mornings."

At the word *violence*, Thea felt a shiver pass down her spine as a tendril of doubt whispered in her mind. *Am I honestly ready to hurt people?* Then she remembered the photographs in the domed room, and Natalie's picture clipped to the easel. Hell yes, she could be ready.

Nixon stopped walking. "And then we have Code Evenings. A Code Evening is where violence will be repaid with violence, along with some of the punishments listed for the lighter transgressions. This is for cases of domestic violence, sexual assault, rape, and murder. I will be with you for your first Code Evening, and you won't be sent on one until I feel you are ready. This is obviously a more complex Balancing, and it takes experience to know how much violence is enough." Nixon paused, rocking on her heels. "This is why over the course of your training I will be picking a team leader. One of the most important jobs of the team leader is to know when to say enough." The girl with the dark eye makeup slowly raised her hand. "Yes, Casey?" said Nixon.

Casey held Nixon's gaze steady. "What about murderers? How do they get what they deserve?"

Nixon's eyes went cold. "The Black Coats are interested in justice. We will repay these men for what they have done and, most important, make them so afraid of us that they will never do it again. We ruin their lives, but the Black Coats do not kill. You are not assassins, and murder is far too messy for this organization." Thea turned this over in her mind, thinking about the implications for Natalie's murderer. Nixon continued. "A Code Evening can never turn into hiding a dead body. Never. Are there any questions?" Stunned into terrified silence, Team Banner sat quietly, no girl daring to raise her hand.

"The Black Coats mostly operate at night," Nixon explained. "Getting in and out of your houses is your responsibility, whether it's saying you are going out with friends or climbing out a window."

She grabbed her black coat from the back of the chair and swung it around her slim shoulders. "Now, I want you to throw those sheets into the fireplace. Training begins now; we are not a group that likes to waste time. Classroom instruction is important, but learning to interact as a team, that is more so. Let's rise, Team Banner." She gestured with her hands for them to stand. The girls climbed to their feet, some slower than others, not at all the synchronized movement that Nixon was expecting. Bea somehow tripped on her desk, and Casey dropped her paper on the way to the fire.

Nixon sighed. "We'll get there someday. Follow me." They filed out the classroom door and followed the snap of her black stilettos down the winding hallway.

As they walked, Nixon proceeded with the lesson. "This house was originally owned by the Texas Historical Commission. Through some tough negotiating by the founding members of the Black Coats, it came into Robin Peterson's possession in 1981. We take pride in this house, and it is to be treated with respect."

Thea was the last in line, her curiosity leading her to appreciate each perfect detail.

Louise spoke quietly. "How much money do these people have?"

Thea glanced at a marble lion guarding one of the doors. "A lot, I'm guessing."

Nixon sharply gestured to a huge door on the right. "And this is where our alumni and luminaries meet: the formal sitting room and library."

Thea poked her head in as they walked past, gasping loudly in amazement and regretting it immediately. Standing in front of a massive bookcase was a black iron staircase that twisted up to a second level, its bannister painted with foxes, moths, and fleurs-de-lis.

Mirabelle leaned over her shoulder. "I bet this is where they ritually murder deserters." She wiggled her eyebrows, and Thea smiled in spite of herself. "Hey, you go to Roosevelt, right? I recognize you," queried Mirabelle.

Thea almost laughed. Of course Mirabelle would barely remember her. *It's hard to remember peasants when you're the queen.* Her tone was dry as she responded, "We have second period together on Tuesdays."

Mirabelle tugged a piece of her hair. "Huh, okay. I guess." Her eyes widened. "Wait, weren't you Natalie Fisher's cousin?"

The words punched through Thea. She froze in the middle of the hallway outside the sitting room, the grief catching her off guard like it so often did. She fought it, every ounce of her self-control working to push away the uninvited shudders that curled up her spine. A sob rose in her throat as she struggled to hold in her tears, embarrassed beyond words. Thea gestured at Mirabelle, choking out her words. "I'm sorry. Please, just go."

Mirabelle shook her head in confusion before moving ahead, leaving Thea standing in the hallway. Thea took a deep breath and struggled to regain her composure, wiping away a hot tear with the back of her hand.

"Now, why on earth do I have a young lady crying outside my room? My, my, my." Thea leaped back at the voice, politely Southern and highly disapproving. On the upper floor of the library, an older woman stepped out of an open door, closed it behind her, and punched a code into a keypad. The door locked with an electronic buzz. She was slight but strong, descending the winding staircase with ease. Elegant crow's-feet stretched out from pale eyes,

67

the lines in her face accented by chin-length gray hair. One hand rested on her chest, while the other clutched a glass tumbler of amber liquor. There was a certain confidence about her, and with each step closer to Thea, the air crackled with intensity. Her voice was not kind. "Thea Soloman, am I correct?"

Thea swallowed, hoping that her voice sounded stronger than she felt. "Yes, ma'am."

The woman circled her, her critical frown taking in every inch of Thea. "Yes, yes, how strange; I was just looking at your file. Student of Roosevelt High, former track star, average student. There was really nothing about you that made you special; in fact, you're quite ordinary, which is why I argued against your placement. However, there were certain qualities that Robin was looking for, and according to her frail mind, you fit the bill."

She reached out and pressed one long fingernail against Thea's chest. Thea stood perfectly still as the woman traced around her heart, the shame of her tears rendering her silent. Finally, the woman moved to touch Thea's cheek. "Look at this skin, like glowing cocoa. My, how the world is changing." She clicked her tongue. "So young, the new recruits. Like babies, sent to do women's work." She took a ladylike sip of her drink before calling down the hallway in a lilting voice, "Oh, Nixon, you've forgotten one of your goslings!"

The president of Team Banner came back around the

corner, her eyes furious. "Go on, Thea. Catch up with your team."

Humiliation flared up Thea's face as she walked away from the two women.

The older woman called out after her, "Team Banner is off to a banner start, I would say, with girls crying in the hallway on their first day." She turned to Nixon, a thinly veiled threat falling like a bomb. "This is your first team. Don't make it your last."

Thea joined the group, who stared at her with barely concealed pity. She raised her head. "Sorry. Sorry," she whispered, wiping her face clean. "Grief is weird."

She felt a hand close around hers, and looked down to see Bea staring at her through her glasses. She smiled as she gave Thea's hand a squeeze. Thea squeezed back as Mirabelle sneered toward the woman. "Who was that, anyway? She's, like, sixty-five years old."

Nixon appeared over her shoulder, her face hard. "That woman is Julie Westing, and she's a founding member of the Black Coats—a luminary. She's one of the two most important people in this house." She sighed before turning to Thea. "And you managed to put a target on our back on day one."

Thea straightened her shoulders. "I'm sorry, ma'am. It won't happen again."

"No, it won't, Thea," Nixon said softly. The meaning was clear.

They were standing in front of an arched door marked with a copper sign that read, "The Haunt." Their president reached out and pulled a beaded chain hanging just outside the door. Warm lights flickered to life, and Thea felt her heart lift. "Now, Team Banner," said Nixon, "let's see what you can do."

SEVEN

Nixon pushed the doors open farther, and the girls stepped inside with gasps of delight. Even Mirabelle looked impressed. They were surrounded by old-fashioned wavy glass windows on every side; it was essentially a greenhouse. Black mats were laid out across the floor. The edges of the room were filled with low farmhouse-style tables and antique chairs in every shade of wood. Outside, Thea could hear the wind rushing through the trees, their leaves tapping harmlessly across the windows.

"Wow!" burst out Bea, pushing her glasses back. "We get to train in here?"

Nixon nodded. "This is the Haunt, and most of your time at Mademoiselle Corday will be spent either in this room or the classroom. You are welcome to use the Haunt anytime you like; it's always open to members and alumni of the Black Coats. It's our common space." Nixon walked over to the open bar area and emerged with a tray carrying steaming croissants and mason jars full of ice water. Thea's mouth watered. She hadn't realized how thirsty and hungry she was; she hadn't eaten or drunk anything since lunch.

Nixon set the tray down on one of the tables. "Now, who would like some of these? The croissants are basted with honey butter, homemade." Team Banner all raised their hands. Nixon proceeded to precisely unbutton her coat, slipped off her heels, and rolled up her sleeves, now wearing only the standard uniform. Then she beckoned to the group before crouching defensively in front of the table. "Come and get them, then. Your first training session begins now." The group stood still, staring at their leader. "I said, come and get them."

After a moment's pause, Louise stepped forward, her small eyes darting back and forth. "Uhh, can we please have the tray, ma'am?"

Nixon shook her head. "No, Louise, you may not, but I like that you thought to ask first. Sometimes the best answer is the easiest one, just not today."

Mirabelle walked up to Nixon, swallowing nervously. When she got close, Nixon shoved her backward, sending her tumbling over her own feet. Mirabelle stumbled and angrily leaped up. "Fine." She charged. Nixon anticipated her actions and stepped aside, spinning her body so that Mirabelle ended up beside her. Then, with a quick lunge, she caught Mirabelle's neck against her arm, clotheslining her. Mirabelle's feet left the ground, and Nixon lifted her up over her shoulder before slamming her down onto the mat, Mirabelle's body bouncing hard.

"Stay down," Nixon breathed. "You're out."

Mirabelle laid her head back on the ground with a wince. "No problem."

Nixon raised her eyes. "Next."

Casey leaped forward, attempting to hit Nixon's knees and knock her off-balance, a better approach than Mirabelle had taken. Nixon stumbled forward, but she was lithe and fast, and before Casey knew what was happening, Nixon had stepped up onto her back and was now pressing her down with both feet. Her hands wrapped around Casey's chin, pulling upward. "Down," Nixon muttered.

Casey closed her eyes but stayed down amid a flurry of ugly curses. Thea and Bea looked at each other with wide eyes. There was a moment of silence before Louise stepped forward, a flush creeping up her freckled face. "I'll try."

Nixon stepped back, making two fists in front of her. She cracked her neck from side to side. "Now this—this should actually be good."

Louise's first series of blows landed, with swift punches to Nixon's stomach and side. She was *fast*. Nixon gasped for breath, but her arms snaked out and yanked back Louise's hair. Thea's team member yelped in surprise as her neck was twisted backward. Nixon leaped in the air before delivering a hard punch to Louise's shoulder. Louise flipped around and threw an elbow into Nixon's cheek, shaking herself free from her grasp. Then she spun quickly and flung her leg out, the roundhouse kick catching their leader squarely in the ribs. Nixon stumbled backward, but she caught Louise's leg on the return and wrenched it sideways. Louise let herself flip in the air, rather than risk twisting her knee, and hit the mat hard. Nixon was on her in a second. "Stay down!" Nixon snapped at Louise. "And that kick hurt. Good job."

Thea decided to use Nixon's momentary distraction against her and darted sideways, shooting forward, toward the water. She easily leaped over Mirabelle and Casey, who lay directly in her path. She reached out for the tray . . . *This victory is about much more than a drink*, she congratulated herself. That was when something hit her so hard that Thea's feet literally left the mat and she flew three feet to the side, her speed making the impact much more jarring. She landed on the mat, and her body instinctively rolled to absorb the shock as she slid to a stop. Her lungs searched for a single breath. Tan feet stepped in front of her.

"You're down," spoke a soft voice. "That's for not noticing your surroundings." Sahil turned away, and Thea gulped in the air around her, her lungs feeling like cracked timber. She raised her head, one arm curled around her stomach.

Nixon and Sahil were advancing on Bea, who simply put her hands up in surrender. "Nope. I'm down." She got on her knees before lying facedown on the ground, her words muffled by the mat. "No croissant is worth that." Nixon grinned as she patted Bea's head once before making her way over to the table. Sahil followed her, stepping over all the members of Team Banner.

"Stand up," their president ordered. Nixon padded over to the glasses of water, grabbing one for herself before gnashing her teeth into the croissant. "Mmm. These are good. Kennedy is a killer baker." She wiped her mouth with her hand. "Now, ladies, what went wrong here?"

"Everything," Casey muttered. "Also, you had help, which wasn't fair."

"No?" Nixon raised her eyebrows. "It's absolutely fair that I brought in Sahil. You know why? Because Sahil is part of my team. You know what resource you never thought to use? Your team. You are still thinking like individuals. I never told you that you had to fight me one at a time. In fact, I didn't tell you any rules at all. You were too worried about being polite. You don't want to look bossy or say the wrong thing. But here, at the Black Coats, we don't have time for that timid female crap. You lost badly, but even worse, you abandoned one another as you watched me take down your teammates. One of you at a time, I can take, maybe even two . . ." She winked at Louise. "But all five of you I would not have been able to control. That's what makes your team so important." She finished guzzling her water and brushed off her pants. "Now, I want you to try again, and this time, I want you to think and move as if you have five distinct talents."

"Some of us do, anyway," muttered Mirabelle, eyeing Bea.

Nixon clapped. The girls came closer. Sahil stepped up beside her.

Thea straightened up. Someone needed to take charge here, and it might as well be her. She had to redeem herself after the awkward scene in the hallway. "Team Banner! Come here." They clustered around Thea as she dropped her voice to a whisper. "Louise, you take Nixon first—you can keep her occupied for a minute or so at least. Casey, Mirabelle, you take Sahil. You won't be able to fight him, but you can at least hold on to him, maybe weigh him down? Casey, go for his legs; Mirabelle, you try to hold his arms. Nixon said you were strong—let's see it. Bea and I will go for the water. We'll flank one on each side. Okay?"

The girls nodded, all except for Bea, who closed her eyes for a long moment as her hands fiddled under her long sleeves.

The girls turned back to Nixon and Sahil, who at the sight of the girls seemed as amused as lions watching antelopes make a plan. Nixon grinned. "Team Banner, are you ready? This time I'd like—"

Thea shouted "Go!" in the middle of Nixon's statement, catching her off guard. The girls swarmed forward. Mirabelle tackled Sahil. He was up in a second, but then Casey was waiting for him and pushed him backward, the weight of Mirabelle holding him down. Thea was running. She passed Sahil and was getting close to the table, where Louise and Nixon were fighting hard. Louise was losing fast; Nixon was fighting dirty, and Louise's martial-arts training had not prepared her for that. Suddenly, Bea appeared in front of Nixon. "What are you doing?" shouted Thea. *This wasn't the plan.*

"Hold her arms, Louise. Behind her. Now," Bea requested quietly. Louise, confused, twisted both of Nixon's arms behind her, thrusting Nixon out in front of her, one foot planted in the middle of her back. Bea stepped forward, moving her hands back and forth in front of Nixon's eyes, like the pendulum of a clock. When she spoke, her voice stopped Thea in her tracks. It was like a river running down a mountainside, a soothing rumble of power, so different from the meek voice Thea had heard earlier.

They all watched Bea in silence as her hands kept moving back and forth in front of Nixon's eyes, her voice lulling them into motionless awe. "You will reach out your hand." Nixon straightened. "Watch my hands. Watch how they move. You are safe with me, Nixon. I am going to take care of you. You can trust me. Are you watching them? Now reach out your hand." Louise let go of her arm, and Nixon reached out. Casey gasped. "Now press your hand against my hand." She repeated the order several times. Nixon's hand began trembling, but finally she did what Bea said, laying her palm across Bea's. "Now close your eyes. Press on my hand and close your eyes."

Nixon's eyes closed. When they did, Bea jerked her hand away quickly and violently, while at the same time ordering: "Sleep." As her hand fell swiftly away from Bea's, Nixon fell sideways, her body following her arm, her face hitting the mat with a soft bounce. "You are falling, deeper and deeper," Bea whispered as she crouched over her. "Deeper and deeper." Nixon didn't move, though the rise and fall of her chest showed that she was, as Bea had commanded, deeply asleep.

Bea walked forward and picked up one of the croissants, looking at it for a moment before taking a huge bite. The team watched in silence as she ate the croissant and drank the water, wiping her mouth messily on her sleeve when she was done. Then she turned back to their president, unconscious on the ground. Bea snapped her fingers. "Wake up!"

Nixon jerked to her feet, her eyes darting from side to side. She looked over at Bea with wonder and pride. "Well done, Bea," she muttered, wiping a droplet of blood from the corner of her mouth. "Well done, Thea and Team Banner."

There was only silence in the room. Sahil's face was a mix of delight and disbelief.

"Holy shit," said Mirabelle.

Nixon clapped her hands. "Again!"

✳ ✳ ✳

After several more tries—some successful, some not—Nixon finally gave them a break. Thea's legs were shaking, and she was dripping with sweat, but at least she wasn't alone. The entire team limped toward one of the low tables and collapsed on the long oak benches that flanked them. Finally, they had earned their reward. The croissants were devoured. The pretense that all high school girls ate daintily was sucked down like the clouds of pastry they were shoving into their mouths. Only Mirabelle turned her pert nose away. "Is that real butter on those? I don't eat dairy," she griped.

Thea chewed on the huge piece in her mouth. "Your loss," she muttered.

Casey raised her dark eyebrows at Mirabelle. "Are you actually allergic, or is that just the new trend for cheerleaders in Texas?"

Mirabelle scowled. "Why would you assume I'm a cheerleader?"

"A lucky guess." Casey snorted.

"Well, I'm not. I'm actually the captain of the debate team. Maybe I should guess some things about you, too." Mirabelle tossed her hair out of her eyes and turned her voice into a pitying whine. "I'm guessing you paint your nails black, just love the Cure, and are biding your time until you can go to Sarah Lawrence."

Casey shoved back the bench, rocking Louise and Thea as she went. "You don't know anything about me." Slowly, she raised her middle finger in Mirabelle's direction, nails painted hot pink, then stalked angrily to a table across the room.

Thea turned to Bea, who was doing her best to disappear into the wall behind the bench. "We have to ask about it, you know. You can hypnotize people?"

Bea played absentmindedly with her locket. "Yes. If they are willing. Nixon could have very well punched me in the face, but she chose to surrender; she wanted you guys to see what I could do."

Thea wiped away the bead of sweat making its way down her hairline and grinned. "It's like you have a superpower! Where did you even come from?"

Mirabelle groaned, obviously eavesdropping. "It's not magic, sycophants. It's carnival nonsense is what it is."

Bea wearily shook her head. "It's actually neither of those things. Hypnosis is a trancelike state, when people have heightened focus. It's science and psychology, nothing else. When people are desperate, they are very open to suggestion."

Thea rolled her hands up her cool mason jar of water. "You pulled your hand back and she fell. Was that part of it?"

Bea smiled. "That's my favorite part. It's called the shock. It's a way of hurtling someone forward into the hypnosis."

Mirabelle pretended to sneeze. "Ahhh, *witchcraft!*"

Bea flinched at the word.

Thea looked over at Mirabelle's impossibly blue eyes. "Well, only one of us was able to get to the waters, and it wasn't you," she deadpanned.

"What is that supposed to mean?"

Thea leaned forward. "We aren't at Roosevelt, and you aren't the queen bee here. You're just as cool as the rest of us, maybe even less so." As the words left her mouth, Thea realized that she would probably regret them tomorrow when she saw Mirabelle at school.

Louise looked up from the end of the table, where she was sitting silently, patting her bruises down with bags of ice that Nixon had provided. "Which, as you may have noticed, is not very cool at all. We suck."

"It's true. For now." Nixon was standing over them, wiping the hint of sweat off her face. She pointed to Casey's table. "Casey, get back over here. You don't leave your team just because Mirabelle said something insulting." Nixon turned back to Mirabelle. "And you, you need to watch your words. The 'face' is the most expendable member of this team, and so far, you've done nothing today to convince me that you belong here."

Mirabelle bit her lip, and Thea thought she saw a flicker of tears in her eyes before she stood up and stormed out of the Haunt. She slammed the wood door behind her so hard that even Sahil, standing nearby, gritted his teeth.

Thea regarded Nixon. "Should I go after her?"

Nixon seemed unfazed. "Not now." She whirled on the remaining team members. "The rest of you can head home. That will be all for today—at least, after you do the dishes."

Casey's head jerked up from where it was lying on the table across the room. "Dishes?"

Thirty minutes later, most of Team Banner was clustered together in a small area in front of a large silver tub, each of them wearing yellow rubber gloves and scrubbing small, delicate china plates. Thea held up her dish, admiring her work. "This is really not what I pictured when I imagined my life of vigilante justice." She sighed. "More Batman, less cleaning."

Bea smiled as she scrubbed. "So, Nixon's terrifying."

"And yet, you made her fall asleep with your hand." Casey shook her head. "That was amazing." She coughed. "It's too bad it wouldn't have worked on Mirabelle."

Louise made a face. "Ugh, Thea, I can't believe you have to see her at school every day."

"Yeah." Dread slithered its way through Thea. Mirabelle could make her life a living hell at Roosevelt.

"The sad thing is"—Casey laughed, a bright smile dissolving her normally scowling face—"she was totally right about the Cure. I love them so much."

Team Banner erupted into laughter. "We're a motley crew," pronounced Bea, plopping the last dish into the sink. "I mean, we pretty much have nothing in common except . . ."

Silence enveloped the group as they each recoiled at her words, each girl suddenly plunged into the darkest corners of her own mind. Finally, Thea spoke up, a small tremble in her voice. "Except the fact that we all lost someone, or had something horrible happen to us."

Bea added, "Even Mirabelle."

The moment was broken as Nixon popped her head around the swinging kitchen door. "Girls. How long does it take to wash dishes? There are four of you. Wrap it up."

Thea turned to Nixon, speaking quietly as the team finished the dishes. "I'm so sorry about the hallway, ma'am, with Ms. Westing. It won't happen again. Sometimes, when I'm caught off guard, I just . . ."

Nixon knowingly put her hand on Thea's shoulder. "Sometimes it's a smell or a song, or perhaps a memory that shakes its way loose at the worst possible time. You can't predict it, and if you could, you still couldn't control it. Grief is fighting an invisible tidal wave."

Nixon had lost someone, too. That made sense.

Thea nodded. "Yes. It's just like that."

"I understand, Thea, but I need you to do something for me in return."

"Of course. Anything."

"I need you to make sure that Mirabelle comes back tomorrow." *Anything but that*, Thea thought, but she nodded all the same.

EIGHT

Later that night, after she scarfed down her mother's chicken casserole, Thea limped up the stairs to her room. The soreness of muscles that hadn't been used in a long time roared back at her. Upon entering her room, she saw her backpack and shook her head with a chuckle. "I actually have to do homework now. Fantastic."

Thea was reaching for her backpack when she heard the shout of a male voice outside. She sprang over to the window and flung open the dual panes. The windows pushed out into the branches of the large tree that dominated their lawn. She looked up and down the street in front of her house and thought, *No, it couldn't be.*

In front of Natalie's house sat a white pickup truck, the same kind that Cabby Baptist drove. Thea inhaled sharply, the very sight of it painful. She reached for the phone, but as her hand curled around it, one of the painters came around from the rear of the house and threw a ladder in the back. As he walked toward the driver's seat, Thea noticed a thin green stripe running around the bottom of the truck and the logo on the driver's-side door. It wasn't even the same vehicle; in fact, now she could see it wasn't even the same model. The painter climbed into the truck and drove off.

Thea sat in front of the windowsill, clutching at her heart, her breaths coming hard and fast. Then she stumbled to the bathroom and clumsily opened her medicine cabinet, reaching for the orange Xanax bottle. One tiny blue pill fell out into her hands. Thea shoved it into her mouth and swallowed without thinking.

"Calm down. It was nothing," she murmured to herself, crossing the room and slamming the window shut.

"Thea, everything okay?" It was her mom's voice, always concerned. Thea was reassured by it.

"I'm fine, Mom. I just dropped my book bag." Thea climbed up into her bed, leaving her homework undone. Instead, she let her mind wander to places it shouldn't, the Xanax calming her breathing but not much else. Her mind swirled like a tornado. A white pickup truck: the object she saw in her nightmares. A trigger, the grief counselor had called it. The last car Natalie had ever seen had been a white pickup truck.

Thea climbed into her bed, helpless as the disputed facts of Natalie's murder flooded her vulnerable mind.

Her cousin had just wrapped up her first year of college when she announced plans to visit. Thea was elated. It was the first year the cousins had been apart, and it had taken an obvious toll on their friendship. While Thea was happy that Natalie was loving college life, the simmering jealousy she felt at Natalie's new adventures with new friends made it hard to talk to her on the phone.

She had felt left behind, and suddenly the previously insignificant gap between their ages was now as wide as the ocean. Thea had friends, but she missed the one who had been an extension of her own body. So when Natalie had come home that weekend, Thea had practically tackled her on the front lawn, both of them shrieking with laughter in a moment of pure joy. It was short-lived, however, as they struggled with normal conversation as the day wore on.

Thea had tried not to care about Natalie's weird political rants and her dismissive attitude about Thea's high school problems, but it didn't work. Natalie announced she wasn't going to come to Thea's practice meet because she was going camping, and that had left Thea bitter and stung. The weekend was awkward, and then, before she knew it, Natalie was leaving. Thea had watched Natalie pack up her car as she stood awkwardly next to it with her arms crossed and heart aching. But just before she left, Natalie had paused and walked over to her, pulling her cousin into her arms. "Hey, girl," she had said. "I'm sorry I can't come to the meet. I'll call you in a few days, and we'll plan for you to come up next month. It will just be us. We'll be okay."

Thea had looked away, knowing she was being ridiculous. But then as Natalie had turned back to the car and stretched out her lean body, Thea had felt a jolt go through her as her cousin's shirt rose up. *Natalie had a belly button ring.* She hadn't even told Thea about it. For some reason, seeing that winking jewel broke something inside her. Tears gathered in Thea's eyes, uninvited and babyish. Her heart gave a painful twist at the knowledge that they didn't know everything about each other anymore. Natalie had moved on.

"I'll see you later, Thea," she had said.

Thea had turned her head away. "Whatever."

The last thing she had said to Natalie was "Whatever."

Thea had headed home, and Natalie had taken off for her weekend in Sam Houston National Forest with her new friends.

A few days later, Thea was stretching her legs on the track, curly hair pressed up against her shins, when she heard a familiar voice. She looked up to see her mom standing next to Coach Vaughn. Her mom's face was twisted in pain, and her coach was covering his mouth, his eyes leaking tears. When Thea started walking toward them, he turned away to give them privacy, and that was when she knew something was very wrong. A sob caught in her throat. "Mom! Is Dad okay?"

Her mom nodded once. "Dad's okay. But . . ." Her mom

pulled her aside and they sat down on the benches, the blindingly hot Texas sun simmering above them. Her mom stared at Thea for a long moment before she pulled her daughter close. "Thea, something happened to Natalie."

Thea looked at her mom's face, knowing the truth even before she asked it. "Is she going to be okay?"

Her mom shook her head, her voice so high-pitched that it was almost a wail. "No, baby, she's not." That's when Thea broke, when the shell that was her happiness collapsed and exposed her raw to every shitty feeling a person could ever have.

Thea drifted through life in a fog for the next few days as details about her cousin's death gradually emerged. They had found Natalie floating in a muddy creek seventy-two miles outside of Austin. Lying facedown beneath a cluster of cypress trees, the top half of her body was almost submerged under their rotted roots, her back coated with wet leaves. The official cause of death was ruled as asphyxiation, most likely involving strangulation, as evidenced by the contusions on her neck. The back of her head showed a large laceration and there were signs of blunt-force trauma as well as multiple bruises on her face. There was no evidence of sexual assault.

The police struggled to piece together what had happened. The investigation later revealed that Natalie had met some friends at a campsite in Sam Houston National Forest on August 6. They'd set up tents and spent the day drinking at the lake. By that evening they had ended up at a dive bar named Bitter Sand just outside the forest. Natalie had met a young man named Cabby Baptist at the bar. According to statements from numerous witnesses, the two of them sat talking and drinking for a long time.

"He looked," reported her friend, who during their flirtation had been off in a corner with a conquest of her own, "like a surfer." Natalie and Cabby had decided to leave together, and her friends had watched her go. Natalie had gotten into her own car and then followed his small white pickup truck out of the parking lot at around 11:00 p.m.

Then she had disappeared. When Natalie didn't come back to the campsite the next day, her friends started calling around. Finally, late in the evening on August 7, they called Natalie's parents, who reported her missing. The police didn't get involved until the next day, but by then it was too late. That same day, an hour's drive away from the bar, near San Antonio Prairie, an elderly rancher noticed his Australian shepherd digging at something near the bank of the creek. He thought it was maybe a snake. It was Natalie. The rancher had quickly called the authorities. Her car was found inside Sam Houston National Forest. It was processed by forensics and came up clean.

According to Cabby Baptist, he had taken Natalie to his parents' cabin, where they ate, chatted, and made out for a few hours before he had walked her back to the car. He swore it was both innocent and consensual. Unfortunately, the evidence was on his side, as a hidden wildlife camera set up by the forest service captured Natalie's car leaving his house around the time given in his statement. His DNA was found on her body, but there was no forensic evidence of his having been in or around her vehicle. The footprints next to the creek bank did not match his shoe size.

Cabby Baptist boasted a clean record. During his interview, it was noted that his hands showed no sign of a struggle. There was also the question of motive: Why would Cabby let her leave his house only to chase her down and murder her later? It made no sense. Everything had happened so late at night that there were no other witnesses to confirm or deny his claim. Cabby had not been ruled out as a suspect, but the evidence was not strong enough to bring charges. After an exhaustive search, the murder was still listed as unsolved. The once-hungry press quickly lost interest, as was sadly the case when a black girl was murdered.

Thea had seen Cabby once, at the police station, his dark eyes staring soullessly down the hallway, slumped over and looking distressed. But when he had walked past Thea with his lawyers, he had given her a knowing smile. It had to have been him. No one else had been with her. It was him; Thea could feel in her heart that he had gotten away with murder.

The week after she heard the news had passed in a dreadful, dark blur, where Thea wondered if she had been the one who died. Everything was a terrible dream that just kept on going: the funeral at a local Methodist church, the closed casket at the front of the aisle, the stench of yellow Asiatic lilies permeating the air, Thea's father struggling with the casket on his shoulder, his sobs loud enough for everyone to hear. The dim church, everyone hugging Thea and telling her how sorry they were, the very fabric of her black dress making her feel like she wanted to peel off her skin. Thea had made it through the funeral before running away from the procession out of the sanctuary, her tears blinding her as she ran all the way home. Her mom had found her lying facedown on Natalie's front porch and cradled her in her arms, both of them sobbing together, unabashed and ugly. *Cathartic.* Thea had focused only on making it through the week, not knowing that the wasteland of grief awaited her on the other side.

Thea had heard nothing about Cabby Baptist in the months that followed, but every time she saw a white truck, her heart seemed to stop. She hadn't told her parents because she knew they couldn't handle the stress of it. They were already hanging by a thread emotionally, and the last thing she wanted was for them to worry more about her. She was cocooned in a shell of her own fear, Xanax her only friend.

Now, back in her bed, she turned over and protectively clutched her arms across her chest, repeating the words to herself: "It was not his truck. It was not his truck."

Instead of thinking about it, she chose to focus on the strength she had felt today, the burning power that permeated the air at Mademoiselle Corday. She felt her breathing return to normal and her hazel eyes popped open. She wouldn't be afraid anymore. No, it was Cabby Baptist who should be afraid. The day she earned her inheritance, she would gather Team Banner—messy as they were right now—and take back what Cabby Baptist had taken from her. She would destroy him.

NINE

The next day, after her last class concluded, Thea made her way through the Roosevelt High cafeteria. Her hands clutched nervously as she approached Mirabelle Watts and her groupies, girls who loved to throw barbs at anyone who dared walk past their table. No one really walked there. Except Thea. Right now. She approached the table. Mirabelle was talking to Jacinda Norton, her hands fluttering wildly around her.

Thea pulled her backpack up onto her shoulder. "Mirabelle, I need to talk to you."

Mirabelle narrowed her ice-blue eyes. "I'm busy. Come back never." She waved her hand dismissively.

She is so ridiculous. Annoyance at Mirabelle's airs lit a fire in her stomach and Thea decided to project her voice. "Okay, but it's about the Historical Society for the Restoration of Victorian Houses."

Jacinda looked from Mirabelle to Thea and back again. "What the hell is she talking about?"

"Nothing. She's crazy! I'll be right back." Mirabelle leaped from her table, hissing "Shut up!" in Thea's ear.

Do. Not. Punch, Thea thought.

Mirabelle marched Thea out of the cafeteria and into an empty stairwell. After checking the area for any stray students, she wheeled on her teammate, grabbing her arm. "What are you doing? You can't talk about that out there!"

Thea raised her hand and carefully brushed Mirabelle's silver-gelled nails off her arm. "I know. But how else could I get you to leave your stimulating conversation?"

"As if I care what you think of me."

"Of course not. But who cares what anyone thinks here?" Thea gestured around her, where posters of motivational quotes covered with occasional graffiti decorated the walls of the hallway. "Aren't you tired of *here*? Of that? Of gossip and being mean?" Thea dropped her voice to a whisper. "The Black Coats offer you so much more than this! Why wouldn't you want to be a part of that?"

Mirabelle shrugged before sitting down on one of the steps with a pout. "I don't know. The team doesn't seem like it needs me." She paused. "Or even likes me, for that matter."

We don't, thought Thea meanly, but instead she sat down beside her. "Nixon picked you for a reason. Don't you want to do something exciting? Do something that matters? Mirabelle . . ." Thea looked into her eyes. "What happened to you that made you angry like this?"

Mirabelle blinked, the sunlight casting a rusty glare on her lovely face. Beneath the perfect veneer, Thea saw a glimmer of pain and felt a surprising rush of compassion. She was right—there was a reason Mirabelle was in the Black Coats.

Mirabelle wouldn't meet her gaze. "Did you know that my parents aren't actually my parents?" Her truth echoed painfully in the stairwell. Thea didn't know what to say as Mirabelle curled in, her arms clenched around her stomach.

"I was six when they died in a car accident on Highway Thirty-Five. They were coming back from furniture shopping. They were really into antiques, and there's a dealer way out of town. They bought a hutch. It was in the back of their truck." She paused. Thea's heart seemed to slow in her chest, her agony recognizing another's. Grief calling to deep grief. "Marc Mitzi was his name, and he was very drunk. Two prior DUIs and let out on technicalities. He was so drunk that the accident report says he didn't even know what happened. Thought he hit a deer." Tears rolled down her face, carving rivers of black mascara through her contoured cheeks. "It wasn't a deer. It was a hutch, shoved through the front seat."

Thea shuddered and reached out for Mirabelle's shoulder. "Don't touch me!" she snapped. "I don't need your pity." Thea pulled her hand back, Mirabelle's anger burning like a flame. "I've been raised by my aunt and uncle. They're nice people, and they've given me every single thing I've ever wanted. But they aren't my parents. They don't *love* like parents."

Thea felt shame. She had always assumed that Mirabelle's mother and father, real estate agents whose glistening smiles graced bus stops and billboards, were her real parents. It was staggering just how little she really knew about her fellow students.

Mirabelle sniffed. "The worst thing is that I was just old enough to remember what my parents were like. I may not remember their faces that clearly, but I remember the love, the feeling of being safe. I remember being part of a real family."

Thea felt the words rise up in her throat. "Then come be a part of the—" She paused. "The Historical Society for the Restoration of Victorian Houses."

Mirabelle looked up at her and they both burst out laughing. She wiped her tears away with a flick of her hands. "It really is the most ridiculous name."

Thea smiled. "I don't know. I kind of like it."

"You would."

Thea leaned in toward Mirabelle. "Come back. Just for today. Give it one more shot. I know you don't feel like you fit in with us the way you fit in there." Her eyes darted toward the cafeteria. "But maybe it's time to let those hungry girls take your place. Breathe. Be uncool for a while." She grabbed Mirabelle's hand. *"Fight back."*

Mirabelle stared at her for a long moment. "Fine. I'll come." She stood up, her golden curls cascading over her shoulder. Then she wiped her eyes carefully. "Don't tell the other girls about this conversation. Or Nixon."

"I won't."

Mirabelle blinked as if waking up. "One condition. If by some miracle we become friends—will you let me help you?"

Thea frowned. "What do you mean?"

Mirabelle gestured to Thea's outfit: jeans, gray flats, and a yellow-and-white long-sleeved T-shirt. "I mean this. What is this even? You're really quite pretty, and if you just tried a little bit more, you could be on a totally different level."

Mirabelle Watts, everyone, thought Thea. She shrugged. "Fine."

"It would probably make sense for us to drive together, after school, to the society."

Thea paused for a second before reaching out to awkwardly hug Mirabelle.

Mirabelle straightened up, her arms rigid. "We don't have to do that."

"Okay. It just seemed like maybe you needed one."

Mirabelle squared her shoulders. "What I need to do is punch some dudes who punch women." She sighed. "I'll ditch this period and meet you by my car in five minutes. Don't touch it." As she walked back into the cafeteria, Thea saw a familiar face heading her way.

Drew's eyes lit up when he saw Thea. "Oh, hey, Thea! I've been looking everywhere for you." Thea exhaled as Drew approached, wide-eyed. "Why were you talking to Mirabelle Watts? She's kind of the worst."

"She's okay, actually." Thea shyly tucked back a piece of her hair as she remembered the hurt on Mirabelle's face, her words echoing in her head. *They don't* love *like parents.*

Drew didn't notice her pause and continued. "So, what should we do this weekend?"

Thea blinked. "Oh, right, our date!" Drew's face fell so dramatically that she couldn't help but laugh. "I'm sorry. I'm excited for it."

His mouth fell open. "Yeah, it seems that way. Don't lie. You forgot about it! I can tell. I'm trained to detect lies that tumble out of the mouths of beautiful girls."

"Is that right?"

He puffed out his chest. "I'm pretty impressive in general. Definitely the type of guy you should remember you have a date with."

Thea nodded kindly. "You're absolutely right. Tomorrow?"

The corners of his wide mouth turned upward, dazzling Thea with his playful, confident grin.

Thea Soloman, she instructed, *do not fall all over yourself.*

She practically floated down the stairs to the parking lot, where Mirabelle was waiting for her in front of the school, her silver Audi convertible purring as it idled. "Come on, come on!" Mirabelle called.

Thea didn't have time to think about it, so she leaped over the side of the car, her backpack landing with a thud at her feet. Her butt had barely touched the ridiculously soft leather when Mirabelle shot forward, the car thundering beneath them. Mirabelle deftly wound them to the highway, and as soon as its wheels hit the pavement, the car practically flew. Thea's curls tumbled wildly in front of her eyes as she struggled to find a hair tie in her bag. "How fast are you going?" she struggled to yell over the roar of the wind.

Mirabelle smiled. "You don't want to know!" she yelled back, gripping the wheel. They passed every single car in front of them, the Audi roaring as it flitted around them, light as air. "I still don't know if I'm going to stay," Mirabelle shouted. "This whole thing is kind of . . ."

"Don't say lame," snapped Thea. "Because it's a lot of things, but it's definitely not lame."

Mirabelle paused for a moment, her blond hair blustering around her head in a halo. "Yeah. It's not lame."

They settled into silence then, the car shooting past the muddy brown fields and bright yellow flowers that blurred in the sun. Before Thea could even relax into the moment, they were pulling up at Mademoiselle Corday. "No wonder you got here so long before me last time," she muttered.

Her legs felt like Jell-O as they uncurled themselves from the car.

Mirabelle looked totally unfazed as she reglossed her lips a peachy pink in the mirror. "Well, at least you can run fast. Or so I've heard." She smacked her lips. "Besides, it's not like you could even go that fast with that piece-of-shit car." With that, she bounced past Thea and through the door of Mademoiselle Corday.

"Just when I start to like you," Thea called after her, "you say something like that." Mirabelle's hand beckoned her from inside the door. Thea dutifully followed, the hint of a smile on her face.

Nixon appeared before they could even make it inside the foyer. "Nice of you to join us, ladies. Mirabelle, are you planning on staying for our entire session today?"

Mirabelle bit her lip, a witty retort no doubt dying on the tip of her tongue. Instead, she nodded. "Yes, ma'am."

"I'm glad to hear it. Don't bother heading to the classroom; we are starting today with individual training and will finish up there afterward. Thea, please head to room thirteen. It's on the lowest level, in the south wing, tucked back toward the end of the hallway. Mirabelle, follow me."

Nixon stalked away from her without a word. Her heart giving a nervous beat, Thea shouldered her bag and headed into the house, wondering what could possibly be in store for her this time.

TEN

Following the room numbers, Thea made her way through the house, marveling at each little touch: a framed painting of an old plantation, a big copper sink functioning as a planter, an antique ladder dangling with small glass bulbs. Deciding to err on the side of caution, Thea ducked into a restroom, smiling at the tin ceiling. Even the bathrooms were lush. She was washing her hands at the sink when the door banged open. Thea jumped as a cluster of girls wearing black leggings and black T-shirts spilled into the restroom. Their voices echoed in the space.

"I still haven't gotten the blood out of my pants from Craig Allen's Balancing last week."

"Try white vinegar, that's what I use."

The girls stopped short when Thea stepped out from behind the sink. Her hands dripping water, she tried to slip past the girls in the narrow restroom.

"Excuse me," she said politely. A solid body stepped in front of her.

"Thea, right?" The voice was older, the woman obviously a president. She was in her midthirties, with huge blue-green eyes and short, chin-length curly hair, striped the color of chestnuts. While shorter than Nixon, it was obvious that she was strong: her muscles pushed against her black shirt, and when she roughly grasped Thea's shoulders to let her team pass by, Thea could feel the strength of her grip.

She swallowed nervously. "Yes, I'm Thea."

"How are things going over at Team Banner?"

"Okay." Thea wanted to wriggle away but instead stood taller. "Actually, better than okay. I was just on my way to individual training."

One of the other girls stepped forward, tossing back her curly black hair. She smiled cruelly, black eyes flashing. "Banner is a team of freaks and spares. What a joke."

The president raised her hand, silencing the girl, who reminded Thea of a barking Doberman. "Valentina. Hush." She circled Thea. "How's your president doing? This is her first team, after all. Nixon, Robin's favorite little pet."

Nixon appeared in the doorway to the bathroom. "I heard my name. Team Emperor, always nice to see you." Her tone expressed a different view. She nodded to their president, who let go of Thea's shoulders with a parting squeeze. "Kennedy."

"Nixon."

In her mind, Thea imagined the tension between them shattering the ceramic subway tiles, but nothing changed. Kennedy leveled her gaze at Thea.

Thea ducked her head. "I'll, uh, be on my way, I guess." Valentina practically hissed at her as she passed.

Behind her, she heard Nixon snap at Kennedy, "Don't speak to my girls unless I give permission. Is that clear?"

Kennedy mumbled something in return that Thea couldn't make out.

Nixon clicked out of the bathroom. "Have a great day, Team Emperor."

Thea smiled to herself. Their team might not be excellent yet, but at least they had Nixon.

She made her way down the hallways, winding deeper into the house. Room eleven was some sort of sitting parlor, and twelve held nothing other than two very deep claw-footed tubs filled with ice baths. Thea shuddered— she knew those all too well from her time in track. She let her fingers trail the walls until finally the plaque appeared: *Room 13.*

It was at the end of the wing, in a dark corner with no other doors around it. Thea knocked. No one answered. She knocked again, harder this time, and there was only the sound of the wind behind it. *The wind?* Thea pushed open the door and gasped.

In front of her stretched an open field. Her feet and

body were in the house still, but if she stretched out her arm, dots of uninterrupted sunlight brushed her skin. Thea couldn't help the stupid grin plastered across her face. Nothing in this house was what it seemed, and room thirteen was nothing more than a door that opened directly to the outside of the house. As she stood in the doorway, a blur of white flashed in her peripheral vision.

Sahil appeared in front of her, pacing back and forth about fifty feet from where she stood. His white linen pants brushed a very expensive pair of neon track sneakers and he was wearing a backpack. Thea looked down and saw a pair of sneakers waiting at her feet—black, marked with gray lightning bolts, just the right size. A spark traveled up through her legs, shaking her whole body with excitement. Sahil's eyes met hers, and the intention was communicated wordlessly. Unable to stop smiling, Thea slipped off her black ballet flats and pushed her feet into the sneakers, her heart pounding. She rolled up the leggings over her brown shins and smoothed the curls back from her forehead. Then she stepped off the hardwood floor and out onto the dirt. The woods were silent for a moment as they stared at each other.

"Catch me," yelled Sahil.

Thea rested her hands on her hips. "Really?"

Sahil beckoned to her and gave her a wicked smile. "If you can." Then he darted out into the field.

Thea flew after him like a bullet from a gun, her muscles

hard at first but gathering warmth as they moved, heat expanding with each step. Then with an amazing surge, they shook off their sleepiness and propelled Thea forward, away from the house. The field blurred beneath her feet as her adrenaline released. Her steps fell into a pace, moving faster and faster, becoming automatic. With each breath, her brain disconnected from her body until she was one with her legs, with her speed and rhythm. Her vision tunneled until everything else was pushed away, and then it was only her and the hard ground and Sahil, tearing away from her through the trees.

God, I love running. She had forgotten the thrill of the chase, the sense of competition that forced her body to rise out of herself and overcome physical pain as she came ever closer to her goal. It was as if she were watching herself from above.

An old dead tree with branches crumbling like bone lay in her path. Thea vaulted over it, her sneakers sending whirls of dirt into the air. Sahil was now only maybe a hundred feet in front of her but moving fast. He was *really* fast. She closed her eyes for a brief second before they entered a swath of trees, loving the warm air rushing past her face. She forced her legs to keep their furious sprint as she shot into the forest, her anticipation at catching him growing. *Closer now.* Her feet thudded across the ground, her mind reaching for something she had intentionally pushed away, a memory that she had locked up inside.

She is running. It is late October, and yellow leaves are filtering down to the ground in lazy circles. She is eight years old. Natalie, two years her elder, is ahead of her, always ahead of her, her hair bouncing behind her as she laughs gaily. "Chase me, Thea!" she screams. Like a ghost, she flies through the grass, almost floating in her pale pink party dress now splattered with mud. "Chase me!"

Without warning, Natalie comes to a screeching halt and Thea runs square into her back, sending them both tumbling forward.

"You okay?" Thea asks, giggling.

"Yeah." Natalie sits up, a branch stuck in her frizzy curls. "Ew, Thea, look!" They carefully crawl over the leaves to where a dead bat stares at the sky. Its wide eyes are pulling back into its head, and its rubbery wings are outstretched, like some sort of macabre sacrifice. Tiny insects are buzzing around its feet. Natalie is fascinated and pokes it with a stick. Thea is scared.

"Let's go home, Natalie. Come on!" She yanks at her arm, but Natalie turns to her with wide eyes.

"But, Thea, he needs to be buried!"

Thea is scared, though, and she runs away from Natalie, leaving her alone in the woods as she runs for the house.

Thea blinked. She was back in the woods now, the trees passing overhead, their spindly arms reaching for her. She ducked under a low-hanging branch, Sahil no more than fifty feet away from her. She pressed out from her core, pushing the memory far from her, pressing only her legs to move faster. *Catch me*, she heard Natalie whisper. A hill rose in front of her, and she crested it easily, soaring over the dry clumps of leaves that littered her path. Sahil was now at the bottom of the hill, so close to her. Thea plunged recklessly down it, her brain connecting a second too late: *I'm going too fast. I'm going to crash!* He was right there in front of her, and she reached out, brushing Sahil's collar with her fingertips. He stepped quickly aside. Moving too fast to stop, Thea's legs cycled and turned and suddenly she was flying through the air, her body gathering momentum as she rolled down the hill. Something violently slammed into her side as she rolled over a rocky outcrop, and her face punched into a thorny bush. Head over heels she rolled three times before her body came to a wheezing stop, her heart racing so loud inside her chest that they could probably hear it at Mademoiselle Corday. Thea rolled over and gave a painful groan. "Oh God. That hurt."

Thea brushed off her bloody hands, which were pricked with pieces of dirt and the occasional thorn, and pushed up to her knees. She felt a blush rise up her face and wasn't sure what hurt more: her aching side or the embarrassment at going ass-over-teakettle in front of Sahil, who was now crouched above her. He wasn't even breathing hard. *Asshole.*

"Thea, are you all right?"

With a shaking hand, she reached out and wearily patted his shoe. "Tag. You're it."

He grinned. "Here, have a drink of water." He handed her a water bottle, and Thea accepted it gratefully before taking a drink and climbing shakily to her feet. Both knees were dripping blood as she handed back the water bottle. Sahil reached into his pocket and pulled out a white cloth. Thea smiled. "It's white. Of course."

He shrugged. "Of course. I must be set apart from the Black Coats in a visual way. I am a part of them, but not one of them. Here, sit down. Let me tend to those wounds."

"I don't think you need white to set you apart, exactly. You're the only male in the whole house."

"This is true."

Thea accepted his outstretched hand and let him lead her over to a narrow tree stump. Thea sat down with a sigh, flexing her long legs and rotating her ankle. "I think I'm okay."

"It is still important to treat wounds as they happen." He crouched before her and traced his hand gently over her shin and under her knee. He reached into his pocket and pulled out a couple of Band-Aids. After putting two little ones over her bleeding wounds, his hands traced again down underneath her shin, squeezing her muscles, kneading them, checking her knees and ankles.

"My legs feel fine."

"Well, take a rest, take another drink, and we will resume in a moment."

Thea groaned. He was obviously not interested, but a little crush was probably inevitable. She surely wasn't the first one to notice him. "Really? Again?"

"You did not complete your task. You were supposed to

catch me, and you did not."

"I kind of did. I mean, I almost did," Thea shamefully answered.

"Almost does not mean anything in this world. You either deliver justice or you fail."

"That is very black-and-white."

"Justice must be; otherwise, it becomes impossible."

Thea raised her head to look skeptically at his face. "Sahil, seriously, who *are* you?"

He shrugged. "I am no one important."

Thea narrowed her eyes. "That's not true. Do you live at Mademoiselle Corday?"

He nodded. "I do. I live in the south wing, just above the Haunt."

"Do you go to school?"

Sahil smiled at her curiosity but didn't say anything. Thea wiped the sweat off her brow. "I'm sorry. I'm just curious. What kind of person lets a bunch of girls beat on him just so that they can gain entry into a society that beats up other men?"

Sahil's smile disappeared. "The kind of person who was born to believe in the cause."

Thea rolled her shoulders, feeling the muscles cramping from her recent tumble. "You avoided my question. Do you go to school?"

"I am homeschooled, here at the house. And before you make assumptions about that, you should know that I am probably smarter than you."

Thea shook her head. "Of that I have no doubt. I go to Roosevelt."

Sahil laughed, a careful sound, as if he didn't laugh often. "Oh, that is not a great school."

Sahil shifted his weight back and forth, his body tightly wound. He reminded Thea of a panther. "How do they feel now? Your ankles?"

Thea tested her ankles; there was no pain. She was stronger than she thought. "I think I'm okay," she said, a little surprised.

"Great! Now let's talk about what to do when you do actually catch someone. You need to know some fast disarming techniques. You almost grabbed me by the collar, which was a horrible idea. If you would have done that, you would have attached yourself to me at my speed and when my feet get yanked out from under me . . ." Suddenly, he was behind her, pulling back on her collar.

Thea couldn't breathe, but he was prattling on like nothing had happened.

"Now, instead of yanking on a coat or a collar, which he can easily slip out of and will also pull you off-balance, pretend you are a defensive lineman on a football team."

Thea grinned. "I have no idea what that means."

"Run from me," he ordered.

Thea had taken three quick steps before she felt his hands close around her waist. Then she was pushed violently forward into the ground. "Use your forward momentum," he explained, "to subdue your subject quickly. You will have a few seconds to take advantage of his discombobulation. Then you begin processing him just as you would any other subject, applying the self-defense techniques you will be learning with Nixon."

Thea's face was pushed up against the dirt, and she had a leaf in the corner of her mouth. She was embarrassed at how easy she had been to take down, and feeling feisty. "*Discombobulation* is a pretty big word for a homeschooled kid," she spat.

Sahil roughly set her back on her feet. "And you are pretty slow for a track star. You need to be training more at home." Sahil crouched down. "Now I am going to run back to Mademoiselle Corday. It is getting late. You will chase me, and you will catch me this time, because you are going to run from here"—he reached down and patted her legs—"and not from here." He tapped her head. "You cannot move forward when you are stuck somewhere else. Grief can hold you back from the places you are meant to go. It is something you will always carry with you, but something you must also leave behind."

Thea sighed. "Thanks, Yoda."

Sahil turned his back to her. "I am tasked with unleashing a fast-and-furious Thea, so you will listen to my words. Also, once again, make sure you look at your surroundings when you are running. That is how you fell, by not being aware of the changing landscape."

Thea barely heard him speaking as she focused on the strength pulsing in her legs and in her lungs. She would catch him. She had to. He left her side without another word, plunging away from her. With a deep breath, Thea Soloman let the memory of Natalie and the bat float away from her like a balloon into the sky.

Then she flew.

ELEVEN

"Crap." Thea's eyeliner wasn't going on straight. In fact, every time she tried to do a smoky eye she ended up looking like a sloppy version of Cleopatra. Her mom had bought her all new makeup for her date, unable to contain her embarrassing, over-the-top joy that Thea was going out with a boy—*a soccer player!* Instead of trying again, Thea hastily wiped her eyes with a cloth, dashed on her new mascara, and dotted her cheeks with a pale cherry blush before heading downstairs.

Her parents were waiting in the foyer, trying to look busy—her dad tapping on his tablet, her mom pretending to rearrange some yellow roses in a mercury vase. Thea sighed as she straightened her navy dress and threw a pair of turquoise bangles in her ears. "You guys. Seriously. I'm not going to prom." Thea raised her hands in surrender. "Everyone in this house needs to calm down and eat some protein."

Her dad looked dejected.

"Will you at least go linger in the kitchen like normal parents? You can easily spy on us from there."

They smiled and dutifully retreated. "I'll be watching," her mom called out.

Outside, a car door slammed, and Thea's heart turned nervously. "Okay! Go!" she hissed at her parents, shooing them away.

She opened the door. Drew gave her an easy smile, leaning against the side of her door. He looked her up and down approvingly. "A dress!" He whistled. "I'm speechless."

"I can't believe that's ever true," retorted Thea. He didn't look so bad himself: tight dark jeans showed off his long legs, and his white linen button-down was just snug enough to frame his chest. The white of the shirt set off his gorgeous olive eyes, though Thea thought there was something different about him. She couldn't put her finger on it.

He held a bouquet of tiny pink and black flowers in one hand. "The florist said these are called anemones. They seemed just right for a girl who probably doesn't love daisies."

"Err, thank you." She glanced up at him with a laugh, finally realizing what was different about him: "You're wearing glasses!" Chunky brown frames sat on the edge of his nose. He rocked back on his feet.

"Ah, yeah. I wear contacts at school, for soccer of course, but on the weekends, my eyes need a break. Are they, um, okay?"

Thea nodded. She liked them. Like, she *really* liked them. He wiggled his eyebrows. "I think they make me look like the guy who never gets the girl in all those vampire books."

Thea took the flowers to the kitchen, where her parents were hiding, and then returned, sliding past Drew to pull the door shut behind them. The night was lovely. A golden sun shimmered against the horizon, throwing long trails of lavender across a dark blue sky. Thea took a breath, willing her nerves to be still. They climbed into Drew's green truck. "So . . . where are you taking me?"

Drew grinned, buckling his seat belt. "After this date, you are either going to be mad about me or never want to talk to me again." Drew rubbed the stubble on his chin as Thea admired his strong profile.

"I'm honestly up for anything," Thea said quietly. Drew nodded once and shifted the truck into high gear as they turned off her street. A white pickup passed them, and Thea sucked in her breath until she saw that an older woman sat behind the wheel.

"What is it?"

She shook her head. "It's nothing."

A change of subject was needed. After a fierce debate in her mind, Thea laid her hand carefully on Drew's. His eyes lit up, but he remained steady, a confident smile lifting the corners of his mouth. Drew turned toward Thea. "So I have to ask: Where do you rush off to after school? I saw you running like a lunatic after Mirabelle Watts the other day.

Why would you do that to yourself?"

"She's not that . . ." Her words trailed off. "Okay, she's kind of bad, but she grows on you."

Drew grinned again. "Not unlike a fungus."

Thea skillfully avoided his question and their conversation continued, light and easy, as Drew drove through the creeping twilight. He turned to her, his olive eyes kind. "So since we're almost there, I feel like you need some history on where I am taking you. My dad knows this weird guy who lives outside Austin. He's been arrested a bunch of times, but only recently for public drunkenness and nudity."

"This," deadpanned Thea, "is already the most romantic date I've ever been on."

"I aim to please. Anyway, he owns a museum downtown. The shady end. It's a museum of weird things." Thea burst out laughing. "It's called Harry's Peculiarium." Drew turned the truck down a dark alley. "I know this seems like I'm taking you somewhere to murder you—" He stopped his sentence as soon as the words were out of his mouth. "Oh, Thea, I'm so sorry. Oh God, I didn't mean that. I don't know why I said that."

I know why, thought Thea. *Because you were making a normal joke like normal people do until you remembered that they found my cousin floating in a creek.* Thea took a deep breath, choosing to smile through the sudden threat of tears. "It's okay. I know what you meant. Go on; tell me more about this weird museum."

"No need to tell. It's right there." Drew parked the car

and pointed through the windshield smeared with a fine layer of brown dust. Small puddles in the alleyway reflected a buzzing neon sign glowing a sickly green: *Harry's Peculiarium*. Thea leaned forward and looked through the windshield. "I'm already intrigued."

"Oh, just you wait." Drew hopped out of the car and came around to her side, helping her down from the massive truck. They ran through the puddles, splashing their way to the door. Drew knocked and then looked at her with a shrug. "I told you this was going to be a weird date."

Thea started laughing, but she stopped when she saw an old man peek through a window. He was heavyset, with greasy white hair that flew in all directions. Above his askew collar a cragged face reflected a long and troubled life. Still, his cloudy eyes lit up when he saw Drew and Thea and his trembling hands reached for the lock.

His raspy voice sounded painful as it passed through his cracked lips. "Hello! Come in! Drew, you brought a girl!"

"Yes, Harry. I brought a girl. Try not to be so shocked."

Harry looked Thea up and down as Thea braced herself for the worst. More common than it should have been, the older generation down here sometimes had a terrible reaction to mixed-race couples. Remnants of racism tended to float through supposedly liberal Austin like dust in the air of an empty house.

Harry paused, his eyes tracing Thea's features before his face exploded into an ecstatic grin. "And she's a lovely one! Together, you will make beautiful babies!"

Drew winced. "Oh my God, Harry, stop."

"Okay, I'm sorry. I had to say it. Come on in."

Thea ducked under Drew's arm and into the tight corners of the cluttered, musty shop. The lighting was dim, and she had to squint to see the corners of the room.

"Well, I'll let Drew give you the tour. God knows he spends enough time here, sadly waiting for his father to come home from saving the world, the poor kid."

Drew rolled his eyes. "Okay, that's enough of that conversation. Maybe next we can talk about my awkward moments during puberty." He turned back to Thea. "Now, shall we?"

Thea grinned. "Please." She was dying to see what was in here.

Drew lowered his voice and leaned forward, his lips brushing her ear. "Welcome to the *weirdest* shit you've ever seen."

The museum itself was just two floors, not much larger than one of Thea's classrooms; still, there were oddities crammed into every available space. Thea and Drew's casual banter fell away as they both succumbed to piqued curiosity. Hanging skeletons, their jaws hinged open, seemed to laugh at the pair as they slowly made their way through the peculiarium. There were the skulls of nomads and balls of bright wax carved to look like miniature brains, as well as a book covered in skin that Thea knew she would see in her nightmares. Not everything was macabre; in one corner alone there were old bottles filled with antique potions promising remedies for "the lady's monthly madness," a collection of large insects forever preserved in glass jars filled with resin, and a torturous-looking device used for childbirth in the 1830s. Each shelf promised weird and fascinating discoveries, and Thea lost herself in the strange items, her reflection distorted in a large glass pane that protected a two-headed taxidermic calf. The ceiling was covered with hanging black butterflies, each one pinned so that they looked menacingly down upon the guests.

"How have I never heard about this place?" Thea wondered aloud, watching the butterflies spin lazily in the air-conditioning.

Drew shrugged as he ran his fingers over a large banana sculpture with an alien erupting out of the center. "It's not really a place they tell tourists to visit. The neighborhood has gone to hell, but Harry has stayed. When he goes, all the stuff will go, too." His face fell, and he ran his foot over the floor. "Although, I'm personally hoping that I get the lobotomy set with matching skull."

She looked over and drank him in: hands shoved deep in his pockets, green eyes lingering on the aluminum spaceship that dangled overhead. She felt propelled toward him, as if he had a gravitational pull all his own. She wanted to be close to him. She wanted to lose herself in this funny ray of sunshine who also smelled *really* good.

"Thea, wait until you see—" He stopped talking when he felt her hands on his face and gently turned it to hers.

Mopey hall-ghost Thea Soloman would have never done this before, not even before Natalie. But something about being in the Black Coats was making her bolder. *Why shouldn't I kiss him when I want to? Why wait for him when this is what I want?*

He paused for a moment before clenching his hands around her waist. He bent down, pressing his mouth hungrily over hers. Light exploded in her vision. His lips were soft, and his mouth tasted of mint. His thumbs softly caressed her cheekbones, his tongue teasing across her bottom lip. Everything faded from her recent memory: the Black Coats, Natalie, her parents, this weird museum. There was only Drew and the way his strong body pressed against hers, the way his hair was falling over her forehead.

His kiss was gentle but wanting, and she could tell he was losing himself in the same way she was. His breath was warm as it passed over her mouth. Thea let her hands crawl up the back of his shirt, the cotton fabric starched and rigid. Drew pulled back before diving in to kiss her again, more passionately this time, this one unafraid. She lost track of time. There was only his mouth on hers, happiness glowing out from every pore. She hadn't felt this way in so long, if ever. Finally, he pulled back with a gasp. Thea looked up at him and started laughing. His glasses were fogged up. Drew let out a long breath, his hands tangling up in her hair, his lips moving from her mouth to her cheek to her neck. He moaned. "Wow. Okay. That was amazing."

He pulled her into a hug and Thea buried herself in the

crook of his hard shoulder, suddenly embarrassed at her boldness. "Sorry. I should have . . ." *I should have let you kiss me first.*

"No. Somehow that was just perfect." He grinned. "Also, we had an audience." Thea turned. On the shelf in front of her, a terrifying doll peered out at them from a wooden bed.

"Oh. That's kind of awkward." Thea grimaced.

Drew reached out with a laugh and spun the clown around to face the other way. "We probably made his day." Slowly, Drew pushed her hair back from her face, his eyes never leaving hers.

"Well, you made mine," said a strange voice from a few shelves away.

"Go away, Harry," Drew said, not moving an inch.

The old man peeked up from behind the shelf before shuffling back to his desk. "It's not often we have people swapping spit in here. Just sayin'. . . ."

Thea closed her eyes. "Annnd there goes the moment."

Drew laughed. "Well, there's still the entire second level of this place." His eyes widened. "We could try it again in front of the stuffed otter upstairs. He's wearing a fedora and holding a machete."

"Take me there immediately," laughed Thea. Holding hands, they headed upstairs, where more oddities awaited them, as well as a few more kisses, each one longer than the last.

TWELVE

The rest of the month passed in a blur. Turning five separate girls into one functioning Team Banner made the days bleed together into an insane mix of running, martial arts, and lectures.

Thankfully, it was a Friday, and they were almost done at Mademoiselle Corday.

Nixon poked her head into the classroom. "Team Banner, meet me in the Haunt. Ten minutes."

The group let out a loud groan. The Haunt meant more physical training, and Thea already felt like her muscles were wiggly noodles.

Nixon shot them a look that could freeze ice. "Anyone want to complain?"

"No, ma'am," Team Banner echoed back. Mirabelle blew a strand of flaxen hair out of her eyes. "I already sparred with Nixon for an hour today."

"Did you win?" snapped Casey sarcastically from her normal perch atop a desk.

"Almost," Mirabelle replied. "But if I have to do it again, I'm just going to run through the greenhouse glass screaming."

Louise curled her arm underneath Mirabelle's. "I'll take her for you."

Mirabelle rolled her eyes. "Thanks for the help. I give you three seconds before she has your face in the mat."

"Five seconds, but this time I won't cry," said Louise.

Mirabelle grinned. "Deal." They shook on it as Team Banner began making their way down the long hallways.

Thea watched them with a smile as she hung back, noting the way Bea casually laced her arm through Louise's, the way Casey yanked on Mirabelle's ponytail when she wasn't looking. The tethers of their individuality were fraying, and a quilt of differing abilities was finally coming together. Team Banner was getting there, one day at a time. *There is a strange magic to this particular group*, thought Thea. *We are healing ourselves.*

Thea was the last one through the doors of the Haunt, the heavy wood slamming shut behind her. The lights were off, an oddity, and Team Banner froze, immediately sure that something was not right in the swallowing darkness.

"Is Nixon going to jump us?" Bea's words faded out. Night fell early this time of year, and through the wavy glass of the greenhouse, Thea could make out the bright light of the moon. Dozens of figures melted out of the shadows and made their way toward the girls. Their hands unfolded and lit candles peeked out of the darkness. Thea saw the illuminated figures of young and old women, each clad in a black coat. Team Banner instinctively clustered together. Julie Westing watched them silently, her wolfish face lit by a golden glow.

"I knew it!" hissed Mirabelle, with a tremble of fear in her normally bold voice. "They are going to sacrifice us for our virgin blood."

"Tell the rest of the world we'll miss them," Casey whispered drily.

Nixon stepped into the moonlight, her black coat turned up at the collar and a dripping beeswax candle in her hand. "Team Banner, step forward."

The girls approached her cautiously, Thea first, and the rest of them following behind her. Nixon held out her hand, bright red lips flickering like wet blood in the candlelight. Their president raised her voice. "Team Banner, over the last few weeks, I believe, has proven themselves worthy of calling themselves Black Coats. They are admirable in their devotion, fierce in their individual training, and noble in their intent to serve the Black Coats with utter loyalty." An amused cough echoed out from the corner. Nixon's glance flitted to where Kennedy and Team Emperor watched silently from the wings, their arms folded skeptically over their chests. Nixon's mouth twisted, but her voice remained steady. "I'll ask you one time. Are you ladies ready to join the Black Coats?"

"Yes, ma'am," they replied in unison.

"Good. There is, however, one thing you must do before you are initiated fully into this society." Thea's pulse raced as Nixon stepped toward them, her voice echoing across the dark expanse of the Haunt. "What if I told you that one of the members of Team Banner was put on to your team as a test? That she was a plant. You may know her as the one who isn't essential to your group."

Thea's mouth fell open. "What?"

Nixon was in front of her now. "Quickly now, Team Banner. Who is it? All your lessons have been leading up to this, all those psychology lessons, all those criminology studies. I have laid out every possible way to find the wolf in sheep's clothing among you. Who is your weakest team member?" Only her sharpest features were lit in the wavering flame.

Mirabelle stepped forward, pointing her finger at Casey. "It's her. It has to be. How much do we need a driver?"

Casey shot daggers at Mirabelle. "I'm not just a driver. I'm a hacker! And I was going to say you. What do you really add to the team? Thea is pretty enough to be 'the face,' and you . . ."

Louise frowned. "I was actually going to say that maybe Thea is the most useless. What does fast do for us?" She gave Thea a sympathetic look. "Sorry, Thea. I like you a lot."

Thea let their voices circle around her, her jumbled thoughts blocking out the accusations. Feelings were being hurt. Bea was almost in tears. *They want to tear us apart.* Thea stepped out of their circle, waving her hands.

"No," she declared loudly. "No. Stop! We've been through so much together. It's not about whose gift is the most useful or the most coveted. It's about how we work together. Each gift in itself isn't enough."

"I agree," whispered Bea. What had Nixon been telling them? Over and over again? *To trust their team.* All their work had built to this moment, and it was close to shattering. Unless, of course, it had been building to the moment where they would sniff out the traitor. Thea's hands clenched once, and then she turned back to her girls.

"No. They wouldn't put us through all that just to pull one of us and make us start again."

Louise straightened her spine. "I agree with Thea."

Mirabelle leaned forward, her pitch rising. "I'm not going to lose out on being a part of the Black Coats because we can't figure out who the traitor is among us."

"Maybe it's you," objected Casey. "Maybe that's why."

"Stop!" Thea's voice was louder than she meant it to be, but all the girls fell silent. Thea reached out her hand, and the girls slowly, one by one, reached out as well until they embraced one another. "We are bonded by the grief we carry, so let's carry it together or not at all."

Finally, Mirabelle stepped forward and joined their

circle. "Fine," she sighed. "But know that I hate you all so much right now."

Team Banner turned back to Nixon and Julie. The latter watched Thea with fascination, her pale eyes sparking like flint in the candlelight. Thea spoke for the team: "Each of us makes up Team Banner. There is no weakness here, only strength."

Nixon closed her eyes for a moment, and Thea was sure that she had made the wrong choice. But then she opened them with a huge smile. "Congrats, Team Banner! Tonight you passed the most important test, more important than all your training. You have shown a willingness to sacrifice your own desires for the good of the team. Some teams here have not been so lucky the first time around." Her eyes darted to where Team Emperor simmered in the darkness.

Julie Westing stepped forward, nodded once, and retreated back into the folds of the Black Coats. "Nixon, you may proceed."

Thea blinked, still in shock, but felt a smile tugging at her mouth.

Their president stepped forward after handing her candle to a Black Coat alumna. "Mirabelle, step forward to receive your coat." Mirabelle was followed by Casey, Louise, and Bea. Thea watched them with her hands pressed up against her lips. She took a deep breath as Bea walked back into the crowd. "And finally, Thea Soloman." She stepped toward Nixon, struggling to control her emotions as Nixon pulled the coat off the rack that had appeared behind her. "Turn around."

Thea obeyed, and Nixon slid the coat onto her shoulders. As soon as she felt the weight of it, she knew that this coat had been made just for her, and it was at once the most precious thing she had ever owned. It was knee-length, with black wool buckles on each wrist. The coat was lined from collar to pocket with large black buttons on both sides. At her hips, the coat flared wide so that leg movement would be uninhibited. *So I can run.* The fabric was smooth but strong under her fingers. The collar hit her just under the chin, reminding her of an old officer's coat.

Nixon gently ran her hands over Thea's shoulders before turning her back around to face her. "Thea, you have also been named the leader of Team Banner." She turned around to face her team, who gleefully nodded their consent, and Thea felt her pride swell. This moment was so much bigger than she was: all these women, all these candles, Team Banner, Sahil's proud gaze resting on her from his place in the corner. She trembled slightly as she took Nixon's outstretched hand. The president jerked her close. "Go carefully into changing waters," she hissed. Then she let go of Thea and raised her arms above her head. "Fellow Black Coats, I give you Team Banner!"

The Haunt erupted into wild cheers, a wave of sound rushing over the space. The candles went out in a collective breath, and when the lights came on, Thea saw hundreds of women, all wearing their black coats. Upbeat music filled the previously silent room, and soon the crowd was swaying to the music, collectively moved by its hypnotic pull. Red wine was uncorked, and the atmosphere turned from a scene of solemnity to one of celebration as older alumni clustered around Team Banner, offering congratulations and telling stories of their glory days in the Black Coats.

Thea sipped slowly from the glass in her hand, wincing at the dry, plummy taste of the wine as she made her way through the endless rounds of small talk. Her heart had finally calmed down when she had the strange feeling of being watched, like a cool fingertip trailing up her spine. Slowly, she raised her eyes to the narrow balcony that overlooked the Haunt, and there, an older woman was indeed watching her silently. She was seated in a wheelchair and had a pink silk scarf wrapped around her head, her own black coat so worn that it had dimmed to a shade of light gray. When Thea's eyes met hers, the woman delicately raised her hand in greeting. Her eyes were tired, the bruises beneath them pulling at hollowed cheeks, and they bored through Thea as congratulations fell around her like rain.

Thea inhaled sharply when she realized who it was: Robin Peterson, the other luminary and creator of the Black Coats. The woman weakly gestured for Thea to join her, and so with a deep breath she made her way up, shyly tucking her hair back behind her ears. When she reached the top of the staircase, she stood for a moment before bowing awkwardly in front of Robin, unsure of what to do with her body.

"You don't need to bow, child." Robin Peterson smiled kindly at her, her calm presence the opposite of the anger that had rolled off Julie in waves. "We're not gods. In fact, I'd say we are almost the opposite." She extended her hand. "I'm glad to finally meet you, Thea Soloman. I'm Robin." Thea gently took her hand in her own, Robin's skin as thin and soft as rice paper. "Thea, it brought me joy to see Team Banner confirmed today. Nixon was a protégé of mine, and to see her leading her own group of young ladies gives me hope for the future of our changing organization—" Midsentence she dissolved into a violent cough and raised a handkerchief to her mouth. She inhaled sharply, and the resulting exhale sent it tumbling onto the floor. "Damn!" Her eyes filled with tears as she struggled to pick it up.

Thea quickly knelt and scooped it up, noting a spot of blood on the yellow embroidered cloth before she handed it back.

"Thank you," wheezed Robin. "As I was saying, I'm happy to see you here today. I fought hard to get you into the Black Coats."

Thea wasn't sure what else to say, so she simply nodded. "I'm so grateful to be here, ma'am."

Robin turned her head and looked at Thea with

intensity, her eyes seeing much more than they let on. She coughed once more. "Tell me, Thea, what do you think is the difference between justice and vengeance?"

The question took her by surprise, and her heart gave a nervous flutter, like the beating of a hummingbird's wings. Was this another part of the initiation? A test? She knew she couldn't wait very long to answer and cleared her throat. "Um, well, I would guess that justice serves others, where maybe vengeance only serves yourself."

The corners of Robin's mouth turned up just a little. "That's not a bad answer—for now. I think you'll find that even the Black Coats struggle with answering that question. And they will especially when I'm gone." She took a mighty breath in, and Thea could tell that talking exhausted her. "When I started the Black Coats, I thought taking revenge would erase the scars on my heart, that it would somehow undo the trauma of my assault."

"And did it?" Thea crouched in front of her wheelchair as Robin looked down at her, her eyes focused on something that had happened long ago.

Robin shook her head. "When a trauma comes from a human hand, it marks you forever. There is a long black road between the assault, revenge, and recovery, and unfortunately, you will walk it alone." Her lips twitched. "In the winter of my life, I've begun to think that scars can't be erased with more scars." Her eyes lit up on something that moved just behind Thea, and she blinked back to reality before dismissing her with a wave. "I'm sorry. Go back to the party and ignore these ramblings of a dying woman. I'm glad I got to speak to you, Thea. Be magnificent for the women we serve."

Thea watched in silence as a strong hand clutched Robin's shoulder, and then Sahil knelt to kiss her cheek. The luminary grabbed on to his hand lovingly, patting it twice. Thea's eyes widened. *Robin Peterson is Sahil's mother?* The resemblance was clear. Though Sahil must have gotten his coloring from his father, he had the same nose and grin as the luminary. Robin reached up with a shaking hand to brush his cheek, and Thea felt guilty for witnessing such an intimate moment.

Robin whispered something to Sahil, and he turned her wheelchair, pushing her back into the folds of Mademoiselle Corday. Thea waited a second before making her way down from the little alcove onto the Haunt floor. There she continued mingling, her mind lingering on Robin's words. *What did she mean, the black road?*

"Thea. Thea." Nixon's voice snapped her out of her stupor.

"Yes, ma'am," she answered dreamily.

Nixon waved to the door. "I must speak privately with you."

Thea followed her president into the hallway just outside the Haunt as older Black Coats passed by them, laughing and swaying to the music. Nixon turned to Thea, her voice dropping to a whisper. "The celebration will be winding down soon. I need you to go and gather Team

Banner and meet back in our classroom. But before you go, I need to speak with you about something. Something not to be shared with the rest of Team Banner."

Thea shifted her weight uncomfortably. "All right."

"As the leader of your team, you are privileged to one essential piece of information that they are not: while each of your gifts is important to your team, there is one member of your team who you need to protect above all, and that's—" Nixon didn't even need to finish.

"Bea," answered Thea, acknowledging something she had long suspected.

Nixon looked relieved that Thea had already made the connection. "Yes. Bea is very important to us here at the Black Coats. We've never had anyone come through here with a gift like that. I fought the luminaries hard for her, even though Julie had other plans. So if ever there is a moment where things get dicey, Bea is always your priority, above the safety of the others. Do you understand?"

Thea stared back at Nixon's dark eyes, anger settling in her chest at the idea that she would leave the rest of her team behind if the chips fell.

"Yes, ma'am," she snapped. "I understand."

Nixon spun on her sharp heel. "Watch that tone, Thea. Round up Team Banner and meet me in the classroom."

With her cheeks burning, Thea turned back to the Haunt.

Ten minutes later, buzzing with happiness, Team Banner burst into the classroom. Bea put her arms out and twirled in a slow circle. "I have never loved anything more than I have loved this coat. Not a single thing."

Thea smiled, feeling the same. The girls admired one another's coats, each tailored perfectly to its owner and her skill. Louise's was extraordinarily light so that her whole body was completely free to move. Mirabelle's coat was short and tight—perfect for showing off her curves—but had pockets inside, perfect for hiding weapons. Casey's had little compartments inside the wrist area for keys and flash drives, along with metal spikes along the shoulders and wrist. Bea's coat was by far the most beautiful and elaborate; it fell all the way to the floor and the back was lined with long strips of ornate black fabric. The garment was hooded, and when Bea pulled her coat on, she looked powerful and mysterious rather than like the bumbling, adorable girl they all knew. It was mildly alarming how well the Black Coats knew them—what to downplay and what to emphasize.

Nixon strode into the room, and the talking stopped. "I won't keep you long—I know we've all had an exhausting night." She stepped up to the front of the room, her eyes softening momentarily. "Team Banner, you made the right choice today and solidified my belief that adding this team was the right idea. Which is good, considering that tomorrow night, you have your first Balancing." Nixon placed the envelope on the table. "I'll see you there, Team Banner." Then she walked out.

The team stood in a circle around the table, staring

down at the envelope. "Are we really doing this?" whispered Bea.

Thea felt the moment turning around her, felt the eyes of the girls resting on her face, the weight of expectations and fears. Then she remembered the picture she had seen of Natalie's body, her long legs tangled up, pale and plastered with muddy leaves, her bare toes blotted with black dirt.

She confidently reached for the envelope. "Yes, we are." Then she opened the envelope, took out the soft paper, and spread it on the table for all to read:

TEAM BANNER, CODE MORNING

TARGET NAME: *Arthur Brewe*

DATE OF BALANCING: *February 28, 10:00 p.m.*

OFFENSE: *Arthur Brewe is a student at Coventry University who has been taking pictures/videos of sexual conquests and then selling them to pornography companies. He blackmails his victims so that they will not press charges, by threatening to release these pictures to their parents, family, and friends.*

BALANCING: *Seduction of Mr. Brewe, followed by a threatening and confiscation of all his technology, as well as any pictures he may have in his possession.*

Good luck!

Signed,

The Black Coats

THIRTEEN

At almost ten o'clock on the following night, Thea was perched on her windowsill, listening with her head cocked to her parents snoring across the hall. The stillness was pierced by Alma, who lifted her head under Thea's comforter on the bed and whined.

"Stay!" hissed Thea. "Lie down!" Alma dutifully obeyed.

Thea heard the purr of an engine outside the window and smiled nervously. Team Banner was here. Her black coat flapping in the wind, Thea leaned out the window, crouching to avoid the gaze of her neighbors. The cul-de-sac was curled up like a sleeping cat; nothing moved.

Thea reached for the tree branch. It was just a short scramble across the branch before she could step onto the roof. She leaped quietly down one level before shinnying across a short drainpipe to the ground. The grass provided a soft landing, and within seconds she was darting across her lawn.

The car door swung open for her, and she squeezed between Bea and Louise in the back seat. "What's up, Catwoman?" Casey laughed. "That was quite a show. I *literally* just walked out my front door."

Thea grinned. "Honestly, it was easier than I thought it would be."

Bea patted her hand reassuringly. "You're awesome, Thea!"

Casey drove quietly down the street before gunning the engine at the stop sign. "Be careful!" snapped Mirabelle.

Casey silenced her with a look. "My job on this team is to drive. Your job is to be pretty."

"And kick ass," piped up Bea from the back.

"Thanks, Bea." Mirabelle rolled her eyes before turning her head away from Casey. "You may be the driver, but this is still my car."

Casey reached out and petted the dashboard lovingly. "And yet her loyalty is already turning." The engine roared, and they shot out onto the dark highway.

There were a few moments of darkness before the dim glow of headlights illuminated the interior of the car. Thea looked back to where a sleek black car followed closely. "Nixon?"

"Without a doubt," answered Casey.

The car was silent after that, the miles stretching out before them. Thea figured she should be giving them some sort of pep talk, but she was just as nervous as the rest of them and knew it would come across as false. How could she inspire when her own heart was pounding? "Does anyone have any questions?" Her words were met with unnerved silence.

Bea swallowed hard next to her. "I think I'm going to be sick."

"Hell no, you will not be!" snapped Mirabelle. "That is custom leather! Get your shit together, Bea!"

Thea reached over and pulled Bea's hood back from her face. "Take a deep breath, okay? Casey? Window?"

"On it." Casey rolled down Bea's window.

Louise smiled. "We're almost there anyway." In the distance, the lights of Coventry University rose over the hill. While its stone walls and secluded corridors were reminiscent of Ivy League schools, its reputation for protecting predators was even stronger. And its local bar, the Railway Scout, was junior Arthur Brewe's preferred hunting ground.

Casey parked the car outside the bar, carefully backing it into a dark corner. Mirabelle ripped open the envelope on the console. A fake ID tumbled out and Casey picked it up with a sneer. "Your name is Ashleigh Smith, and you're from Big Sur, California."

"Yup, that's home." Suddenly, Mirabelle's thick Texas accent was replaced by a cool Californian tone. Even her posture changed: tightly wound Mirabelle relaxed into Ashleigh, slumping against the seat, her shoulders down. Thea was impressed. As Mirabelle then uncurled herself from the car, her thin T-shirt rode up over her torso. Dark blue jeans rode low on her hips, and long gold earrings flashed in the light.

"Nice outfit," deadpanned Casey. "You look like . . ."

Mirabelle raised her eyebrow. "An easy mark?"

Casey leaned back. "Yeah, actually. You look just naive enough."

Mirabelle snarled. "See now, you saying that is part of the problem. I should be able to dress however I want and not be able to attract a predator. Whatever you wear and whatever you do at a bar does not give someone the right to take what he wants, which is exactly what Arthur Brewe does. Ugh." Mirabelle flipped down the car mirror. "This lipstick is the wrong color. Anyway . . . Louise, you coming?"

Louise climbed out of the car. She was nondescript, wearing simple jeans, a black T-shirt, and her black coat, practically invisible next to shining Mirabelle. Thea felt like she should say something and leaned forward, pulling in her team.

"This is it, ladies. Let's do it." She took a breath in. "*Soulevez-vous, femmes de la vengeance,*" she whispered, butchering the French. They repeated it after her, as the two girls stepped away from the car. "Good luck, Mirabelle. Louise."

"It's Ashleigh! And I'll be fine." Thea was reassured by Mirabelle's unwavering belief in herself as she tossed her mane of golden hair over her shoulder. "Bradford Dorm, room three-o-six, one hour."

Casey drove off, leaving two of their team members

behind in the dust. It felt strange. There was only silence as Casey drove a mile down to the college, parking in a leafy spot beside Bradford Dorm. Part of Casey's job was to know the layout of each and every location that they visited, and so far, she was flawless.

"So, we just wait now?" Casey turned the car off and began nervously tapping her nails.

"Yup," piped up Bea from the back, her voice quaking.

Thea's body was tense. It felt wrong to be in the dark while Louise and Mirabelle were out there starting a Balancing. Whatever they were doing, it couldn't be worse than just waiting. She turned to Bea with a smile. "Someone, please talk."

Casey ignored her and instead pulled out a tattered copy of *The Perks of Being a Wallflower.* "I've got homework. Talk among yourselves."

"So, Bea . . ."

Her friend let an embarrassed smile pull at the corners of her mouth. "I know exactly what you want to ask."

Thea gave a hollow laugh. "Okay, so apparently you are psychic as well?" Bea groaned as she continued. "I don't have just one question; I have *all* the questions. When did you learn how to hypnotize people? How did you learn? Where . . ."

Bea looked down shyly, her frizzy dark hair falling over her forehead.

"Well, it runs through the Hopwood women, really. My grandmother was the first member of my family to show

140

signs of the gift. This is really cool—she actually traveled around with the circus, though they will deny it if you ever ask about it."

Thea sat back in her seat. "Wow."

Bea grinned. "Yeah, I love our history. In her later years, my grandmother became a big proponent of hypnosis in terms of behavioral conditioning in children and rehabilitation for prisoners. My mom is a social worker at a counseling center here in Austin. She occasionally is called on to use hypnosis for victims of domestic abuse, but she really lives for the social-worker part of her job. I've grown up with stories of women and kids with black eyes, bloody noses, and broken wrists."

The dark of the car swallowed Bea's quiet voice as a burst of wind rustled the leaves overhead. Thea patted Bea's knee.

"So that's why you're here, on the Black Coats."

Bea nodded. "I've seen too many women hurt by broken men. I was taught very early to use hypnotism. I'm not as good as my grandmother was, but I'm better than my mom. I am, however, quicker than both of them. I can get people out pretty fast." She sighed. "My mom says it's because I'm a product of my impatient generation."

Bea's eyes shone in the streetlights. "But for once, I feel like I belong somewhere. I want to use hypnosis to help people, to—"

"Quiet!" interrupted Casey, her eyes darting to the

rearview mirror. "They're here."

Thea pressed back against the seat, trying her best to blend in with the gray leather. Bea ducked, and Casey sat still as a stone.

"That was fast," Thea whispered. *Really fast*. Through the window she could see Mirabelle making her way to the front of the dorm, her arm linked loosely around Arthur Brewe's shoulder and her body swaying drunkenly with each step. Louise was standing nonchalantly out of sight on the opposite side of the dorm, sweaty from her run.

"You're up," whispered Casey, but Thea was already slipping out the back door. Crouching in the shadows, she gently shut the car door, silently measuring the distance from the car to the front door. Mirabelle's loud laughter swallowed any sounds. Thea stared intensely at Arthur Brewe as he struggled to get the door open. Mirabelle stumbled against him and his key card slipped from his hand onto the ground. They looked at each other for a minute before dissolving into hysterical giggles.

"You're so drunk!" slurred Mirabelle. "I got it; I got it." She bent down, giving Arthur a generous view down her shirt. Thea saw her switch the cards and watched as the real card fluttered to the ground behind Mirabelle's back. The eye of the motion-sensor camera followed Mirabelle and Arthur as they slipped through the door to Bradford Dorm. Thea burst out from behind the car, quickly closing the distance between the car and the door. The camera was already turning back in her direction, but Thea was fast, scooping the card up in her palm before racing back to the car, just beyond the view of the camera. As soon as she reached the vehicle, she exhaled. "Got it."

Getting his key card was of utmost importance. The key-card sensors for the dorm were high-tech; visual security was not. Cameras were situated only by the main entrance, leaving the back vulnerable—as long as she could unlock it. She felt the key card, warm in her palm. "Casey, take us around. Let's not leave Mirabelle with that treasure of a man any longer than we need to." The car pulled up to the back of the dorm, and Louise poked her head in the window.

"Are we ready?" she asked nervously.

"No," Bea said flatly.

Casey wiggled her shoulders. "Absolutely."

Thea pulled her collar up over the sides of her face. "Either way, it's time."

Team Banner grabbed their black backpacks from the trunk and, on Thea's signal, swiftly approached the rear entrance of the dorm. They were covered by a thick canopy of stone, and as she reached the door, Thea grinned at the irony: Coventry's grandiose architecture had inadvertently given them the perfect cover.

"Allow me." She ran Arthur Brewe's card over the lock. It snapped open, and Team Banner made their way into Bradford Dorm. Casey took the lead, and they followed her through a winding set of back staircases and tight hallways of dorms.

Bea reached up and covered her nose. "It smells disgusting in here."

"It's definitely making me rethink dorm living," whispered Louise.

The small unmarked staircase sat at the end of the hallway, jutting out between the laundry room and a wide window that overlooked the campus. Silently, the team slipped up the stairs, the blackness of the hallway swallowing their forms. Mirabelle had left the door unlocked, as promised, and they slipped in easily, Thea closing the door and bolting it behind them.

His room was unsparingly gigantic, with a giant king-size bed in the middle of it. Multicolored Christmas lights blinked in the dark, displaying the bottles of liquor that sat half-empty among piles of unwashed laundry, textbooks, and video-game controllers. The only neat spot in Arthur's room was his immaculately clean desk, glowing under the reflection of a behemoth monitor and two expensive black server towers. Thea's eyes found the bed where Mirabelle was dancing on the mattress fully clothed, a bottle of vodka in her hand. Vodka that happened to actually be water. Arthur was lying underneath her legs, a look of predatory delight across his surprisingly boyish face.

"That's it, girl, let me see . . . such a tease you are."

The team watched silently, waiting for him to notice them. He gave a hysterical giggle. "Now, hold on, pretty girl, what's your name? Ash? Aggy?"

"That's right, Aggy," purred Mirabelle.

That was when he noticed the four black silhouettes in the shadows.

"What the hell?" Arthur reared back, ready to leap up from the bed, but Mirabelle dropped her knees down onto his arms, pinning him beneath her.

"Sit still, you bastard," she hissed. "It will all be over soon."

He bucked his torso once before Mirabelle pulled out a knife and held it to his throat, her ice-blue eyes lighting up with power.

Thea felt her stomach drop and said, "Steady . . ."

Mirabelle nodded and exhaled. "I'm okay."

Arthur went still, his breathing becoming panicked.

"What do you want? Money? I have it! Tons of it. We can go to the ATM! My father—"

Thea cut him off, stepping boldly into the light. "We know exactly who your father is. In fact, we know everything about you, Arthur." Her eyes combed over his dorm room. "So no, we don't care about the mounds of money you've made selling pictures of your conquests to porn websites."

His face paled. "Those are just licentious accusations! I haven't been charged with anything! I'm innocent."

Mirabelle grinned, the drunken girl gone and in her place a woman who stared down at her prey like a starved lion. "Oh, I don't think so. I think you planned on doing exactly to me what you did to those other girls." She nodded to Team Banner. "Get it done."

"Quickly now," hissed Thea. Two Black Coats swept past her, as Bea searched his shelves and Casey attacked his computer.

"What are you doing?" Arthur snapped. "Don't . . . don't touch that!"

Casey pulled out a small USB stick and inserted it into his tower before she began typing like mad, her voice steady. "I'm guessing you're pretty smart, Arthur. Smart enough to hide the files on these poor girls. Do you know, when I was in middle school, a sixteen-year-old girl started sending me messages? I told her things, things I wasn't ready to tell my parents. After a while I agreed to meet her at a department store because I liked her. I took the bus like she told me to, and when I got there, there was no one in the parking lot, no one except for a forty-five-year-old man with a gray van. As soon as the bus pulled away, he tried to grab me." The entire room was frozen, listening to Casey's story. "I fought, and then I ran. I escaped, but I will always see his face in my nightmares. So you could say I have a particular hunger for men who prey on women online."

She leaned back in Arthur's chair. "I'm guessing you have your victims in an innocent-looking folder, encrypted with a . . ." She laughed. "Ah, here. Found it. Did you know you can hack hidden files by setting an attribute to extract them? It's like the opposite of a virus."

Arthur's face was turning red as he stared up at

Mirabelle. "How dare you? You stupid whore—"

Mirabelle clamped her hand down over his mouth. "Yes, we're all whores when we call you out on your bad behavior. I'm *so* done listening to you talk, Arthur. Twenty minutes was more than enough for a lifetime."

"Careful," warned Thea. "Don't block his nose." She was suddenly hyperaware of how quickly this could all go wrong. So many variables were at play here. She realized in that moment why they had so many classes, so much training, because Arthur was a cat in a cage. She watched now as his hand grasped at the covers, searching for a weapon.

Louise pinned his hand under her foot. "Nope."

Bea shrieked with delight from his bookcase. "I think I found something!" Mirabelle lifted her hands to clap.

Thea stepped over to join Bea, who was running her fingers along a strange piece of wall behind the bookcase. She gave it a push and a shoe-box-size portion of the wall came crumbling out. Bea flicked a flashlight out from the sleeve of her coat, and Thea let a grin spread across her face.

"And what do we have here?"

Arthur was beginning to sweat. "Don't touch that! That's mine! You . . ." He dissolved into a series of demeaning curses, words that normally would have made Thea flinch, but now she didn't even blink. The coat stretched across her shoulders protected her, and she let the words bounce off its wool as she pulled everything out of the hole: a dozen USB drives, along with three heavy file folders filled with photographs and what looked like emails and contractual agreements. There was also a gun. *Oh my God.*

Her motions easy, Thea switched on the safety and unloaded the chamber before slipping the weapon and every item from Arthur's secret trove of blackmail material into her backpack. The Black Coats didn't ever use guns, but they did know how to handle them. She turned back to the boy, who was now crying fat tears as he begged Mirabelle to let him go.

"Please, this isn't my fault!" he sputtered. "I owe someone money, and I needed to—"

"We don't care," spoke Louise quietly.

Casey snapped her gum over at the computer, where she was digging into Arthur's files. "You blackmailed women. You took advantage of intoxicated girls by filming your encounters and selling them. You're a predator."

Fury was rising in Mirabelle's face. "Are you sure this is a Code Morning?" She squinted at Thea. "I think maybe just a punch or two, just to knock out some of these pretty white veneers."

"No." Thea didn't even look up. "Not one scratch."

"Fine."

"Got it! Is that it?" Casey pulled out her USB drive and leaped up from the desk and began unplugging the computer from the wall.

Thea nodded. They had been in the room less than ten minutes, but it already felt too long.

Casey stood up from the computer desk and swiftly made her way past Thea, Arthur's computer towers in her arms.

Arthur let out a cry. "Wait, what are you doing with that? Do you have any idea how expensive those are? *Stop!*"

With a wink, Casey opened his window and then looked back at Arthur. "Oh, you mean these computers? I actually *do* know how expensive they are."

Thea leaped forward to stop her, but it was too late; Casey shoved both computers out the window. The resounding crash of metal and plastic exploded up through the windows.

"You bitch!" he screamed.

Casey stared at him. "Oops."

Thea pulled the backpack onto her shoulders. "We need to move! You girls, go now! Get the car. Dammit!"

Arthur turned his head to the side, defeated. Mirabelle continued to hold him down as Thea bent over him, her lips brushing his ear. "Just because they were drunk, just because they were high, just because they were naive doesn't make this okay, you human piece of garbage. We're going to make sure that you never, *ever* do this again. Dear Daddy is going to get all of this: videotapes of you with these girls, your contracts with the porn websites, and your emails back and forth with the bros who helped you."

She pulled back from him to look into his wild eyes. "Look for a campus-wide email soon."

Arthur's lower lip began quivering. "Why are you doing this to me?"

Mirabelle rolled her eyes as she climbed off the bed. "Ugh, you are possibly the most revolting person I've ever met."

Thea's hazel eyes caught Bea's, and she nodded. Bea stepped forward and knelt in front of Arthur. With the black hood pulled up and her glasses removed, she looked like some sort of mysterious druid. "Arthur?" He sat up and looked at her, his eyes red-rimmed and his face desperate—signs that it was the perfect time to move Bea into place. Arthur needed an ally, and she was going to be the good cop to Mirabelle's bad one.

"Hi, Arthur. I know you're having a bad night. I'm here to help you. Can you take a deep breath?"

He took a jagged breath, followed by a choked sob. "Yes."

Thea almost felt bad for him. In this moment he seemed like a scared child. Then she remembered some of the photographs she had seen in the file, and her stomach turned. Empathy melted away.

Bea gave Arthur a kind grin. "Can you press on my hand?"

Arthur reached out his trembling hand, laying it on her own. "Close your eyes." Bea waited a moment before violently yanking her hand away from his, speaking the word "*Sleep*." Arthur fell backward onto the bed. "That's it. Deeper, deeper, all the way down the rabbit hole. One, going even deeper now. Two, you, Arthur Brewe, are never, ever going to do this to women again. You won't even be able to imagine doing this to a woman. You are going to turn yourself in, leave this college, and never come back to academia."

Bea placed her hands on either side of his head. "Three, in a few minutes, you will wake up with a very fuzzy memory of what happened here tonight. You did this to your room when you were drunk." She gently released him, childlike snorts changing to moans as he rolled over on his side. Bea nodded at Thea. "It's done."

Mirabelle shook her head. "I was hoping for more magic."

Thea was the last one out. She paused, her eyes resting on the clock above his bed. It had been fifteen minutes since they'd pushed through his door. *Fifteen minutes, and they had changed for the better the lives of one terrible man and dozens of girls.*

Thea shut the door behind her, and Team Banner made its way through the dorm and out into the parking lot. There was the roar of an engine behind them and they were bathed in headlights as Casey pulled the car forward. Thea didn't need to wait for direction. She spun, throwing open the back door before shoving the girls inside, her momentum sending her skidding across the soft leather. Thea's door wasn't even shut before Casey was pulling out of the lot and onto the open road that bordered it. Thea let out a breath of relief when her back sank against the cool leather. As they soared home, the car was bursting with joy and disbelief.

"That was *amazing!*" Casey punched the steering wheel.

"Did you see his face," laughed Bea, "when Mirabelle told him to sit still?" Casey opened the window and leaned her head out. "Team Banner! *Yeaaah!*"

Thea leaned against the seat, letting the warmth of their bodies hold her tight as Casey opened up the roof, her heart intoxicated with excitement. She wanted to do it again. And again. She lifted her voice in a cheer as Team Banner soared out into the night, their coats flapping in the breeze.

FOURTEEN

"Hey, what are you thinking about?" Drew poked her with a sandaled foot.

It had been two weeks since their first Balancing, and finally Thea was getting some time with him. This perfect day found them lying in her backyard on a plaid throw, soaking in the sunshine and studying for their upcoming Spanish test together. *Well*, thought Thea, *one of them was anyway*. Claiming he was hot, Drew had lost his shirt and was now lying on his stomach, his head bent over the decaying textbook and his body propped up on muscled arms. His skin was tanned gold and dotted with a few freckles, and as he studied, her boyfriend somehow turned into a sun-drenched god. He looked over at her and smiled before flipping over onto his back, his arms stretched above his head so that his ab muscles were on full display. *Good Lord.* Thea almost laughed. *This was getting ridiculous.* She sat back on the blanket and took him in, sunglasses thankfully covering her eyes. Not only could she let her eyes appreciate him more than they should, but the shades also masked her emotions as she relived the last two weeks.

The Black Coats consumed her every thought. Even now, when a superattractive male—who also happened to be one of the kindest people she had ever met—was stretched out next to her, her mind returned to Arthur Brewe's Balancing and the ones that had followed swiftly behind it. She had a bad habit of going over every little moment, evaluating what they had done wrong and what they had done right, trying to figure out how to best lead her team for the next one.

Four times now, Thea had waited at the window, the sound of Mirabelle's car coming down the street raising her arm hairs in anticipation. The adrenaline of the Black Coats was potent, and the righteous feeling of serving justice was addicting. Thea felt like she was a live wire, sparking with excitement.

From far away, she heard someone calling her name. She felt a warm hand touch her shin. "Thea, where are you? Hey!" Drew reached out and leaned against her calf.

Thea blinked. "Sorry. I'm just drifting off here. I've been so tired lately."

"I can tell." Drew sat up as he gently pried off her sunglasses. "You've got some dark rings under these gorgeous eyes." With a devastatingly handsome smile, he leaned forward and kissed her cheek.

"Boo, that was chaste," pouted Thea, disappointed. "Are we courting now—*Sense and Sensibility*–style? Is this your way of telling me to start our English homework?"

Drew looked toward the house. "More like, I'm pretty sure your parents are watching us out the windows."

"Don't worry about my dad," answered Thea before pausing dramatically. "Worry about my mom."

"Yeaaahhh . . ." Drew lay back on the blanket, scooting away from her. "I guess I can handle a little space right now, even if you are making it very hard in that thing." He gestured to her torso, barely covered by her shirt. "Is that a bikini top? Half a bathing suit? Like, what is that? You know what, it doesn't matter, I love it."

Thea blushed. After class had wrapped up at Mademoiselle Corday last week, Mirabelle had surprised Thea by taking her shopping. To her further surprise, she actually loved the things that Mirabelle had picked out for her, including this outfit of a black-and-white-swirled retro crop top dotted with tiny black umbrellas and paired with high-rise white shorts. When Thea had put it on, she had felt like a sixties' pinup. The white shorts were just right for showing off her long, muscular, copper-brown legs, which were now crossed in front of her.

Drew let out a whistle, and Thea reached for him. "I know my parents probably are watching us, but you can at least hold my hand."

"It could be improper. You could be scandalized. Your dowry could be at risk!"

"I'll take that chance. It's probably only antique radios anyway."

Drew curled his fingers around hers. "Okay, seriously, though, why are you so exhausted? Is the Tolkien Houses for Societal Reconstruction taking up that much energy?"

Thea laughed at his butchering of the name. "No, I mean, yes. It's a lot of work. It can be quite physical, restoring things." She shielded her eyes, mixing a truth with the lie. "It's more rewarding than you could ever imagine, though. It's probably how you feel about soccer. It becomes a part of you."

Drew pushed himself up to look at her with a surprising intensity. "But aren't you, like, painting chandeliers?"

Thea bit back a smile. "That's part of it, but it's also being around the other girls. I haven't been exactly social these last six months and it's nice to have . . ."

Drew finished for her. "A team."

"Exactly."

"Could I ever come with you?"

She kicked her leg out toward him, narrowly missing his arm. "No! They have pretty strict rules. Besides, it's women only."

Drew stared off into the distance, his eyes focusing on the horizon. "Huh." He paused. "Well, I have a wig," he finally muttered. "I think I would look great as a redhead."

"You would." Thea raised her glass of sweet tea and stole a glance at the boy who had captured her heart one afternoon at a time. She scooted up next to him, relishing his warm skin pressing against hers, the sun bathing them both in its generous heat. Thea brushed her nose across Drew's. "I love being a part of my team there." She placed both of her long hands across his stubbly cheeks. "But I'm not lying when I say that there is nowhere I would rather be in this moment than right here with you." Thea raised her lips and pressed them against his. *Sorry, Mom.*

Drew kissed her hungrily and then pulled back with a groan. "Now you're making this really difficult." He wrapped his arms around her, Thea feeling the hard lines of his rib cage against her own, their hearts beating inches apart, everything about him warmed by the sun, warming her from the inside out.

From somewhere on the blanket, her phone buzzed. *No, no, no.* Thea ignored it, sinking deeper into his kiss, into Drew himself, into the way his hand traced across her hips. The phone buzzed again. Thea shifted, and the moment was broken. Drew sat back. "Want to turn that off?"

Thea frowned. "Yes, it's probably just . . ." She looked at the phone. It was from Nixon.

BC. One hour. Meet at Mademoiselle Corday.

"Oh no." Thea let out a nervous sigh. "I am so sorry, Drew. I have to go. This sucks."

His head jerked back. "Are you kidding me?"

"No. It's an emergency."

He sat up. "Is everyone okay?"

"Yes. Sorry, not that kind of emergency." Thea pushed her hair back from her face with aggravation. "Everyone is okay. It's just, you know, my team."

He gave her a look of extreme disbelief. "Thea, what kind of emergency could a two-hundred-year-old house have? The sudden onset of oldness? Too much quirk in the drawing room?"

Thea was already packing up her books, avoiding his gaze. "I know. It's stupid, I just have to see this commitment through."

Drew stood awkwardly, his movements betraying his quiet anger. "Thea, I'm trying to be cool about this, I really am, but we were supposed to have today together."

The hurt in his voice gave her pause. "I know." She took his wrist and dropped her head in frustration. "I really don't want to leave you. That kiss was just getting good."

He shook away from her. "It was, and still somehow I don't entirely believe you." He looked into her eyes. "I can tell you want to go, you know."

It was impossible, and yet Thea did. She wanted to be both with him on that blanket and in the car with Team Banner. She raised up on her tiptoes and kissed the tip of his sunburned nose before wrapping both arms around his neck. "We should probably head inside anyway; you're getting sunburned." She kissed him softly. "Tell me how I can make it up to you."

He sighed, pressing his tongue on the inside of his

cheek. "Okay, but you'll be sorry you asked. Come meet my dad sometime soon? He's been asking about you, and I've been putting it off, but he's getting annoying and also"—he swept her up in his arms, lifting her off the ground and resting his forehead against hers—"I really, really like you, Thea Soloman, you with the mysterious side job restoring Edwardian furniture."

"Victorian houses," she whispered, "and the feeling is mutual."

Team Banner could wait for a few more minutes, she figured, and she pressed her mouth to his for one last taste of sunshine before she began her descent into the electrifying dark.

The target's name was Jonathan Samper, and he worked at an upscale farm-to-table eatery called Pear, near downtown Austin. They parked Mirabelle's car outside the restaurant right before closing time.

"They are going to hate us. People who come to restaurants right before closing are the worst," muttered Louise.

Casey shook her head. "Only you would worry about being polite during a Balancing." She turned to Thea. "Do you have everything?"

Thea nodded, pulling a tiny black vial out of her pocket. "One powdered dose of Rohypnol, generously supplied by the luminaries."

According to their Balancing sheet, twenty-one-year-old

Jonathan Samper had been accused of drugging and date-raping not one but two of his girlfriends. Because they didn't go to the police immediately, there was no physical evidence to charge him. He remained in good standing both at school and at work, while the two women he raped suffered the shame of their reputations. That was all about to change.

Team Banner was dressed nicely today; under their Black Coats they each wore a dressy outfit to blend in at Pear. A bunch of girls all dressed in head-to-toe black would have drawn attention, and that was the last thing they needed.

"This is on Mademoiselle Corday, right?" asked Casey, standing at the door. "I looked at the menu last night and it's pretty pricey."

Thea nodded. "Yes, but don't go crazy. No duck. Sandwiches all around."

"Or salads!" suggested Mirabelle cheerfully.

Thea's fingers curled around the vial in her dress pocket. She was nervous, and the setting sun was beating down on her coat. She couldn't stop seeing Drew's disappointed face in her mind. "Let's do this, Team Banner."

The meal was quite delicious and the company divine. Even when they were on a Balancing, Thea was surprised by how much she loved hanging around these girls. They watched with careful eyes as the restaurant slowly cleared out, and soon they were the only ones left besides Jonathan—their waiter—and the bartender, who was glued to his phone. Thea signaled to Mirabelle, who raised her arm in the air. Jonathan zipped over to her side, his eyes on her chest.

"Hi." She casually laid her hand on his arm. "We just need our check, and also I was wondering: Would you want to have a drink with us? We're celebrating our friend's promotion! It's on us." Jonathan's eyes lit up as he took in the group.

"Yeah, I mean, cool! Let me go ask the bartender for a round. You're the only ones in here, so that's no big deal." He practically hopped away, excited by his luck and Mirabelle's attention. She tilted her head and smiled coyly.

He soon reappeared with bottles of beer for each of them, plopping down between Thea and Mirabelle. When Casey stood to go to the restroom, Thea used the sound of her chair to cover the noise of her popping the top off the vial. Quick as a fox, she dumped the powdered contents into her beer and gave it a swirl. Jonathan's eyes were still on Mirabelle, who was telling a funny story about some people she had met on a bus. Thea then switched her bottle with Jonathan's. When Mirabelle concluded, Jonathan reached for his beer. Thea was incredibly disturbed at how easy it was.

Thea raised her drink with a sexy wink. "Shall we go bottoms up? Maybe to sharing things?"

Team Banner watched with smiles on their faces as he finished the last of it.

✳ ✳ ✳

Thirty minutes later, Jonathan Samper lay across their legs in the back seat of the car, his head on Thea's lap. Mirabelle's car hurtled forward on Highway 71, out toward Barnpiper Park: a thirty-three-acre plot of land that included playgrounds, camping sites, and a big patch of woods right at its center. Getting him there was easy: the drug rendered the taker compliant, incapable of resisting. It also produced a sort of amnesia, which was what made Rohypnol the drug of choice for men like Jonathan.

He was conscious, but only partly. He was quite attractive, with thick black hair combed back from a handsome face combined with strong eyebrows, flawless skin, and an earnest smile. Thea could see why women would fall so easily for him. Here on her lap he looked innocent, occasionally babbling on about this or that, but she knew he was anything but. In his drug-induced euphoric stupor, Jonathan was reaching up and touching Thea's face every few minutes. She repeatedly slapped his hand away in disgust.

"How's he doing?" whispered Louise.

"Drugged," responded Thea. "I would almost feel bad for him were it not for the fact that he raped women who were in the same state that he's in right now." She lifted his head. "Jonathan, do you consent to jumping off a bridge?"

He nodded sleepily, his words badly slurred. "If that's what you guys are doing."

Thea's eyes narrowed. "See? How can you consent in a

162

state like this? The women he raped were like pliant children. That's what the drug does."

Casey gripped the steering wheel hard. "He'll learn his lesson soon enough. We're almost there."

Thea checked his pulse again; it was strong. They had been lucky—sometimes people who were roofied became aggressive and excitable. *That would have been a problem.*

Casey slowed the car, and Thea watched as the headlights bounced off the visitors' center at the Barnpiper Park entrance. It was almost midnight, and the park was closed and empty. They passed the playgrounds and parking lot and neared the curb where the park turned wilder, accessible only by a walking trail. Old ash junipers rose up on either side of them as the car moved farther into the darkness. Thea winced as the tires bounced over the rugged terrain. "Not too far in," she said softly.

"Why?" snapped Casey. "We don't want to make this easy for him."

"We won't, but I don't want him to die," said Thea firmly. "Remember what Nixon said: a Balancing cannot turn into hiding a dead body. What if he finds his way to the highway and gets hit by a car?"

"Or steps on a rattlesnake. Or walks into a river," added Louise.

Casey braked hard. "If he had been as concerned for the women he raped as we were for him now, those girls' lives would have gone on as usual. He's in a park. After he wakes up, he'll think he's in the woods for about an hour or so until he makes his way out and is greeted by moms holding sippy cups."

"This is my call, Casey," Thea said firmly. "Drive in maybe another half mile." She expected a fight but got none. Casey respected her position and stayed silent. The car continued through the black night, the only illumination the car's headlights rolling over the trees around them. It was as if the eerie stillness of the park had swallowed them whole.

"This seems a little like the beginning to a horror movie," uttered Mirabelle, saying what everyone was thinking.

Casey gripped the wheel. "Yeah, except this time we're the things people should be afraid of."

"I'm not afraid of you!" crowed Jonathan, drugged out of his mind. "I think you're my friends. You're my *best* friends."

"We're not," replied Louise, pulling her hair back. "You're actually terrible."

Thea sat forward as they drove past a long-abandoned set of wooden benches. "Here! Stop here, this is good. Yes! Let's roll him out."

Casey screeched the Audi to a stop. Mirabelle flung open her door and ran around to Thea's side of the car. When she opened the door, Jonathan flopped over onto the ground, hanging his head. "I like you guys, but I don't think you're good." He moaned, but when Mirabelle told him to get up, he did it so obediently that it made Thea's heart hurt.

The rest of Team Banner climbed out of the car. "Walk over here, Jonathan," Louise ordered. He shuffled his way over to where Thea was standing. He leaned heavily on Casey, who turned her head away from his alcohol-soaked breath.

Jonathan walked up to the park bench. "You guys aren't leaving me here, right?"

Bea followed behind him, her voice low. "Jonathan, take off your clothes." She raised a hand, but there was no need. Grinning like an idiot, Jonathan began unbuttoning his pants. Everything he was wearing fell to the ground. Bea spun and looked at Thea, her face reddening at his sudden nudity. Thea had a hard time not laughing at her teammate's utter shock. Bea turned back to him. "Lie down," she commanded, "and stay there." Thea watched for a moment before raising her eyes to take in the incredible sky. There were no lights out here; the stars blazed so brightly that it was like she had never seen them before.

As she watched, a memory came, uninvited:

She and Natalie are camping out in her backyard, looking at the stars until they fall asleep. Their sleeping bags are huddled together, the girls whispering back and forth in an effort to avoid sleep.

"Do you think we'll be safe out here?" Thea asks, worried about sleeping away from her parents.

Natalie takes her hand. "As long as we're together and we have Alma, we'll be safe." They both look over at Alma, then still a puppy and lost in a pile of blankets, before bursting into giggles.

Thea blinked away the sudden tears. "Let's head out," she ordered, but the team didn't move. Mirabelle was twisting her hair; Bea softly shuffled her feet on the ground.

"It feels weird to leave him," Louise finally said softly.

Thea nodded, glad that someone had vocalized what she was feeling. She stepped forward, gathering the girls around her. "Look, at ten tomorrow I'll call from the burner phone to make sure someone found him. I know he seems vulnerable and innocent right now, but he's not." Thea stepped over to him, brushing aside the lock of hair that had fallen over his forehead. "When Jonathan wakes up with no clothes on and no recollection of what happened to him last night, he'll be as scared and feel as violated and confused as the girls he raped. That's what happened to them; that's what he did. And unlike his actions, we did him a kindness: we didn't hurt him, though we could have. Trust me, Jonathan Samper has gotten a very gentle taste of what it's like to be roofied."

Without another word, she walked over to the car, popped open the trunk, and grabbed a piece of plastic sheeting. She threw it over his body. It was a warm Texas night, but she couldn't risk exposure. Still, it was a mercy Jonathan didn't deserve. After that, she walked over to a nearby tree and snapped off a small branch before turning to the red dirt in front of the bench. Then she flung the stick into a nearby bush and dusted off her hands as she climbed into the car. She found her team staring straight ahead, out the windshield, not speaking. "It's done. Now, let's hurry home because I have homework."

"Yeah, about that . . . ," Mirabelle started.

"No can do," laughed Casey. "How about tacos instead?"

"I vote tacos," added Bea. "And we need our *entire* team to get tacos, Thea."

Louise spun around in the front seat to look at Thea. "Yeah, be the leader we need, Thea, not the one we deserve."

At her intense expression, Thea burst out laughing. "Okay, fine. Tacos it is." She looked behind her as the car pulled away, out of the park. In the light of the moon she could make out the huddled lump that was Jonathan and the message she had left in the dirt for him:

Roofie again and we'll kill you.

She clenched her hands as they rolled into the night, ignoring the sharp sliver of guilt passing through her. Justice may have been delivered, but she knew she wouldn't sleep much that night.

FIFTEEN

He didn't know she was watching him.

That morning, while her parents thought she was over at Drew's house, Thea had driven into downtown Austin hoping that she would see him: Cabby Baptist, the man who had killed her cousin. Two months of Balancings had made her quite bold; she had created some aliases to follow him on social media, hoping to find any clue, but his social media game was almost nonexistent. He never posted, and nothing had been gained. Except for last night, when a single picture of an oozing cinnamon roll popped up, the caption underneath it reading, "Will be eating one of these tomorrow!"

Thea knew exactly where he was talking about. Elizabeth's Café in downtown Austin was famous for their rolls. She couldn't explain to herself exactly why she needed to be there, but she did. She had waited for an hour and a half before he showed up, but her patience paid off: at 9:36 a.m. his white pickup truck puttered to a stop in the parking lot.

Sitting on the hood of her car, Thea put down her own delicious roll and raised her binoculars.

She felt adrenaline rushing through her as she watched him; she hadn't seen this man since the police station, and there he was, grinning at the young cashier like he hadn't killed a girl her age nine months ago. Thea ground her teeth together as she watched him, elaborate fantasies playing out in her mind in which she smashed his head on the glass tabletops and dragged him into her trunk. She took a long sip of her coffee, her hands shaking just a little. He disappeared into the folds of the restaurant and was seated at a table where she couldn't see him very well. Dammit. She wiped her hands on her pants and eyed his car. Maybe if she could jimmy the lock . . .

Her phone buzzed and she glanced at it with a sigh. A Balancing. Of course. She narrowed her eyes at Cabby's car. *I'll be back for you later*, she thought.

Mademoiselle Corday loomed above the trees as Thea parked the Honda in the driveway. The face of the house stared menacingly down at her while Thea trotted inside, buttoning her black coat as she went. Team Banner was lingering at the front door of the house, waiting patiently for her. "Hey, ladies!" She crowed.

They responded with silence, their bodies all clustered together in the foyer.

"What's wrong?" Thea asked.

Bea finally looked up and motioned Thea over, her soft

face drawn in with concern. "Look." Thea made her way into their circle, where Team Banner stared down at their Balancing sheet lying on the entry table. When she read the first line, Thea felt her stomach drop.

TEAM BANNER, CODE EVENING

TARGET NAME: *Raphael Amadoor*

DATE OF BALANCING: *May 9, 4:30 p.m.*

OFFENSE: *Mr. Amadoor is a well-known plastic surgeon living just outside of Austin. He is also a habitual wife and child abuser who has escaped the justice of law due to his high status in the community, as well as his connections with corrupt law enforcement. He has been accused of beating two women at a hotel. His wife and daughter have recently fled Texas for the safety of Guadalajara.*

BALANCING: *Please make sure that he is unable to hurt any woman ever again.*

Good luck!

Signed,

The Black Coats

"Are we ready for this?" asked Louise, always so thoughtful.

"Hell yes!" snapped Mirabelle. "I've been ready for this for a long time."

Casey frowned. "Me, too, in theory. It's just . . ."

"Terrifying," finished Thea, her hands curling around the paper, taking in as much information as she could.

Some photographs slid out from behind the Balancing sheet: graphic photos of the marks he had left on his wife: blackened eyes, cracked and bloody lips, a broken nose, her face shaded in purple bruises.

"Who does this to another person?" whispered Casey.

Thea felt her fear dissolve into a churning anger. "Let's pack up," she ordered. Their supplies were already sitting by the door.

Thea dropped the Balancing sheet into a nearby fireplace and followed her team out of Mademoiselle Corday. Nixon was standing in the driveway. "Listen up, girls. The Balancings that Team Banner has been assigned so far have been specifically chosen for the nature of the man. Arthur, Jonathan, and all the others you have attended have been pushovers. These were set up so that you could experience a Balancing without an imminent risk of danger to yourselves. Men like Raphael are different. Be on your guard." Nixon took a deep breath as she climbed into her black car. "As this is your first Code Evening, I'll follow you there, but I won't be coming in with you."

"Do you want some company on the drive?" asked Bea brightly.

"No," responded Nixon, slamming her car door shut.

"I could have told you that was going to happen," deadpanned Casey. "C'mon, circus freak, get in the car. You belong with us."

They rode in total silence, their thundering hearts swallowing all possible conversation.

***

Raphael Amadoor's Mediterranean-inspired house sat on a high bluff overlooking a wealthy community just outside of Austin. Stunning views of the town below were visible from the portico in front of the enormous circular driveway. Casey pulled the car right up to the front of the house and parked. Thea leaned over. "You hacked the security cameras already, right?"

Casey nodded. "It was so easy. His password was one-two-three exclamation point. Now all that will be on there will be the loop from this morning."

"He's expecting us, remember?" Thea ignored the pounding of her heart.

"Right."

"Let's take off our coats." As Thea's slipped off her shoulders, she felt naked and exposed. Without her realizing it, her black coat had become her armor.

"But . . . ," protested Louise.

Mirabelle shook her head. "No house cleaners wear coats like this."

In their black shirts and leggings, all it took was a few name tags to make them look like an expensive team of maids. Casey grabbed a mop from the trunk, handing a broom and a bucket of chemicals to Bea. Mirabelle and Louise each carried buckets, though inside theirs was a lot more than cleaning supplies. Thea stuffed their coats into a large empty bucket and covered it with a rag. She looked up at the house for a moment while ignoring the doubt that was raging through her mind. She was a black girl about to assault a white man in Texas, and the consequences if they got caught would most likely not be doled out in equal measure. Thea took a deep breath, focusing on the job ahead; she was the team leader and needed to act like one. This was not a time for fear, no matter how justified.

"Thirty minutes, in and out." She glanced over at Nixon's car, parked beside the house. "We'll be fine. We're not alone."

The team made their way up to the doorway. "Slouched posture!" Thea hissed at Mirabelle, who walked everywhere like she was on a catwalk. "Don't look so haughty!"

Team Banner sagged. "Does everyone have their gloves on?" Thea asked. They nodded, and Thea knocked on the gigantic wooden door. They waited a few moments, and Thea shrugged and knocked again. The door was yanked open violently.

"Jesus, I'm here!" Raphael Amadoor stood before them with round glasses perched on the end of his nose and a bushy black beard. His short, stocky build reminded Thea of a bulldog, as did his face. He looked the girls over. "Come in. I have guests arriving in an hour, so you better work fast."

They stepped inside. As Thea reached back to close the door, she took one last glance at Nixon's car, which unexpectedly sped down the driveway and disappeared into a cloud of dirt. Her hand tightened on the doorknob: they were alone. She turned to her team, each girl eyeing her. She would not tell them, not now.

"What's wrong?" asked Casey.

Thea plastered a fake smile onto her face. "Nothing!"

"Enough chatting!" snapped Raphael Amadoor coldly. "I'm not paying you girls to talk. The party will be just through here."

They followed him down a set of wooden stairs into the loveliest room Thea had ever seen. It was designed with four open doors, where billowy white curtains led out to an enormous patio. Through the doors, tiny flecks of sunlight danced on his teal pool as olive trees shook in the wind. The garden was walled on every side. "Your house is beautiful," muttered Thea, not having to pretend to look impressed.

Raphael's eyes moved uncomfortably over her. "I know that, girl. I got this land for a steal about ten years ago. Good investments, knowing the right people, a little bit of naughtiness . . ." He winked at Mirabelle. "You look like you know a little something about that."

Gross, thought Thea.

"We're in high school," whispered Bea.

Raphael licked his lips and held up his hands. "Hey! I didn't say anything improper. I'm just a friendly guy having a party. But if you all feel like staying around afterward, I know that my soon-to-be ex left some very pretty dresses upstairs. I'll show you girls a really good time, and what's more, I'll pay you for it—much more than Shiny House Cleaners pays you."

He took a step down into the living room. Mirabelle stepped forward, seductively biting her fingernail. "Maybe you could give me a private tour? I would love to see the bedrooms. Unless anyone else is here? I just want to make sure . . . I'm kind of shy."

Raphael's eyes lit up like he couldn't believe his luck. Thea felt anger rising inside her, and she could see it in her team as well—the way Louise stiffened, the way Casey's eyes simmered. "Well, I would be honored, Miss— What's your name? You know what? It doesn't matter."

Mirabelle reached out her rubber-gloved hand. "Shall we go?"

Raphael turned away from the girls, with his focus on his young conquest, and that was all the distraction they needed. Thea nodded once and then watched in silence as Louise pulled the head off the broom, twirled the stick once, and brought it crashing down against Raphael's turned head in one swift movement. He slumped to the ground. The very stones beneath Thea's feet seemed to shake as she looked down at this man, realizing that Team Banner had crossed an invisible line. There was no turning back from here, not from this. A small splatter of red blood was leaking from his temple onto the floor. The Code Evening had begun.

Thea checked his pulse. "Okay, he's down. Now, let's get ready for the party." Thea grabbed his legs as Mirabelle and Louise dragged him by his arms over to an expensive chaise longue and propped him up against the back, his body slumping forward like a rag doll.

Casey popped out the bottom of the Shiny House Cleaners bucket and pulled out a roll of duct tape, wrapping it around him and the chair several times. She then checked his breathing. "We're still good. Go."

The team went to work after slipping their coats back on. From their tubs of chemicals, they pulled out folded posters of the faces of Amadoor's victims: his wife, his daughter, and the women from the hotel. Giant photographs of eyes swollen with blood, of lips gashed, of hair that had been ripped out, X-rays of broken ribs—every single one went up on the wall. The luminaries, as always, had done their prep work perfectly. The names of the officers who had let him off with warning after warning were spray-painted across his priceless pieces of art in huge black letters: *Officer Ramses, Shame on You. Officer Lee, You Were Supposed to Protect.* They hung up posters everywhere: his foyer, the living room, the patio, and one right above his bed. Thea made sure another photo was pushed deep into his one-thousand-thread-count sheets. As she rolled out photo after terrible photo, the Balancing sheet popped up in her mind: *Make sure he never hurts anyone again.*

As they worked, Casey was on her custom Black Coats laptop, uploading the lists of his crimes and the pictures of his victims to all his social media sites, including his business website. Thea was spray-painting a list of his assaults onto his patio glass when she heard Louise give a shout: "He's waking up!"

Thea ran back into the living room, where Team Banner circled around Raphael, each staring down at him in pure hatred.

Mirabelle grinned when he opened his eyes. "Good afternoon, Mr. Amadoor."

SIXTEEN

Raphael looked down at his restraints. "What the hell is this? Untie me this instant!"

"Yeah, I don't think so," said Thea menacingly. "We are here to make sure that you are unable to hurt women ever again. That's what pathetic men like you do, you see? They use their money or their strength to exploit those who they should protect. Neither your money nor your power is here to protect you now." She leaned forward. "And we do not bend."

She nodded and stepped back but was still surprised when Louise flew forward to punch him hard across the face. Thea jumped, hearing the crack of Louise's knuckles connect with his cheekbone, feeling deep inside her chest the snap of Amadoor's neck as it bounced off the back of the chair. *Oh. My. God.*

"You . . ." He blinked in shock.

"Whatever you are about to call us, we've heard it before," snapped Casey. "It's amazing how powerless those words become when you decide they have no power over you."

Amadoor was looking around the room now, the beginnings of panicked fear showing on his face. "Are you here to kill me?"

Thea waited a few seconds longer than she needed to before answering. "No. Not today. But your reign of terror over women you claim to love is coming to an end."

Raphael spat blood onto the floor. "They deserved every bit of it."

Thea went to open her mouth but was suddenly shoved violently aside by Louise. "Move." Thea looked over at her, surprised at the animal fury plastered across Louise's normally cheery face.

"Louise?" she whispered, not recognizing the person before her.

With a snarl, Louise leaped onto the chair, planting her heeled boot on Raphael's chest before letting her momentum push the chair backward. It hit the marble floor with a violent crack, shards of wood spinning away from them. Louise snarled in his face, the sharp point of her boot pressing deep into Raphael's chest. He yelped in pain as she twisted her foot back and forth. She brought her hand across his face again with a quick slap and then squeezed his chin with one hand, bringing her face down toward his own, angry words tumbling from her mouth.

"I know men like you, Raphael. I've known them all my life: my father and his brothers, all cruel men like you. Do you know what I remember from my childhood?"

Raphael's lip quivered. "Are you going to kill me?"

Louise ignored him. No one breathed as she continued. "I remember hiding in our hall closet, pressed up against one of my mother's furs, stuffing it deeper and deeper into my mouth to keep from screaming as my father hit her again and again and again." A hot tear dripped down her face. "Did you know, Raphael, that when I get a fever, I still taste those furs, that horrible mix of smoke and animal on my tongue?" She bit back a sob before boxing his ears with both fists. Raphael cried out, and something uncomfortable twisted inside of Thea. "My father stole my childhood, and the childhood of all my siblings, just so he could feel bigger about himself, feel like a man. I will always be broken because of what he did. I will never be able to love normally because of what he did." She took a jagged breath that tore at Thea's heart. "Just like you, he always had an excuse for it. *Said we deserved it.* Then one glorious day, they found his body under a highway bridge, because he messed with the wrong person." A smile crossed her face beneath her dripping tears. "Do you know what we did that night we got the news that my father had died?"

Tears were streaming down Raphael's cheeks as he stared into Louise's twisted face, his eyes unblinking and terrified.

"We ordered pizza." Louise leaned back. Her anger was

so potent, Thea felt it washing over the team. Thea met Casey's gaze. She gave a slow nod to Casey, acknowledging that she would step in if she needed to. Raphael was muttering some prayer, his sloppy sobs filling the room. Louise looked disgusted. "Don't you dare cry in front of me. I'm not the one who deserves to see your tears." With that, she brought her elbow down hard across the bridge of his nose. A loud crack resonated across his defaced living room.

Thea leaned forward. "Calm down." Her stomach turned uncomfortably for a reason she couldn't understand. Wasn't this what they had prepared for?

Mirabelle gently pulled Louise back, but not before Louise grabbed Raphael's face and turned it to the side, the blood from his nose pouring out onto his expensive rug. "Look at those pictures." Raphael let out a cry as she forced his eyes open. "Look at what you did to the women you swore to love."

He was screaming now, his eyes closed. "I'm sorry! I'm sorry! You're right! I didn't mean to hurt them, but I did. They left me because I deserved it!"

Louise's hands were lingering over his neck now, tracing over the jugular. "You deserve to die, you know."

Raphael let out a wail, his tears mixing with blood and snot as they poured down his face, his mouth distorted, his pathetic howls reminding Thea of a wounded animal. "I'll do better; I swear that I will."

Louise was gritting her teeth now, her body coiled and

ready to strike. Thea put her hand on Louise's shoulder.

"Enough." *Louise could break his neck if she wanted to.* "I said, that's enough," she whispered, turning Louise to face her. "He deserves it. But it's not ours to give."

Raphael let out a moan. "Oh, thank you, God! Please have mercy on me."

With a cry of surrender, Louise let Thea turn her away. Casey had stepped toward Raphael when they heard a loud thud from upstairs. Team Banner went silent. Terror shot through Thea. "I thought you said no one was home!" hissed Mirabelle.

Raphael leaned his head back and laughed, his lips curling to reveal his bloodstained teeth. "They'll save me, I'm sure of it!" He laughed some more, his mind lost to fear.

Thea looked up the stairs, her eyes searching for a shadow, for movement. There was nothing. She motioned silently to Casey. "Come up with me. You guys, stay on him." She pointed to Bea. "It's time to make sure that he never does this again. You're up." Thea stepped onto the first stair, the antique wood creaking under her feet as they circled up the staircase.

"What do you think it is?" At Casey's voice, the sound stopping suddenly. *Someone was inside.*

With Casey following close behind her, Thea ran up the stairs and burst into the hallway. She began kicking open every door, with nothing in her hands to defend herself. After seeing a few over-the-top bathrooms, Thea stepped back into the hallway when she heard the sound again—a hollow thump, like someone dragging something. Thea froze, her eyes on the door at the end of the hallway. Behind her, Casey slipped on her brass knuckles. "No," Thea ordered. "Put those away! We are here only for him. He is the only one who pays today."

"Arggh!" Casey muttered, slipping the knuckles back into her pocket.

Thea paused outside the door with her heart thudding in her ears, her hand hovering over a blown-glass doorknob. Nixon's voice played in her head: *Indecision is not your friend. Pausing can mean losing control.* Thea took a deep breath and slammed her foot hard against the door. It flew violently open, scaring the daylights out of two fat black cats that were seated just inside the door.

On the floor, an unfazed orange tabby paused from batting a hanging rubber ball against the wall. She looked at Thea with annoyance before returning to her ball. *Thump. Thump.* One of the black cats darted down the hall while the other turned and hissed at Thea. She hissed back before stepping through the door. Casey gave a hearty laugh. "He has a room just for his cats. Unbelievable. Beats his daughter, spoils the kitties."

Thea had opened her mouth to reply when a huge crash from downstairs interrupted her thoughts. Everything after that happened so fast. There was the sound of glass breaking and a hard thud, followed by Bea screaming, "No, no, no . . ."

There were the sounds of chaos and then Mirabelle's loud voice, rising over the commotion, screaming her name. *"Thea!* Oh my God, *Thea!"* Then words that cut through her like a knife: "He's running!"

Bea's voice: "He's outside!" Thea ran forward into the cat room, shoving aside an overstuffed sofa to look out the south-facing window. From there the tiled roof slanted downward and ended near the pool. Directly below her, Thea saw a flash of movement: Raphael. He was bolting away from the house in a white shirt spotted with blood. His movements were frantic and desperate.

Before Thea said a word, Casey was already at her side and ready to provide a boost. Without a second thought, Thea stepped onto Casey's palm and was promptly heaved up and over the ledge, her body tumbling out the window. Thea shoved her feet out in front of her and then she was sliding down on her bottom, her body flying over terra-cotta tiles, which broke under her weight, shards of red clay slicing through her black leggings. A stream of pebbled tiles went before her, plunging off the edge of the roof as Thea tried to find a way to slow her momentum. She was going to fall, but it wasn't far, and she didn't even have time to take a breath before she was on the edge of the roof. Using the training that Sahil had taught her, Thea leaned forward and the moment her toes hit the ledge she leaped, using her speed to twist her body in midair, giving herself the pause and the control that she needed. A second later, Thea landed hard on her feet and then on her knees, and the impact of the pavement ricocheted up her legs. Pain sliced through her like a hot wave through her hips, her ribs, and finally her teeth, which ground together with a painful crack. Then it was gone. Thea gave herself a shake. She was okay, and Raphael was ahead of her now, running toward the latched gate at the end of the pool. Thea let a nasty smile curl across her face as she crouched down. Fear had made him fast. *She was faster.*

She shot forward like an animal released from a cage, her feet flying underneath her, her coat flapping as she pounded past the pool, gaining on him easily. Raphael was crying, his hysterical sobs rising as she gained speed, until she felt the ground disappear underneath her feet. The chase intoxicated her. *Come closer,* she thought, *I've got you.* Compared to Sahil, Raphael was practically a snail. The gap between them was closing.

Jagged breaths tore at her rib cage as the pool chairs passed by in a blur. *Closer.* Her legs were cycling in a fury, no rhythm, just speed, everything in her pushing faster. Raphael was almost at the end of the property now. His shaking hands had just reached out for the latch when Thea snarled in his ear. He turned just a moment too late, and it was all she needed. Her speed propelled them forward into the stone gate. Thea put out her hand and twisted them both sideways, protecting them from the impact of the stone. Using that same momentum, Thea grabbed his collar and spun her body, flinging him backward, her power lifting him off his feet. He flew into the pool with a guttural scream as she roared in return. The water around him turned crimson as the blood from his nose and chest seeped into the pool. Raphael waved his hands once above the surface before he sank underneath the water, his head disappearing in a cloud of red. Thea leaped in after him feetfirst, her body plummeting into the deep end.

After the initial shock of the cold water, she kicked her legs and swam toward him as he flailed below the surface. A small pocketknife in his hand waved around desperately. Thea paused underwater, watching the cruel irony of the situation unfold. Raphael Amadoor, a man who had hurt God knew how many women in his lifetime, now needed one to save his life. His pleading eyes were on her now, his body jerking in fear, his mouth open and swallowing water. She could leave him there, watch him sink ever lower, drowning in the weight of his many sins. *But I won't.*

She gestured to the knife and he dropped it without hesitation. He reached for her desperately, and her hand met his own. Thea quickly wrapped her arms around his waist and let them sink down for just a moment, just enough so that her feet touched the bottom of the pool. The second she felt the sea-glass tiles brush her boots, she pushed up with all the remaining strength in her muscled legs.

They surfaced a second later, both greedily sucking air as Thea pulled Raphael over to the side of the pool, her arms wrapped firmly around his limp form. In her blurry peripheral vision, she could see her teammates running to the side of the pool. Thea spun Raphael around to face her. He looked defeated, his skin bloated and pale, his body quivering with exhaustion. "You saved me. You didn't have to and—"

Thea let her fist fly, the way Nixon had taught her, connecting with Raphael's jaw. He slumped against her in the water with a moan. Mirabelle reached her first, pulling them both out of the pool. Thea leaned over, her hands on her knees, trying to catch her breath. Casey and Bea struggled to pick Raphael up. "Is everyone okay?" Thea sputtered.

Mirabelle's face fell. "Not really. He had a knife in his back pocket; we didn't know. He must have cut his hands free when Bea started working on him. He could have killed her! Thank God Louise saw him move and threw her arms out to protect herself." She shook her head. "He cut her forearm, but it's not too deep. She's not going to die or anything."

Leave it to Mirabelle, Thea thought, *to minimize a stabbing.*

They carried a limp Raphael back inside. Louise sat by the door, a towel wrapped around her bloody arm. She shook her head when she saw Thea. "This is my fault. I shouldn't have lost control."

"This is no one's fault," reassured Thea. "Only his." Mirabelle slammed him down into another chair, his body limp, defeated. His eyes opened partway, his whole posture sagging when his eyes met Thea's. She recognized the look; all the fight in him was gone. She knew exactly how that felt; it was the way she had felt before the Black Coats had come along.

Casey glanced up at the clock. "There are maybe twenty-five minutes before his guests start arriving. We needed to be gone ten minutes ago."

Bea stepped forward, her brown eyes blazing. "I only need three. And he's going to get a very special gift from me." She pulled up her hood and kneeled before Raphael, her voice changing to its commanding cadence. She thrust her hands out toward him. "Raphael Amadoor, look at me. Do you trust me?" He nodded. "Then surrender." This time, without hesitation, he did.

They left wearing the same cleaning uniforms that they had arrived in, leaving behind a house painted with a man's guilt and that same man sleeping peacefully inside. At the end of his driveway a black sedan lingered. Thea approached the window, which lowered just enough to see Nixon's dark eyes. "Anything to report?"

Still dripping wet, Thea tilted her head, preparing to give the full details of the near disaster that had just occurred. Then she thought better of it. "Team Banner handled all conflicts. The Balancing is complete."

Nixon lowered the sunglasses perched on her head over her eyes. "Good. See you girls on Monday." Then she gave

Thea a sly wink just over the tinted glass. "I was never far away. And, Thea—nice sprint."

A happy flush ran up Thea's cheeks. "Thanks."

Team Banner pulled away from the house, Casey quickly putting as much space between them and the Amadoor residence as possible. The team was giddy with delight as the golden Texas sun set in their dusty windshield. Mirabelle cranked up the music and they flew back toward Austin. As Mirabelle began singing along with a country song, Thea turned to Bea in the back seat. "What exactly did you do to Raphael?"

Bea smiled. "It's complicated. He won't remember the events of today, only that he had a nervous breakdown over his own guilt." She grinned. "Also a little extra present: Raphael will find himself violently ill at the thought of hurting a woman."

Thea leaned her head back against the seat with a sigh. "You're amazing, you know." Thea's mind was churning as the car flew down the highway, the noise of her team fading to a background din. All she could see were Raphael's eyes on her underwater, desperate and afraid. She had seen herself reflected in his eyes, and ever since then, doubt had pressed uncomfortably against her chest: *Was what we just did to Raphael justice? Or was it torture?*

As their car sped back toward Austin, Mirabelle spun around, reaching for each of their hands. "Something has changed," Mirabelle whispered. "Can you feel it?"

Thea pushed her negative feelings aside and leaned forward, her eyes like embers in the dying light, the last strangled rays of gold passing over her strong features. Her voice was soft but strong when she spoke.

"We're not Team Banner anymore. We're Black Coats."

PART TWO

SEVENTEEN

The sunset is stunning from here, Thea thought. Only a month had passed since she and Drew had lain on the blanket in her yard and in that time it seemed like an entire season had changed. Beyond her view, a yellow horizon hovered under a cluster of dusty-blue clouds. Underneath it was the wide stretch of land belonging to Drew's father. Wind swirled around her shins, lifting her white sundress momentarily before it settled around her. Thea wiped the sweat from her brow, unsure if she was sweating because of the ungodly hotness of this evening or because she was about to eat dinner with Adam Porter—Drew's dad—who was incredibly intimidating.

"What do you think of our patio, Thea?"

Thea turned back to Drew's dad, a handsome man in his early fifties with salt-and-pepper hair and eyes that looked just like Drew's. He was standing at the edge of the porch, his rigid posture intimidating. One hand was shoved in the pocket of his khaki shorts, the other clutched a beer. In all honesty, it seemed he was a bit nervous, too.

Thea cleared her throat. "It's lovely out here. Is that the end of your property there? By the horse?"

Adam Porter smiled. "Oh, you mean Applejax? He's got one foot in the grave, but we keep him around to trim the fields, I guess. A goat would probably do a better job."

"True," acknowledged Thea. "But then you would have to have a goat."

Mr. Porter laughed before pointing at her. "I like you, Thea."

Drew came out onto the patio, carrying a steaming platter of barbecue. "Okay, the beef is sauced, and I think we can all prepare ourselves for the meat sweats." He set it down on the splintered wooden table next to corn on the cob and homemade honey buns, courtesy of Thea's mom. The three of them settled around the table. After a quick grace, they dived in. Thea ate delicately while the two men attacked their ribs.

"So, Thea, how exactly did you and Drew meet?" asked Mr. Porter between bites.

"Dad." Drew shook his head. "This isn't our engagement party. Chill out."

Mr. Porter slapped his son on the back. "Don't be embarrassed, Drew. I'm just curious how a goofy guy manages to win the heart of a very interesting girl."

This is going well, Thea thought happily. On the drive

over, she had had nightmarish visions of his dad—what if he was a bigot, a racist? What if she said something that accidentally offended him? What if he hated that his son had begun seriously dating someone right before college? What if, what if, what if . . .

Thea was happy to see that her fears were unfounded, when upon opening the door, she had been greeted with a friendly bear hug from Mr. Porter. Now, as Thea sat at their table, across from the men, she felt content and nervous at the same time.

"So . . ." Mr. Porter leaned forward, a meaty rib in his hand.

"Oh yes, how did we meet?" Thea cleared her throat.

Drew didn't let her answer. "Thea was swimming in a fountain outside of school."

Mr. Porter almost choked on his beer. "I'm sorry?"

"When I met Thea, she was swimming around in the Bucket," he continued.

Mr. Porter's eyebrows raised. "That disgusting fountain outside the school? Oh, Thea, why? That water is not even close to blue. Why on earth were you in it?"

"It's still a mystery." Drew raised his eyebrows as he squeezed a lime over the corncobs. "She says she dropped her schedule, but I have my doubts."

Thea leaned back in her seat, her heart beating a little faster than she would like. *Think of a lie. Quick.* "Okay, you got me. I had dropped something else. A ring."

Drew tilted his head, his eyes narrowing. "A ring? Why didn't you say so?"

Thea's heart ached at what she was about to say. "It was Natalie's. I didn't want to talk about it."

The silence could have cracked the wood table in two. Drew put down his corn, his eyes full of sorrow. "I'm so sorry, Thea. I didn't know."

"It's okay." *You lying cow,* Thea reprimanded herself. *What am I doing?*

Mr. Porter leaned back in his chair, his eyes sympathetic. "Drew told me about your cousin. I remember when it was all over the news. I'm so sorry that you had to go through that. I'm sure it's been really hard on your family."

Thea clenched her napkin under the table, willing herself not to cry. There was something about the kindness of these two men that threatened to break her. "It hasn't been easy," she mumbled, looking for an out.

Mr. Porter must have seen her struggling for a change of subject and decided to help. "So Drew told me that he took you to Harry's on your first date?"

Thea looked at him gratefully. "He did, and it was quite the experience."

Their conversation blossomed out from there, easily darting from one subject to the next. To her surprise she found herself enjoying the evening, tossing secret smiles Drew's way, laughing at the funny relationship Drew had with his dad—Drew groaning at his dad's jokes, Mr. Porter taking such obvious pride in his son's accomplishments.

After a spectacular meal, Thea stood to help clear the table but was intercepted by Mr. Porter. "Sit, sit! We'll do that later. You are our guest! I insist."

Thea smiled, shyly tucking her hair back behind one ear. Drew's dad paused. "So, Thea, tell me about this club you're in! Drew said you flip houses?"

Drew stared hard at his father. "No, Dad, that's not what I said. She *fixes* old houses."

"Oh. That makes more sense. I was going to say, that's a lot of work for a high schooler."

Thea clenched her teeth, losing track of the lies. "We take old Victorian houses and slowly restore them with a team of other high school girls. It's intense work, but it's very rewarding."

Mr. Porter's eyes narrowed. "It's so interesting! How did you ever find out about this kind of thing? Is it offered at Roosevelt? They seem like more of a bread-and-butter athletics kind of school." He nodded at Drew, who was lazily tracing his fingers down Thea's arm. "No offense, son."

"None taken. The place is kind of crappy."

Mr. Porter raised his beer. "So how do you like this society?"

Thea let a deep truth pour out of her. "You know how when you see something deeply broken, you just want to fix it? Well, sometimes you can't, because you don't have the resources, or you aren't strong enough. But these houses, which are sometimes filthy places, crawling with rats and waste, you can fix them. You can do something about it."

She sighed. "That's why I love it. Because as I restore these houses, I feel like . . ."

"You're restoring yourself." Drew was looking at her now, his green eyes seeing everything about her except the truth.

Thea took a jagged breath and lay back against the crook of his arm. "Yeah."

Adam Porter watched her with curious eyes. "So do they let dads join?"

Thea and Drew started laughing. "No, they don't, and you're the second dad to ask about it. My father desperately wants in."

Mr. Porter patted his full belly. "Well, maybe your dad and I will have to get together to find our own houses to restore."

"That's not fair," muttered Drew. "All I have is soccer, and I don't care about that half as much as you care about this."

"Son." Mr. Porter's eyes bore down on his son. "Don't ever sell short your abilities. You're amazing out there."

"I have to agree," intoned Thea. "I've heard about your amazing abilities myself."

"And yet, you've never seen a game." Drew's voice carried a sharpness that surprised Thea, though she knew she deserved it.

"Well, we will have to change that, won't we?" she said, softly resting her fingers on his elbow.

"Will you bring pom-poms? Say you will."

"Drew Abraham Porter!" His dad stood. "Stop teasing the poor girl and get her some peach cobbler."

Thea grinned. "Yes, get the poor girl some cobbler, please."

Drew leaped up from the table. Adam Porter watched their visitor in the waning sun. "Can I ask you something, Thea?" She turned her head. His eyes burned into hers, curious and intense. "How is Drew doing? With his mom leaving and all."

Thea swallowed. "To be honest, he hasn't really talked to me about it. A mention here and there but nothing more."

Mr. Porter nodded. "That's about what I get, too. It's got to be hard. His mom already had two feet out the door when he turned ten. Mothering was just too much for her. She was . . . not like you."

Thea tilted her head. "How do you mean?"

"You're strong. I can see it. A girl doesn't make it through something like her cousin's murder without a spine of iron." He shook his head. "Nasty world we live in, where people take things into their own hands, lean into their most selfish desire. People like that destroy lives." His eyes lingered on Drew happily doling out a bucket's worth of whipped cream on top of each dessert. She squirmed uncomfortably, remembering the blood that had dashed over her knuckles the night before. It hadn't been her own. "Thea, I sure hope they caught the bastard who did that to your cousin."

In the background the strains of Johnnyswim began playing over the kitchen radio. Adam Porter smiled and stood up from the table. "Thea, it's been a while, but would you dance with me? I love this song."

Thea offered her hand, and Drew's dad took it, twirling her around the patio. When he stomped his feet and began clapping, Drew joined in. Thea lifted her feet and threw out her arms, letting the happy beat echo through her. It was the opposite of what she had expected: meeting her boyfriend's dad had somehow turned into a truly lovely evening. Thea spun in the twilight, letting a carefree delight wash over her: a new feeling for a new time.

Thea returned home a few hours later, hoping to slip into the bed she was beginning to miss so much. A light was on in the kitchen, and when she entered the room, the solitary figure at the table made her leap backward. "Oh my God! Mom! You scared me. What are you doing up so late?"

"Oh, sorry, honey." Her mom rested her arms on their worn kitchen table. "I was just making some tea for your friend."

Thea shook her head. "Drew stayed home with his dad. He's not here."

"Not Drew, honey, your other friend. Mirabelle?" Her mom's voice dropped to a whisper. "Is that the one you and Natalie used to talk about?" She checked behind her. "You know, the mean girl?"

Mom, Thea thought, cringing.

"Well, she's here." Her mom raised her eyes. "She's upstairs in your room, and pretty upset by the looks of it."

Thea nodded, inwardly sighing. An emotional Mirabelle was going to be the opposite of sleep. Thea's mom handed her two steaming mugs of tea. "Quick, tell me—how was meeting Drew's dad?"

Thea sighed. "Good. I really liked him, actually. We had a good time. They have a horse."

"Interesting. Is his dad a rancher?"

Thea shook her head. "No, he's some sort of public defender, I think."

Her mom patted her cheek softly. "You've got your color back, girl. It must be Drew." She raised her eyebrows with a smile.

"Mom, stop." Even as she said it, Thea knew that she didn't mean it. Seeing her mom smile was a gift that she would never again take for granted.

"Okay, I won't keep you. Go see Mirabelle." She shook her head with a laugh. "Wonders never cease."

Thea made her way up the stairs, the smell of honey and chamomile tea making her eyes water. With her foot she pushed open the door. "Hey, Mirabelle, what's—" She stopped when she saw her face. Her teammate looked destroyed. Mascara had run down her cheeks in long black rivulets. Her normally bright blue eyes were red and glassy, and her perfect mane of hair was piled into a tousled bun on top of her head. Thea put the mugs down on her bookcase before turning to Mirabelle. "Oh my God. What happened? Are you okay?" She pulled her into a quick hug before stepping backward.

Mirabelle reached into the pocket of her hooded sweatshirt and pulled out a folded piece of paper. She handed it to Thea, her hand giving a slight tremble. Thea carefully unfolded the tearstained paper.

Mirabelle Watts Inheritance
Dear Mirabelle,
As a luminary, it is my job to decide when it is the appropriate time for you to earn your inheritance. I feel that the time has come for you, Mirabelle Watts, to take yours. With my permission, you may commission your team for this Balancing. Both the target and the severity of the punishment are up to you. All the information you need is provided here.
Signed,
Julie Westing

Thea struggled to find her breath. *An inheritance? Already?* It was crazy. Did that mean hers was on the way, too? She shook her head. "What are you going to do?"

Mirabelle leaped up. "What do you mean, what am I going to do? I'm going to take it!" The streetlight cast shadows across her sharp cheekbones. "Marc Mitzi stole my parents from me. He paid a three-thousand-dollar fine and was in prison for a very short time for reckless endangerment." She spun around, her eyes flashing. "A slap on the wrist, for taking my entire life!" She curled her fist. "We are going to make him bleed. Tonight."

"No. Not tonight. Not tomorrow night. We need time to plan, and I'm not letting you go out when you are in a state like this. Look at you. You're a train wreck, and it's understandable, but you are not in the right frame of mind for a Balancing. No way." She reached out for Mirabelle, who was sobbing into her hands. "I know you want to go right now, because you've been waiting for this your entire life, but tonight is not the night. Say it."

Mirabelle took in a painful breath before she choked out the words. "Tonight is not the night."

Thea curled her arm around her friend's shoulder. "Okay. We will do this. Today is Saturday. How about Wednesday night? We'll leave straight after school for Mademoiselle Corday, grab our gear, and then go. But, Mirabelle, you know it can't be you. Hitting him. You're too invested emotionally. It has to be us."

Mirabelle nodded, her voice now stripped of all emotion. "I'll stay in the car."

Thea doubted it, but that was something to worry about later. "Mirabelle, we'll get him, okay? We just need time to plan." Thea eyed her bed with longing. "Why don't you stay here tonight? I'll sleep on the floor. I used to do that all the time with—" She lost her voice halfway through the sentence.

"Natalie?" Mirabelle turned to her with haunted eyes.

Thea nodded. "With Natalie." Mirabelle pressed her forehead against Thea's, their grief uniting them.

"Why do other people think they can take *our people* away from us?" Mirabelle sniffed.

Thea closed her eyes, willing the tears away. Tonight was Mirabelle's night to cry, not hers. "I don't know," she whispered. "But it's not fair. We'll make it right, okay?"

Mirabelle nodded. "Okay." She stepped back from Thea, wiping her eyes. "Thanks for letting me stay." She looked at the bed. "Also, do you have any fresh sheets? Because gross."

Thea let out a relieved sigh. "Good to have you back, Mirabelle."

Mirabelle glanced at Thea's one-eyed teddy bear. "I mean, it's not the Ritz, but I'll make do." After Thea had turned out the light, Mirabelle fell asleep within minutes, exhausted by her emotions. Her mouth was halfway open, and she snorted with soft snores, one arm clutched around the teddy bear that had once been Natalie's.

Thea lay awake on the floor, watching the shadows glide across the ceiling as cars passed on the street. *An inheritance. Why would they give Mirabelle hers so early?* There was no explanation, except one that only the luminaries understood. She turned over, cracking her neck and wincing at the pain of the floor pushing up against her hip as her friend breathed comfortably above. There was, however, a strange reassurance in Mirabelle's snores. Thea had forgotten how oddly comforting a sleepover could be—that feeling of not being alone in the world. If only Natalie could see her now, lying on the floor with freaking Mirabelle Watts in her bed, she would die laughing. *She had died.* Thea watched Mirabelle for a minute before turning over. *They have taken so much from us,* she thought, *and we will take it all back.* She settled down into her sleeping bag. *Our vengeance is finally beginning.*

She had almost surrendered to sleep when her phone buzzed underneath her pillow.

"Turn it off!" grumbled Mirabelle, rolling over with a huff. Thea ignored her and let the light of the phone wash over her face. It was a text from Nixon:

I am saddened to share that this week one of our founding luminaries, Robin Peterson, surrendered to the breast cancer that she bravely fought for years. All teams must be at Mademoiselle Corday promptly by 10:00 a.m. tomorrow to attend the funeral.

"Oh no." Thea let her head sink back against the pillow, sad for the woman with whom she had spoken so briefly at the Team Banner celebration. Robin had seemed wise and strong, the kind of person who wore her trauma with grace. Thea turned over. *What does this mean for the Black*

Coats? What does this mean for Sahil? After another half hour of tossing and turning, Thea finally was taken by sleep, where hazy dreams of long roads and black soil tore violently at her subconscious.

Early the next morning, after sending Mirabelle home to change, Thea pushed open the door to her closet and reached for the dress that she had sworn she would never wear again: a simple black cotton dress with lace cap sleeves. Thea shuddered as she pulled it out of the closet, remembering the last time she had worn this dress, the way it had pressed against her throat as she watched her dad struggle with Natalie's coffin. Unfortunately, it was her only option with this short notice; she couldn't very well show up in a cheery yellow dress or jeans and a blouse. No. It had to be this dress. Thea pulled it over her head, noting the sour smell at the armpits, wincing as it fell over her hips. *Don't think about it.* Over the dress she threw on her black coat, twisted her messy curls into a loose side bun, and dashed on mascara before heading downstairs. Her mom was in the kitchen, humming a quiet song while she fixed eggs for Thea's father.

"Hey! Is your friend here? I hope she likes . . ." Menah stopped when she saw Thea in her dress and coat. Her eyes narrowed. "Why are you wearing that?"

Shit. I should have snuck out and left a note, she thought, too late. Now there was going to be a conversation.

"Umm, well, my friend's mom died from breast cancer. She asked me to come to the funeral."

Her dad dropped his book on the table. "Oh, Thea, that's horrible! Who was it?"

Thea shook her head. "You don't know her. She's in the restoration society with me." *So far, no outright lies. This is good.*

"What is her name?" he asked with concern.

Thea swallowed, saying the first name that came to mind. "Bea."

"Oh, honey!" Her mom wrapped her arms around Thea in a stifling hug. "I'm sorry, honey. I'll be honest, I was looking forward to seeing you this morning, but this is more important." She pulled back to look at Thea's face. "It might be hard to go to another funeral. Do you want to borrow one of my dresses?"

It was tempting, but Thea eyed the clock above the stove. She was already cutting it close. Sometimes she swore lateness was in her DNA. "No, I'm okay. Really." Her dad was staring at her with sad eyes, no doubt thinking of Natalie. Thea berated herself. This was too much for them. *God, why did I wear this stupid dress?* "I have to go." Thea grabbed her purse from the counter and gave her mom a quick kiss. "I don't know how long I'll be."

"Thea." Her dad's strict voice filled the kitchen. It wasn't a sound she heard often. "We haven't seen much of you lately, and I don't like it. I think it's great you are going to support your friend this morning, but tonight you will be here for dinner, and then you are hanging out with your two lame parents, watching a movie of their choosing. This is not a request."

Thea nodded. "That's fair."

"Good." Her dad snapped open the paper. "I'm going to choose the most awkward movie I can find. That'll teach you to ignore us."

The door slammed behind Thea as she made her way to her Honda, thankful that she had parents who cared but also nervous about their growing curiosity about her activities. She turned the key and flew out of her neighborhood, wondering just how long she could keep this lie going.

EIGHTEEN

A half hour later, Thea pushed open the front door of Mademoiselle Corday to absolute silence. Where was everyone? She stepped forward, straining to hear anything. Quietly, she tiptoed her way through the house, clutching her purse, wondering if she was the victim of a final bizarre hazing into the Black Coats. At last there was something: a whisper coming from the kitchen area. *The kitchen?* She wound her way into the huge room, ducking under the hanging copper pots. The sound of women's voices singing some sort of dirge was coming from the pantry. *The pantry? What the hell was going on here?*

Thea pushed open the door and was met with a familiar sight: canned milk, jars of honey, and bags of flour. She stared for a moment before her eyes caught it, tracing the line of the ceiling down toward the shelves. There, invisible if someone wasn't looking for it, was the faint outline of a door. *A secret door.* Although it probably wasn't all that secret if everyone had gone through it already.

Thea snuck through the door and started down a steep brick staircase that wound deep into the damp earth. At the bottom, the staircase opened up to a sliding barn door. Voices tumbled out of the opening while Thea ducked down into her coat, hoping no one would notice that she was late. The room was full of bodies, so many bodies that Thea soon found herself crushed in a horde of shoulders, each of them wearing a black coat. Rising to her toes, she spotted her team, tucked away in the left corner of the room. At the front of the room was a long wooden table, and upon that the coffin of Robin Peterson ominously loomed over the proceedings, her black coat draped over it. Beeswax candles dripped in every possible corner, and the air was thick with incense. Near the coffin, Julie Westing was directing a small choir of Black Coats through a song that Thea actually knew: "God's Gonna Cut You Down," the Johnny Cash cover version. Her dad was a Cash fan, and, apparently, Robin had been, too. The Black Coats' voices rose through the basement, filling the cold room with sound and raising the hairs on the back of her neck. Of course they had perfect harmony. Casey caught her eye with a disapproving glare and motioned her over. Thea had started toward them when she saw Sahil, seated behind Julie at the front. It wasn't the fact that he was curled over with his hands on his eyes, so obviously broken by grief that hurt her

210

heart. It was what he was wearing. Gone were the white linen tunic and pants, the only outfit Thea had ever seen him in, and in their place was an immaculate black suit. A properly pressed black suit for his mother's funeral. As she watched, he raised his dark eyes and stared at the coffin, his eyes dull. Thea knew from her experience that he probably wasn't even processing what was going on right now. He was deep within himself, watching all of this like an out-of-body experience and telling himself in some small, comforting way that this wasn't actually happening to him.

Thea felt tears pooling at the corner of her eyes. She didn't really know Robin at all, but she knew what it was like to lose a loved one. After that, life's never the same. As the song came to a close, Julie cut off the choir and raised her hands for the crowd's attention.

"Robin loved that song. I know, because she played it on repeat constantly." The women gave a polite chuckle. Sahil looked like he was going to throw up. "Many of you know this already, but for those new team members who don't, Robin and I started the Black Coats after she was raped in 1972, just outside of Grapeland High School." Julie turned toward Robin's coffin, sorrow distorting her face. "She was a friend, a confidante, and a partner. We disagreed constantly, but that didn't change the fact that we built the Black Coats together." Some in the crowd gave a quiet clap.

"It hurts to say goodbye to her. Robin had an unbridled enthusiasm for life and optimism that she poured out onto all of us, for justice and for the Black Coats. She will be missed by so many—sisters here, sisters afar, and by her son, Sahil. I know she was most proud of him, a man who will *always* do what needs to be done to protect women." Sahil looked away from the coffin, his face a violent struggle. Julie's eyes narrowed, and the candlelight flickered off her hollowed cheeks.

"But for now we must look forward, to the future of our organization. As the sole luminary I will do my best to lead this group. We will cut out our weaknesses. I will work to secure what we have and plunge us firmly into the future of this great city. We will rise from Robin's loss stronger, a group of women who will be feared and respected. We will stand against those who oppose us, and to those who hunt us"—she paused—"we will join you on the black road." The Black Coats erupted into thundering applause.

The three presidents stood rigidly near the body like guards protecting a king. Nixon stood perfectly still, but tears crawled down her face. McKinley faced forward, her eyes darting from Robin's coffin to Julie and back. Kennedy was smiling at Julie with a worshipful expression.

The luminary continued, "And now, Robin will sleep in the cradle of the place that she loved so well, as we send her on with prayers for her eternal rest." Julie carefully laid her hand on the coffin. She ran her palm over Robin's coat with a nostalgic look on her face. Then she turned back to the Black Coats. "Please head upstairs to the Haunt, where we will toast our Robin with her favorite drink—a gin and tonic—and other refreshments. Thank you all for coming."

Thea pressed against the wall as the crowd moved past her, a cold look crossing Julie's features when her eyes met Thea's. Then she was gone, followed by a pack of Black Coats all making their way up the stairs.

Mirabelle sidled up next to Thea, elbowing her softly. "Way to be late to a funeral, team leader!"

Thea shook her head. "I know. I'm sorry. My parents were difficult this morning."

"Don't worry, I think only Julie noticed," Casey said softly.

Louise was red-eyed. "It was so sad! Robin wasn't even that old!"

"More reason to live for right now," said Bea as she squeezed Louise's arm.

Casey fiddled with her collar. "Speaking of, I'm going to attempt to get a gin and tonic. Who's going to card us *here*?"

Mirabelle looked over at her with exasperation. "Of course you would be thinking about that right now."

Louise leaned in. "Did you hear what Julie said about cutting our weakness? Is that us? Are we the weakness?"

"I don't think she was talking about us. I think she was talking about someone coming after the Black Coats. I've heard whispers that they are worried about that," Mirabelle replied.

Louise shook her head. "Who would be that stupid?"

Thea saw that Sahil had not moved from his spot on the chair. "You guys go on ahead. I'll be a minute." The team looked at Thea with raised eyebrows before heading upstairs. Thea walked over to Sahil and rested a hand on his shoulder, dully aware of the fact that there was a dead body a foot from where she stood. "Hey," she said gently.

"Hey." His voice was ragged and dry, probably from all the crying he had done. Thea didn't say anything. Sometimes it was best to just let the other person feel, to be open to whatever came out of his mouth. "She was sick for a long time," he croaked. She nodded. Sahil went on, "She was ready. We were ready. Everything was prepared, and yet . . ." He let out a sob. "I don't feel ready for this."

Thea shook her head. "No one is."

He wiped away a tear with a half laugh. "How creepy is this place down here?"

"Yeah, it's pretty bleak. Is this where they keep all the bodies?"

Sahil's head jerked up. "What do you mean?"

"Nothing. It was just a joke. Bad timing. Funerals make people do weird things," said Thea. Sahil cracked a smile, but it wasn't honest.

Thea looked at the floor. "It gets easier. I never thought I would say that, but somehow it's true. I thought I would never laugh again. It was like a grenade was dropped onto my entire life and yet I laugh. I smile. I look forward to things."

Sahil raised his eyes. "Like our training?"

Thea shook her head. "Well, I wouldn't go that far."

"Thanks for talking to me. Everyone is acting like I'm either invisible or made of glass." He pushed up from his chair. "I should probably go upstairs. Julie will be waiting for me to pretend I'm supportive of everything she does. My mom's body is barely cold for three minutes and she's already changing things." He sighed. "I just want to run. Far away from here. From everyone and everything."

Thea took his hand. "Anytime you want to run, I'll run with you." She paused. "As long as you don't run out of the state, because that won't work for me." He smiled, and this time it was real. "I'll see you upstairs, okay? Take your time. Everyone else can wait." She gave his hand a squeeze.

As she climbed the stairs, the light growing brighter with each step, she was at once sorry for Sahil and thankful that she wasn't lingering in that kind of darkness anymore. There was no way through it but time.

She found Team Banner seated outside, spread over a picnic table just outside the Haunt's open doors. Inside the Haunt, the sounds of a polite reception filled the space, whereas outside the air buzzed with the sound of bees seeking sweet nectar. Mirabelle had lain down on the picnic table, a pair of bright yellow sunglasses perched on the end of her nose. "How was Sahil? I didn't know you were hot for him."

"I'm not," snapped Thea. "He's a friend, and someone who could use more friends, frankly."

"Mirabelle!" Bea snapped. "He's grieving! Give it a rest!"

Mirabelle sighed. "Okay, but only because I know what it's like to lose a mom." She pushed herself up on her elbows as Louise took a sip of sweet tea. Thea parked herself next to Casey. "So did you wrangle a gin and tonic?"

Casey fiddled with her key ring. "Nope. Damn Black Coats, following the law only when it suits them."

Mirabelle snorted. "Hey, how long do you think we have to be here?"

Thea drummed her fingers on the tabletop, half listening, her mind on Sahil's grief-wracked face. "I'm not sure, but here comes Nixon to tell us. Sit up, Mirabelle. Now!"

Mirabelle scurried to a normal sitting position. Their tired-looking president approached the table. She had obviously been up all night. "Nixon," started Thea, "I'm sorry for your loss."

Nixon raised a hand to silence her. "Thank you for your condolences. I've just been informed by Julie that Mirabelle has been given her inheritance." The rest of the team sat forward in surprise. Nixon shifted on her feet. "This is the earliest Balancing I have ever seen. Much too early, I think, for your team. However, the Black Coat bylaws state that this is Mirabelle's choice and not mine. Therefore, I would urge you, Mirabelle, to be patient."

"No." Mirabelle stood, her eyes filled with defiance. "If it's not your choice, then I will choose to do it now. I'm not meaning to be disrespectful, but this is something I've been waiting ten years for. I will not wait a minute longer than I have to."

Nixon shook her head. "I believe that's a mistake, but it's still your mistake to make. Just make sure you take the entire team." Her eyes met Thea's as she turned around with a sigh. "Now go mingle. I'll not have my team out here looking like the reject table at a high school."

Casey waved her arms around. "Um, hello—we *are* the reject team and this *is* our table." Thea thought she saw a ghost of a smile on Nixon's face, but then she turned to go, with an order. "I'll not ask again. Mingle or leave."

The team looked at one another, no need to even speak.

Casey tossed her car keys in the air. "Let's go hang at Mirabelle's and get slushies."

"Beatrice?" The sharp voice caught them by surprise. The team turned. Julie Westing stood before them, statuesque, her eyes on Bea. She didn't seem to even notice the other team members. "Hello, Beatrice, I'm Julie. I'm one of the luminaries—" She stopped midsentence, blinking. "No, I'm sorry. That's not right. I'm *the* luminary." For a moment, Thea thought she saw a sliver of humanity in this woman, but then it was gone, just like Nixon's smile. "I would be delighted if you would come have a drink with me."

Bea fidgeted nervously. "Well, actually, we were just about to leave."

"I'm sure they won't mind." Julie's eyes met Thea's. "If your team leader says it's okay."

Thea knew better than to object. "Of course that's

fine." She turned to face Julie. "I'm sorry for your loss, Ms. Westing." *Sorry, Bea.*

Julie raised her chin, and her eyes went cold. "Thank you for your condolences, Miss Soloman." She put a hand on Bea's back. "Now, if you come with me, I'll show you the best seat in the Haunt. It's my favorite place to sit and think." Bea gave the girls a desperate look before disappearing back into the thick crowd of Black Coats now filtering out into the yard.

Mirabelle watched her go. "What's so great about Bea?"

Casey shot her an annoyed look. "Do you really have to ask?"

Thea was standing still, watching Julie turn Bea around like a prized pony in front of some Black Coats alumni. "She is very important to them."

"But us, too," piped up Louise. "She's a part of Team Banner."

Probably not for long, Thea noted silently. That was the last thing her team needed to hear right now. The sun was high in the sky, another scorching day on its way, and Thea felt a bead of sweat drop down her neck. "Let's head out."

Something about this funeral was making her very uncomfortable. *Where would Robin's body go? Why was Nixon so stressed?* They piled into Mirabelle's car. Bea's empty seat stared up at Thea as Casey turned the car out onto the gravel roads surrounding Mademoiselle Corday.

"Who wants to go really, really fast?" she whispered.

"Me," said Thea, leaning against the seat. "Let's fly."

The car shot forward with a roar. Thea looked out the window just in time to see a flash of black dart through the woods—a blur, something moving between the trees, something dangerously swift. She leaned her damp forehead against the window to see more clearly. It was Sahil, running through the woods. He was racing as though he could outrun his sadness, as if grief wasn't chasing him like a hungry animal. She pressed her hand up against the window, feeling empathy wash over her. She knew that feeling all too well, and sadly she knew the truth: grief would run him down every time.

NINETEEN

Wednesday came too quickly, and Thea found herself walking as slowly as possible to her locker after her late-morning chemistry class. Normally, she anticipated the rush of administering justice, but something about Mirabelle's Balancing was making her uncomfortable. She was quietly switching her books in the locker when she felt arms wrap around her waist. "You better be my boyfriend, otherwise . . ."

She heard Drew chuckle behind her. "And what if it wasn't?"

Thea spun around, her lips against his ear. "I would slam my head backward into your nose, stunning you. Then I would spin around, knee you in the junk, slam your head against my knee, and throw you on the ground. Then I would put my foot on your neck to keep you down."

"Uhhh." Drew stepped backward, his hands in the air.

"That's more than a little terrifying. Are you a serial killer in your free time?"

Thea shrugged, though she was smiling. "I don't know, I always thought Dexter was on the right side of things."

Drew shook his head with a laugh. "Yeah, vigilante justice isn't justice, though." He said it so easily that she felt his words bruise her like a plum.

This conversation was on the verge of getting messy quickly, so Thea leaned forward. "It's a good thing I like your arms around me, that's all I'm saying." That wasn't a lie.

"No kidding, psycho. Hey, I have something for you."

"Oh yeah?" She smiled.

"So because a guy at my dad's old work got food poisoning"—he raised his hands with a woot-woot and Thea burst out laughing—"my dad has two Andrew Bird tickets for tonight and get this: they're going to have an ice-cream-waffle food truck there. Thea. Ice cream waffles. Are you hearing me?"

Thea's mouth opened and shut. "I can't. I have . . ."

Drew raised his eyebrow. "I'm sure you can miss one day of house restoration for this amazing date." He let out an exasperated sigh. "Hot fudge on a waffle, Thea. You are coming with me."

Thea took a long look at his face, realizing that this might be a make-or-break moment for their relationship. He had been patient with her chaotic schedule and broken dates so far, but she could see that it was wearing on him.

"Okay, yes. I'll see what I can do. I have to rearrange some things. Can I at least meet you at the concert to give me more time?"

"Yes! Absolutely." Drew hugged her with a delirious grin and spun her around. "It's a date. Music and waffles and you. A man could not ask for more, truly."

Thea laughed in spite of her growing panic. "If I'm going, I'm getting extra sprinkles. You should know I have a thing for rainbow sprinkles."

"Yeah, you will!" Drew high-fived her and then kissed her hard on the lips. Thea's heart tilted and spun, realizing what had been sneaking up on her; Drew made her so happy. His excitement about life was contagious, and he looked at her differently from how anyone ever had. It was as though he reflected her own light back to her. It was extraordinary.

"I need to let my friends know. Can you send me the concert info?" she asked.

Drew gently took his fingers and trailed them up her neck, lifting her chin. "Yes. You have made me very happy today." He kissed her softly, the tip of his tongue trailing gently along her bottom lip before whispering across her mouth, "Maybe it's the waffles, though. I can't tell."

"Take it down a notch, you two. You're not getting married." Mr. Parrot passed by them in the hallway, a reprimanding look on his face in response to their PDA. They pulled back from each other.

"That guy." Drew shook his head. "I'm going to put a dead fish in his radiator before I graduate."

"You will do no such thing." Thea waited until the teacher turned the corner and kissed Drew on the cheek. "Okay, I got to run. But I'll see you tonight."

Drew raised his eyebrows. "Thea, wear something . . ." She raised a quizzical eyebrow, daring him to finish that sentence. "That can get hot fudge on it."

Her smile dazzled every person she passed on her way to the door. Once she got into her car she whipped out her phone, texting the team that Mirabelle's inheritance was going to need to start early—in fact, it needed to start pretty much now. They would all be skipping the remainder of school today. Everyone seemed okay with that.

Since Mademoiselle Corday was out of the way, they decided to meet at a park near Marc Mitzi's house in one of Austin's older neighborhoods. The houses were tiny and crammed together, which would be an issue for their exposure if this was the sort of neighborhood where people cared about that sort of thing. Luckily, it was not. Mirabelle sat bursting with nervous energy in the front seat, Marc's file spilling out over her lap. There was a small window when Marc would be home—from two thirty to five in the afternoon.

Casey drummed on the dashboard. "Are we sure we want this to be a Code Evening?"

Thea looked squarely at Mirabelle. "I don't know. And I still don't think you should come inside with us."

"Like hell I'm not." Mirabelle's eyes flashed angrily. "Thea, are you going to stay in the car when we go find Natalie's killer?"

Thea let out a long breath, her chest tightening at the prospect. "No."

Mirabelle crossed her arms. "That's what I thought. Also, if anyone asks me again, I swear to God, I will punch them in the face."

No one asked again. At 1:45 p.m., Casey pulled the car into the small alleyway behind Marc's house. They silently climbed out of the car and made their way up to his back gate. With a hoist from Bea, Thea reached over and unlocked the gate, and they filtered into his backyard. It was surprisingly nice for the neighborhood it was in, with a trim lawn and flowering bushes lining the fence. Thea motioned them forward, and the girls moved quickly to the back of the house. Thea knelt at the back door and pulled a crowbar out of her backpack. "Move aside, ladies," she whispered.

"No need." Bea grinned. She pushed the door inward with a creak. "It's open."

Casey shook her head. "People are ridiculously trusting."

With Mirabelle in the lead, they made their way inside. Thea was the last one in, shutting and locking the door behind them. The back door opened up into a galley kitchen, cluttered but clean. Within seconds, Mirabelle was walking near the sink, her fingertips trailing over plates and forks, her eyes red.

"He eats here." She turned to the team. "He gets to eat, every day. He gets to laugh and have dinner and watch TV, and my parents don't. Just because he felt like having a drink that night." No one said anything.

They all jumped when a car door slammed outside. "Shit! He's home early!" Thea looked around the kitchen. "Everyone in the back bedroom! Now!"

They moved down the hallway, shutting the door halfway behind them. Thea looked around the room. It was basic: a bed, a dresser, and not much more. There was a framed picture on the wall of a misty forest scene, and a Dallas Cowboys hat hung on the bedpost. Thea, however, became fixated on another item: a well-loved stuffed unicorn with tattered wings was propped up against a pillow.

"Stay here!" she ordered, and darted out of the bedroom, making her way down the short hallway. She threw open a door—a bathroom. The next door was a closet. Finally, she flung open the last door, hoping to find storage or perhaps a rack of dead bodies, anything other than what she was seeing. There was a bunk bed in the kids' room. The decor indicated that a boy and a girl shared the room; a *Frozen* comforter was crumpled on the floor alongside a heap of giant Transformer action figures. Kids' drawings covered a small table where untouched goldfish crackers sat in a bowl. *No, no, no . . .* This was wrong; it was all wrong.

Thea rushed back up the hallway, shutting the door quietly behind her. Team Banner looked at her with alarm. "We have to leave. He has children! We can't be here!"

Mirabelle suddenly pushed Thea up against the wall, her arm pressed against her neck. *God, she was strong.* "He killed my parents!" she hissed at Thea.

"Mirabelle." Casey was looking over at the dresser, where, in a framed picture, two kids leaned against their dad. They had fishing poles in their hands and toothless grins on their faces. "We can't. What if the kids are with him?"

"They won't be! The luminaries would never have given us his address if that was the case." Louise looked around the room. "He's divorced. Nobody else's clothes are in the closet."

The garage door began closing. Thea made the call. "We need more time to figure this out. We can't do this inheritance right now."

"I'm not leaving!" Mirabelle shoved Thea sideways as she shot toward the door, but Louise blocked her with an outstretched arm and spun her around so that she was caught in a headlock.

"Mirabelle. Take just a minute! Calm down!" whispered Louise. "I don't want to hurt you."

"Let me go, you don't know! You don't know how it feels."

Thea bent over to look in Mirabelle's eyes. "I *do* know.

We all know. Mirabelle, it seems like maybe he has his life together! What else could we ask for?"

"Justice?" whimpered Mirabelle, losing her composure. "For my parents."

Casey's voice rose from the corner of the room. "He's a dad."

"So was Raphael Amadoor." Mirabelle hiccupped, and Louise loosened her grip.

"That was different," Thea hissed.

"Is that up to you to make that call?" Mirabelle snapped. "Is it you who gets to decide?"

This was getting murkier by the second.

"No. Yes. I don't know exactly, but what I do know is that we can't do this right now," Thea said, taking Mirabelle's shaking hands into her own. "We have to leave. Let's take some time and decide together what to do about this."

Mirabelle nodded. "Fine." She took a breath. "I'm okay."

Thea made her way over to the window. "Good. I think we can just leap out of here, really quick. Mirabelle, go first."

But Mirabelle was spinning now, her fist landing squarely across Louise's jaw, her strong body pushing past Casey, who went flying into the closet. Bea leaped for her, but it was too late.

"Mirabelle, *stop!*" Thea yelled, but by the time the words escaped her mouth, Mirabelle was out the door and down the hallway. Thea flew after her, skidding into the hall and running to the back door. She turned into the kitchen. *Oh God.*

Marc Mitzi was standing at the kitchen counter. The bag of groceries he had been carrying had been dropped at his feet, and peaches rolled to a stop on the tile. Both of his hands were out in front of him and his voice was shaking. "Calm down. Whatever you want, I'll give it to you."

Mirabelle loomed in front of him, her impassioned figure trembling. She was bigger than he was, and she was pointing a large kitchen knife in his direction. Thea slowly walked into the kitchen behind Mirabelle. Marc's lip quivered when he saw her. "Please don't hurt me. I have two children."

"That's rich!" sputtered Mirabelle, waving the knife as she spoke. "Are you worried about them being orphans?"

Marc stepped backward as Mirabelle took a step toward him. "Yes."

Mirabelle's eyes widened and pure fury crossed her face. "Well, you made an orphan of *me!*" she screamed, flinging herself at Marc with the knife outstretched. Thea lunged forward and caught Mirabelle around the waist, flinging her against the table. Together they bounced hard off the back of a chair and spun to the floor. The knife skittered across the tile. Marc picked it up and stepped toward them.

Thea held out her hand in surrender. "She's okay. Mirabelle, you're okay."

Mirabelle was sobbing now on the floor, her anger dissolving into desperation as she deflated in Thea's arms.

"You killed my parents. You took them from me," she wailed.

Marc's expression changed from fear to shock as he looked down at her with disbelief. "Mirabelle . . . Watts?"

Mirabelle raised her head. "You know me?"

Marc dropped a trembling hand. "I think about you every day."

Thea sat back on her knees. The rest of Team Banner, she knew, waited silently in the hallway to see what happened. She stared down at Mirabelle. "Can I let you up? Are you going to do something stupid?"

Mirabelle shook her head. "No."

Thea reached out to Marc. "Give me the knife." It wasn't a request, and he swiftly obeyed. Thea stood and watched as Mirabelle curled her body up from the ground. Thea tossed the knife out the back door.

After a second, Marc reached forward and took Mirabelle's elbow. "Here. Come sit in here." Mirabelle simply nodded, letting Marc Mitzi lead her into the living room, where she sank into a comfortable recliner. "I'll get you some tea." He gestured to Thea. "You?"

"No, thank you," Thea said.

"I'd like tea." Casey's voice was sharp, and Marc leaped backward as the rest of Team Banner stepped into the room.

"Oh God, there's more of you. Y'all are really here to kill me, aren't you?"

"No." Thea shook her head. "We're not. We're just friends with Mirabelle."

He raised an eyebrow. "She must have good friends, who would break into a house with her."

Louise raised her chin. "She has good reason to hurt you, you know."

Marc shook his head as he reached for the kettle, his voice achingly sad. "I know it. What kind of tea would you like, Mirabelle?"

Mirabelle's exhausted voice drifted in from the living room. "Any kind."

"That leaves me too many options." Marc opened a cabinet to reveal what was easily thirty tea boxes. "Since I don't drink anymore—" He gestured to the cabinet. "I need options. You could say that I've become a tea snob." As he reached for a lemon ginger, Thea noticed the tremor in his hands. *Marc Mitzi is still very scared.*

After settling a tea bag into a red mug, Marc turned to Thea. "Do you think I could talk to her?"

"Yes," answered Thea, "but we won't be leaving here without her."

Marc eyed them wearily. "How do I know you won't hurt me when we're done?"

Thea looked deep into his light brown eyes. "You don't."

Marc nodded for a moment and then with a sigh headed into the living room. The kettle began bubbling on the stove. Thea took a seat near the door, where she could hear every word. She heard Marc settle on the chair across from Mirabelle, his voice already choking.

"On November sixth, the night before your parents died, my girlfriend at the time had left me. . . ." Thea heard the whole story, unfolded over two hours. She heard how Marc was so drunk that he had sideswiped another car even before he plowed through Mirabelle's parents' truck. How he woke up on the side of the road with some mild bruises, two broken legs, and a million paramedics around him. How when he learned what he had done, he wished for death. He had tried to commit suicide twice, before his short prison sentence. He told Mirabelle about the strange blessing of prison—that it had allowed him to become sober for the first time since he was sixteen years old. He told Mirabelle about his childhood, about his own neglectful parents, who were gone most nights and spent the days passed out on the living room couch.

He talked about marrying, and then separating from his wife. Spoke then of his children, of how they gave him purpose. Team Banner sat stiffly in the kitchen as he retrieved a box and brought it into the living room, showing Mirabelle everything: the newspaper clippings of her parents' deaths. His court documents. A small mention of her in the newspaper as Miss Teen Austin Runner-Up. They were all nestled together in Marc Mitzi's box of shame. Through Mirabelle's sobs, he begged for her forgiveness, his own cries echoing through the kitchen. Tears clouded Thea's eyes. Casey was staring at the ceiling. Bea and Louise were openly weeping.

Thea found her mind shifting from what she thought she had known. Men like Raphael Amadoor wouldn't change unless someone forced them to. But Marc Mitzi? His justice was somehow worse: a living hell made of his own guilt, one that he would carry with him until the day he died. Thea realized that no justice they would have brought to this man would equal the disgrace he felt now, bowed at Mirabelle's knee. This man would pay for his crime in his mind for the rest of his life; did they even need to be here? *Maybe,* she thought, thinking of Mirabelle. *Maybe this was needed in a different way.*

Casey was drumming her fingers on the table when Thea grabbed them. "Enough. You're driving me crazy."

Casey coughed and leaned back. "Sorry. I just keep thinking—why did they allow Mirabelle to do this? Seriously, why would they? The luminaries always do their research. Why didn't they know that he had children who could have easily been in the house?"

Louise bit her lip. "Robin died. Maybe they didn't have time to do any research. Things fell through the cracks?"

Thea bit her lip. "Maybe. But does Julie Westing seem like someone who makes sloppy mistakes? An inheritance is a very purposeful thing." The group was silent. Thea ran her fingers over her lips. *Could the Black Coats make mistakes? Was anyone checking on that? Had this been a mistake, or something else?* She shook the thoughts loose from her head, trying to focus on her team.

They were interrupted by a shuffle in the living room, and before Thea could leap to her feet, Marc and Mirabelle came through the door. They both looked totally wrecked.

"I think we are through for today," he managed. "Having you girls waiting in my house was definitely not what I expected, but I can't say that I'm not glad." His eyes met Mirabelle's. "This was a long time coming. We'll be in touch, yes? I mean it. Coffee maybe, next month? I'll bring my daughter?"

She took a long look at his face, and then, without a word to her team, wearily made her way out the back door.

Thea waved toward the rest of the team. "Go to the car. I'll be there in a moment."

Team Banner filed out the door as Thea turned to Marc, who was standing nervously near the stove. She raised an eyebrow and took a step forward. "You cannot tell anyone that we were here. Ever."

Marc's eyes reflected his exhaustion, but he still managed to square his shoulders as he looked into her face. "I won't, but you can never come here again. If my children had been with me this would have turned out very different. There is nothing I would not do to protect them." This was a threat, and she took it as such.

"I understand." She paused. "You seem like a good dad."

Marc turned away from her. "I'm trying to be." He opened the door for Thea to walk through. "What do you call yourselves?" He gestured to her coat. "What is this?"

Thea paused in front of him, taking a moment to look directly into his tired face, and she knew he wouldn't tell anyone. The shame ran too deep. She cleared her throat. "It's just a coat, and we're just good friends."

The door slammed behind her, and she heard him mutter, "Like hell you are."

In the car, Mirabelle sighed and leaned her head back against the seat, her body slumping from emotional exhaustion. "How do you feel?" asked Thea.

Mirabelle looked out the window for a long time before raising her voice, even then only a whisper. "Better."

TWENTY

It was dark outside when Thea remembered Drew.

She and Bea were lazily curled up on Mirabelle's Adirondack chairs overlooking her aunt and uncle's private lake, gazing at the stars. After dinner and a swiped bottle of wine from the liquor cabinet, the night had passed quickly.

Bea rolled over with a groan. "Do you think Mirabelle's servants can get us breakfast in the morning?"

Thea giggled. "I don't think she has actual servants, just, like, maids."

Bea yawned. "Well, either way, I'm requesting pancakes and eggs."

Breakfast. Pancakes. Waffles. "Oh my God!" Thea shot to her feet. "Shit! Oh God!"

Bea sat up, a muslin blanket falling to her feet. "What's wrong?"

Thea stumbled to her bag, rooting around for her

phone. Her hands closed around the case, and she drew it out, her face furrowed in distress. Seven missed texts. The feeling of drowning was instantaneous. She had forgotten about Drew, forgotten about the concert. She quickly scrolled through them.

> I got us amazing seats. I'm pretty sure we will be
>   able to see the drummer's leg hair.
> Looking like a creeper who comes to concerts by
>   himself. I promise I have a girlfriend.
> Thea, where are you? Are you okay?
> I'm getting worried. Where are you?
> I'm freaked out and calling your parents.
> Your mom said you were with the restoration
>   society. At least you're not dead.

Finally, the last one:

> FYI, Thea, waffles suck by yourself.

Drew had been waiting for her at the concert, all night. There was only one call, a voice mail she put on speaker. She ground her teeth when she heard his weary voice, full of disappointment. "Thea, we need to talk." Then the line went dead.

"That didn't sound great," Bea said honestly.

Thea put her phone down and sucked in her breath. "Dammit. What is wrong with me? Drew's pissed. I stood him up at a concert tonight. How did I completely forget about him?"

Bea wrung her hands. "We had a crazy emotional night;

it wasn't totally your fault."

Thea sat down, hanging her head between her knees. "This is bad. He's been tolerant so far, but this was . . ." She ran her hands up her arms, feeling the goose bumps raised across her copper skin. Her heart felt like it was being sucked into a black hole at his words. *We need to talk.* He was going to break up with her. She began folding her blanket. "I can't be a nice girlfriend, the one he deserves, not while I'm a part of this."

Her friend looked at her through long black eyelashes. "But you're really into him, right?"

Thea thought of the way Drew's lips would gently trace the spot behind her ear, the way he left her little presents in their secret spot in the library. She waved toward the three other girls, currently skipping rocks on the lake and shoving one another into the water. "This gives me purpose. The Black Coats gave me life. But he makes me feel happy."

"Well then, what are you going to do?" asked Bea.

Thea rolled up on her toes and back down, something she had always done before a race. "I think I'm going there."

Bea shook her head. "It's, like, eleven o'clock."

But Thea didn't even want to wait a second more. "Tell the girls I'm going to Drew's house." And with that she sprinted down the driveway.

Thea pulled up in front of Drew's house a half hour later. She climbed silently out of the car, watching as a passing cloud made darkness swallow the house. She made her way across the yard, pausing on the side of the house. *Am I imagining it, or is that something rustling?* She searched, but there was nothing; it was only the old oak trees stirring in the breeze. Thea straightened her shoulders and reprimanded herself for being so jumpy.

Drew's room was on the south side of the house, bordered by some azalea bushes. She pushed her way through its branches to one of Drew's two windows. She reached up and rapped quietly, once and then again. Silence. After a minute, she pulled out her phone and texted him:

I'm outside your window.

She waited. The wind whistled around her body, blowing her coat outward. She had reached out to knock again when the window slid open.

"Thea?" Drew's hair was adorably messy, his eyes swollen with sleep. "What the hell are you doing here?"

"Can I come in?" Thea whispered. "Is your dad asleep?"

"Yeah, I don't hear the TV." He looked at her for a long moment. "Fine, come on up, I guess."

They reached for each other at the same time, their strong arms clasping. Thea felt his arms tense, and then he yanked her upward as she scrambled up and through his window. Her momentum was too fast and they both tumbled, landing squarely on the bed. Thea's legs straddled Drew's waist.

"Hi," she breathed.

He pushed her hair back from her face. "Hi."

She bent forward, running her hands over his bare, muscular chest, his skin burning beneath hers. "Drew, I'm so sor—"

He sat up underneath her. "Don't. Don't say sorry. I know you're not, so you don't get to apologize."

Thea waited a moment. "I am, though. Truly sorry. I hate the thought of you sitting alone at the concert."

"Oh, I wasn't alone. I met hordes of women. And they all wanted waffles. And my body. My body covered in waffles."

"I deserved that," whispered Thea, overcome by the sudden need to touch him, to lose herself in Drew Porter as they burrowed together in this quiet, protective dark. Slowly, she pulled off her black coat and dropped it to the floor before wrapping her arms around his neck.

"I keep telling myself that you're bad for me," whispered Drew. "Then I see you, and I can't even stay mad at you." He kissed her, his tongue dancing with her own. He pulled back again, Thea shuddering as they separated. "But I know you're lying to me about something, Thea. I know you're not restoring houses."

Thea leaned her head against his, surrendering her will to what she needed: him. "You're right. I'm not."

Drew was tracing a path of fire down from her cheek now, his hands finding the soft skin under the bottom of her shirt. "Okay, next question." He kissed her hard and pulled her up against him. "Are you with another guy?"

"No," Thea whispered, noting how deep into her core the answer went. There was only Drew. Her heart had been frozen so long in the loneliness of grief, but each time Drew touched her, she felt it melting into something warm and strong. She felt carved out by his hands, the same hands that were now trickling up her spine, driving her *mad*. "No other guys. There is only you. I swear."

"Okay." Drew said softly, "Are you a drug runner?"

Thea laughed. "No more guessing. Not tonight. One day, I'll tell you, I promise.

"Soon?"

Thea pressed against him, losing her mind to the whole of him. "Yes," she whispered.

"Good," he growled. "Because I can't keep myself away from you, no matter what you're doing." With one hand, he wrapped her close to him and flipped her around so that he was on top of her. He looked down at her, emotions clashing across his face. "When I first met you, I didn't understand what it would be like. I thought I could keep myself separate somehow, protected from the feelings that I would have for you." He looked at her now, and Thea felt like he could see through her skin, right into the secret parts of her. "I never dreamed that I would fall in love with you." He almost didn't finish his sentence as Thea pulled him down onto her, their lips meeting. *God, I have never wanted anything the way I want him right now.* They clung desperately to each other as their passion pulled them under, secrets forgotten in a wave of lust.

Two hours later, Thea was tracing patterns onto Drew's hip as he snored quietly beside her. She watched his chest rise and fall, his sleep unburdened by the cares that kept her awake. Silently, she tiptoed out of his bed and pulled her shirt back on before picking up her coat and slipping it over her shoulders. She eyed the window again but decided that going out the front door would probably be easier. Thea took one glance back at him, smiling at the way he nuzzled his pillow. Moving quickly, she turned and headed down the pitch-black hallway. Drew's dad's room was just up ahead, and so she didn't even breathe as she turned the corner to make her way into the living room. But instead of moving to the door she bumped dead-on into a body, moving rapidly in the opposite direction.

Instantly, Thea was thrown roughly to the floor. The attack that followed was brutal: a swift punch to the stomach and before she even could figure out what was happening, her arm was wrenched behind her, her face smacked against the floor. Thea's training kicked in, and she thrust a leg out behind her, meeting with the attacker's shins. The person gave a grunt as they grabbed ahold of her hair and yanked her roughly to her feet, her hands flailing uselessly in front of her.

"Mr. Porter?" she mumbled, her heart pounding.

Then Thea felt minty breath wash over her in the darkness. A dim light flicked onto her face, blinding her momentarily as she squirmed in the tight grasp. Then she heard a gasp of shock and the hand holding her hair abruptly let go. Thea fell to the floor, still not understanding what was happening. She blinked and her eyes adjusted, the moonlight giving off enough of a glow for her to see what she was looking at. Even then, she didn't believe it.

In front of her stood an imposing figure, clad all in black, with a dark linen mask covering the top half of the face. The full lips, slashed with red, were familiar.

"Nixon?" Thea blinked again as the figure pulled the mask up. Was she dreaming? Was she still in Drew's room? But no, there was Nixon, looking just as confused as she felt, her hair pulled back in a tight bun, her black coat buttoned to her chin.

"Thea?" Nixon reached down to steady Thea, a sign that the president was indeed as shocked as she was. That moment was where the kindness ended. Nixon looked at her for a long moment before suddenly shoving her roughly back against the wall, her whispered voice full of confusion. "What the hell are you doing here? Tell me immediately."

Thea angrily pushed Nixon's arm away from her neck. "What the hell am I doing here? *This is my boyfriend's house.* What the hell are you doing here?"

Nixon stepped back. "What did you just say?"

"I said this is my boyfriend's house."

Nixon shook her head. "No. Wait—what? Your boy-friend?"

"Drew Porter. From school?" Thea stepped forward, everything about this situation raising alarm. "Nixon, seri-ously, what are you doing at Drew's house?"

Her president's eyes focused on Thea's face, and Thea saw a tiny twitch in her lip. A second later, Nixon turned away from her, her face shrouded by the dark. "I don't like this. I don't like this at all." Her voice was low, and then she was touching her ear, speaking into a tiny microphone. "M-One, back down. Subject has been compromised. I'll say it again, M-One, abort immediately."

There was a quiet buzz back, and a female voice responded. "Say again, N?"

"I said, immediate abort. Do you copy?" There was a long pause. Nixon held up her hand to silence Thea.

"We'll meet you at the drop point. Message affirmed," came the reply.

Nixon dragged Thea across the living room. "Listen to me and do exactly as I say. This is important." Some-thing in her voice stopped Thea cold. For the first time ever, Nixon seemed scared. "Go out the back door. Silently. Take an immediate left and go around the side of the house under the carport. Hug the walls. Stay there, on that side of the house. Wait for ten minutes, then run—don't walk—to your car. Go right home and wait for my instructions. Do you understand? Do not say a *word* about this to anyone else, especially not Team Banner." Nixon grabbed Thea's chin and leveled her eyes at her. "Thea, do you understand? I'm trying to save your life right now."

Thea stepped back, suddenly very afraid of whatever this was, whoever Nixon was at this moment. "Yes," she whispered.

"Good. Go. Now."

Thea headed for the back door. Cracking open the screen, she slipped out into the night and around the side of the house, her heart pounding with each step. Pressing herself against the siding, she slid down the wall until she was lodged between the carport and the fence. After a moment there was a tiny screech, the whisper of a window shutting. Thea froze. They were exiting the house just a few feet away from her—a slight footstep here, a crunch of a leaf there, the rustle of pebbles underfoot. Whoever it was moved almost silently; it was nothing that would ever wake a sleeping person. Thea kept her head down, resisting the urge to run back inside and check on Drew. *Why would they be here?*

In the distance, she heard a car door slam and the purr of an engine. Headlights illuminated the fence across from where she huddled. Two soulless eyes peered back at her and she jumped, but it was only a deer skull, its macabre grin staring at her as a black spider scuttled out of its eye socket.

Thea counted to sixty before she burst from the carport,

sprinting as fast as she could to where she had left her car. As soon as she slid into the car, words exploded from her mouth as she turned over the ignition.

"What the hell?" Thea slammed her hands against the steering wheel as she drove. Her phone buzzed; Nixon's number popped up. Thea let out a sigh of relief, hoping to get a text message that explained everything, even though she knew that was completely implausible: *Hey, I got drunk with some friends of mine and we decided to dress like Navy SEALs and party in a random house, and it just turned out to be Drew's, no big deal, see you tomorrow!*

Instead, what Thea got were numbers; that was it. Thea stared at her phone, her hands shaking. "What?"

481542

There was no answer, and when she tried texting back, her phone replied that the number was no longer valid.

When she pulled up in front of her house, she was no closer to understanding what she had witnessed in that dark living room or *whatever the hell Nixon meant with these numbers.* She shook her head as she climbed up the tree to her window, whispering to herself, "You're crazy. You're thinking crazy."

Was she? Once she was in her bedroom, Thea shed her clothes and curled up onto her bed. Her mind kept returning to the same question: *Would Drew lie to me? Maybe.* Or maybe she thought that because she constantly lied to him.

Sleep wouldn't be coming, she knew that, but she turned

out the light anyway and was left alone with her swirling questions. Why would the Black Coats be interested in Drew? Or was it his father? Had they hurt someone? Was that Team Emperor that she had heard there? Why was Nixon with them?

What did *481542* mean?

And finally, *what the hell was M-One?*

TWENTY-ONE

Everything is normal. She repeated the phrase to herself the entire drive to Roosevelt High the next morning, the cement behemoth simmering in the sun. Thea managed to avoid Drew most of the morning but he found her at lunch, this time sitting in the busy cafeteria.

"Hey!" He set his bag on the table before kissing her on the forehead. Thea stiffened. "I've been looking for you all morning."

"Hmm . . ." Thea chewed. "I've been busy."

Drew turned his head. "Are you okay?" He reached for her hand, his eyes suddenly petrified. "Are you feeling uncomfortable about last night? I know that got intense pretty fast, but we can absolutely slow things down in the physical department if you want to."

"No." Thea forced herself to meet his eyes, his perfect olive eyes. "It's not that. I promise. I have no regrets." How easy it was to let Drew's lightness of being wash all over her. Thea pulled her hand away. "But have you ever done anything you regretted?"

Drew's eyes narrowed before he shook the moment off and reached for her. "Yes. I mean, I wasted years not knowing you. And I maybe wasn't the best boyfriend to some of my exes. I could have been kinder, I suppose." He blew out a breath. "Anyway, do you have plans after school today?"

She nodded, but her mind was elsewhere: she was remembering Nixon's face when she had seen Thea—utter disbelief mixed with guilt. Nixon hadn't been in control of that moment. Thea stared at her boyfriend, her brain reeling. *Who are you, Drew Porter?* If only there was . . .

She sat up in her chair.

Oh my God. A record. The records room. Thea blinked.

I was just looking at your file. Julie Westing had said those words that day in the hallway. It was right after Thea had seen her locking the door behind her, when she had heard the buzz as the door sealed shut. It was the only electronic lock that she had ever seen at Mademoiselle Corday; the rest were opened with old-fashioned keys.

And that one, the records room, had a numerical code.

The numbers Nixon sent.

But why? Why would she want Thea to go into that room when she could go into the room herself? Unless she couldn't.

Everything Drew was saying faded into the background as Thea's mind quickly weighed her options. She wouldn't be able to do this alone. She looked across the cafeteria to where Mirabelle was sitting before leaping to her feet. "Drew, I have to go." She stood so fast her knees knocked the top of the table.

"Thea, what—I just sat down. We are literally in the middle of a conversation. Where are you going?"

"I'm sorry, Drew, I'm not feeling well; I just need to go."

"Thea! Did I say something? Thea, talk to me!"

She ignored his pleas as she made her way through the sticky cafeteria to the Core, where Mirabelle held court with two other girls. The queen bee stood when she saw Thea, dismissing her minions with a wave of her hand. "I'll see you guys at debate. Hey, what's up?"

Thea bent over to whisper in Mirabelle's ear. "I need you to help me break into the records room at Mademoiselle Corday after training today."

Mirabelle grinned; there was a happiness in her that hadn't been there the day before. "I'm so in."

"You didn't even ask why."

"Oh. Why?"

"I'll tell you on the way there." Mirabelle looked sadly at the ancient clock that ticked above the lunch line.

"We still have three more hours of class," she whined, but Thea was already walking away from her, forming a plan in her mind.

On their drive to Mademoiselle Corday, Thea told Mirabelle everything about the night before. It was a secret she couldn't keep, couldn't understand. Afterward, Mirabelle leaned back in her seat, her blue eyes flashing with mischief. "So you spent the night at Drew's house?" She clicked her tongue. "Naughty Thea."

Thea leaned forward. "That's what you took away from that?"

Mirabelle grinned. "Sorry. I mean Drew's worth it, right? Doing this?"

Thea nodded. "Yeah. He is."

"Wow." Mirabelle was silent for a second, before her face twisted up like she'd licked a lemon. "Well, I hope for your sake he's not a serial killer. What's the plan?"

Thea tapped her teeth, something that had once driven Natalie nuts. "After training, we'll hide out in one of the bathrooms. When Mademoiselle Corday closes for the night, I'll sneak into the records room and look for something on Drew or his dad."

Mirabelle sighed, tossing her hair out of her eyes. "You remember that there are some presidents who live at Mademoiselle Corday, right? On the upper floors. Kennedy and McKinley, I think. Julie probably sleeps upside down in a coffin upstairs."

Thea gave her a small smile. "I'll be quiet. Besides, I'll have you as a lookout."

"I'll do my best, but if we get kicked out of the Black Coats for this . . ."

"We won't." Thea felt like she was reassuring herself. "Something is off."

Mirabelle frowned. "I feel it, too. Something changed when Robin died. It's like, before, the Black Coats had a clear purpose. Now it's just . . ."

"Anger," Thea finished.

Mirabelle parked the car in front of Mademoiselle Corday. The house looked especially insidious today, her black eaves stabbing the soft clouds that lingered above her.

Mirabelle threw her bag onto her shoulder. "Here we go."

Together they walked through the door, Thea noticing again the names etched in gold underneath the arch:

JOHNSON • HAGEMAN • ZINN • CLEARY

Why had she never thought to ask what had happened to the ladies who bore those names? As she passed into the foyer, she looked around her, feeling for the first time like a thousand eyes were watching her.

Mirabelle looked back at her. "Come on, slow poke— you're stalling." Thea hoisted her bag up and followed Mirabelle down the winding hallway to their classroom.

The rest of the team was waiting for them: Casey perched in her normal spot, doodling on a notebook; Louise looking rapt with her hair neatly tied back in a pink ribbon; and Bea, who looked beyond exhausted.

"Yikes," Thea said as she sat down next to Bea and reached over to grab her shoulder. "No offense, but you look terrible. Is everything okay?"

Bea just shook her head miserably before looking the other way. The classroom door banged open and Thea looked up, expecting to see Nixon's hard scowl and prepared for whatever false friendly interaction they were about to have, when all she wanted to say was, *I saw you there, at my boyfriend's house. Why were you there?* Maybe Nixon would actually tell her. Maybe Thea could just go home after this.

Except it wasn't Nixon who walked into the room. It was Kennedy. Thea's breath caught in her chest.

Casey looked up from her notebook. "Umm, where's Nixon?" Kennedy gave Casey a withering gaze before grabbing the notebook out from under her pencil. "Hey!" shouted Casey.

"I don't want you to have any distractions." She tossed the notebook into the trash before brushing her hands off as if the notebook was dirty. Her blue-green eyes narrowed in on Thea, as if she knew exactly who was to blame for this group's weaknesses. However, instead of laying into her, Kennedy took a perch on the wooden desk in front of them. Her hard outer shell melted away as she smiled at the group. It caught them unawares, the warmth that Kennedy could project when she wanted to. "I'm afraid that President Nixon has stepped down."

The team gasped. Mirabelle caught Thea's eye. Unfortunately, it was just long enough that Kennedy noticed. She went on. "She has decided—voluntarily—to erase herself from the ongoing legacy of the Black Coats." She adjusted her seat on the desk, her own black coat falling over the sides. "This actually happens quite frequently in the Black Coats. As you well know, being on a team or even running one can be physically and mentally exhausting. What we do here is so important, but it does take its toll, especially on the weaker members."

She shook her head, as if the news was devastating to her as well, but Thea could tell she was lying. She swallowed the rising panic that threatened to show itself any minute. The world was swirling around her, the weight of unanswered questions pulling her down. *I'll never know what happened. Nixon is gone.*

Louise was staring at Kennedy now, her eyes clouded with tears. "Does this mean you're dissolving the team?"

"Oh, no, my dear." There it was, the false kindness again. "I'll be taking over Team Banner as your president. It's my privilege to lead such a special group of young girls. We will keep moving forward as if nothing happened. Any objections?"

Thea gripped the edge of the desk. What she wanted to do was to walk out of this cold classroom and into the light, but she couldn't let her feelings compromise these girls' futures in the Black Coats. Thea cleared her throat and stood, looking at her team members. Bea wouldn't meet her eyes, but Casey's hard glare told Thea all she would need to know. She turned back to Kennedy, disgusted by the look in the president's eyes as she stared hungrily at Bea. "We will stay on under you."

"Good, I'm glad to hear it. Now, where were you in your lessons?"

Louise raised her hand. "Compliance versus the criminal mind."

Kennedy grinned and picked up a piece of chalk. "One of my favorite subjects."

The hours ticked by. It turned out that Kennedy was actually a pretty good teacher. Still, Thea could barely sit still. She needed to run, she needed to *do* something.

Finally, the girls were dismissed for general training in the Haunt. Sahil was waiting for them there, sitting cross-legged on the mat and exuding his normal demeanor of calm and control.

"Hey, Sahil!" Mirabelle threw down her training bag, a routine familiar to them all.

"Do not put that there," he snapped, opening his black eyes. "Put it where it goes, in the cubbies."

"Whoa." Mirabelle shook her head. "Someone woke up on the wrong side of his yoga mat."

"I am not in the mood for your attitude today, Miss Watts. Put your bag in the correct place and then come over here. Today we will be working on clinch fighting." The entire team groaned. "I do not want to hear it! You may run before we start. Thirty laps around the Haunt. Go!"

Sahil was unhinged. He screamed at them while they

were running: to lift their knees, to jump, to stop in the middle of the workout, plank, and then leap back to their feet. Bea looked like she was going to throw up, and Casey was close to revolt. When the running finally stopped, they did a brutal clinch-fighting training, where Sahil fought more than trained, leaving them bruised and sore. Louise took the worst of it, since she was his best match, but even then it wasn't close; Mirabelle was next for the brunt of his anger and ended up getting slammed stomach-first onto the mat, the wind knocked out of her.

When Thea stepped up next to spar, Sahil actually rolled up his sleeves, something he had never done before. Within seconds of Thea rushing forward, Sahil had her in a headlock and she was unable to use kicks, punches, or any sort of melee weapons. When she finally got her feet underneath her, Sahil swept them away, and Thea landed hard on her right side. It wasn't even a fight; it was more of a takedown. She submitted gracefully, laying her head flat on the floor. Sahil was bouncing on his toes, ready for more, sweat pouring down his neck. "Get up, Miss Soloman."

"No." Thea did not rise.

"I said get up."

Thea pushed off her knees with a groan, stretching her sore side. "And I said no. You're not training us, you're just taking out whatever it is you're going through on my team, and I won't allow it. We're done for today."

Sahil stopped moving, his eyes narrowing. "You can't decide that."

She stared him down. "My job is to watch out for my team, not to please you. Girls, go ahead." Team Banner limped toward the door, grumbling about their day, terrible from beginning to end.

Thea stepped toward Sahil. "You're not ready," she hissed. "It takes a long time to be ready for anything. I didn't leave my house for two weeks after Natalie died. I couldn't even step outside without feeling like every part of me was going to shatter and blow away in the wind."

Sahil raised his hands to his head. "It is not that. I mean it is, but—" He spun away from her. "I cannot talk about it." A long breath escaped from his lips. "You were right to send the team away. I should not have been training like that. They were not learning; they were just defending themselves." He fell to his knees, and leaned forward, his head resting against the floor. "I'm a monster sometimes."

"You're not!" She leaned over beside him. "You're grieving."

Sahil exhaled. "Yes, I suppose that's it. Thank you for stepping in. You are dismissed." Just like that, he was done with her, just like so many other times. Without a backward glance, he walked out of the Haunt, disappearing into the trees and the open fields beyond the house. Thea didn't chase after him. If he wanted to talk to her, he knew where to find her. In the meantime she needed some answers.

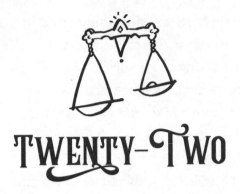

TWENTY-TWO

"Okay. We haven't heard anything for an hour. I think it's safe to say no one is here," whispered Thea, her voice echoing off the antique tiling. She and Mirabelle had been hiding in the bathroom in the alcove under the stairs for the last two hours, waiting for Mademoiselle Corday to go silent.

Mirabelle stood and stretched out her long body. "Good. Because I cannot sit in this creepy bathroom with you for one more second."

Thea pushed open the door and looked over the foyer. The house was still. Together they ran up the hallway, past their classroom, and out into the main area of the house. They paused for a few seconds, nervousness pushing against Thea's stomach as she waited for an alarm to go off, but there was nothing. She motioned to Mirabelle, wordlessly communicating exactly what to do, something that

Nixon had taught them. Mirabelle moved in front of Thea, leaning out to check the hallway ahead of her, which led to the formal sitting room and library and, inside that, the locked room. After a moment, she turned back and shook her head, her cornflower-blue eyes alarmed.

"Camera, above the door," she mouthed.

Thea's heart sank, and she turned to go.

"Wait!" Mirabelle grabbed her arm and pulled her close, whispering into her ear. "I think I know how to shut off the power here. Remember that day when we had to lay mousetraps and sweep the cellar after training? When I was down there, I saw the breaker for the whole house. Each part of the house was labeled. I can go turn it off, maybe for just ten seconds, not long enough that it will seem like anything other than a flicker or a power surge. Can you get into the door in that time?"

"Yeah, I think so."

"As the fastest person I know, you better." Just as Thea was about to dart away from her, Mirabelle grabbed her arm. "How are you getting out?"

Thea's whisper was nervous. "After I get what I need, I'll just go out the window of the records room—I've seen it from the outside. Then I'll meet you down the street from Mademoiselle Corday, by the black mailbox at the end of the lane. I should be there in twenty minutes."

Mirabelle saluted. "You better move your ass, Thea." She gave her leader a quick hug, sharp notes of some pop star's latest perfume enveloping Thea. Then Thea watched her friend disappear into the darkness.

Breathe in; breathe out. She counted the steps from here to the door of the sitting room, reviewing the layout in her mind. Thea took a last look at her phone. Two missed calls from Drew and one from her parents, whom she had told she had a society function tonight. Her hand paused over the screen, considering what to text Drew, running over options in her mind.

Sorry I'm being so rotten; it's just that I'm a
member of a secret society of vigilantes.
P.S. I ran into a friend of mine inside your
house at one in the morning, so tell me more
about you, Drew.

The lights gave a short flicker; that was Mirabelle's warning. Thea tucked her phone into her bag, pulled her hood up over her head, and crouched back on her heels. Her feet flexed in anticipation. *Boom.* The lights went out and everything around her plunged into darkness. Thea shot forward, her feet barely touching the ground as she zipped underneath the camera.

She counted in her mind, knowing that she had ten seconds before the camera turned back on. *Two, three, four.* She was through the door to the library.

Thea made it to the bookcase. *Five, six, seven.* The staircase spiraled up and away from her, and Thea ducked under the small chain that blocked it off. She could see the keypad now, its numbers glowing green. *Eight, nine.* Her hands fumbled against the keys, her mind racing from one horrible possibility to the next: Maybe this wasn't the code. Maybe Nixon didn't even mean to send that text to her. What was she doing here? She had made a mistake.

She punched the keys: *42815* . . . No, that was wrong. "Calm down," she mumbled to herself in the darkness, waiting for it to reset. Her lungs constricted and Thea held her breath. *Do it right this time.* The lights gave a preliminary flicker and then she heard something even more terrible: murmurs in the hallway. Thea's fingers frantically pushed the keypad. *4. 8. 1. 5. 4. 2.* She held her breath. There was a buzz and a click, and the lock kicked backward. *Thank God.* Thea opened the door and shut it behind her, the lock buzzing again as it relocked itself. The lights flickered on behind her, and Thea leaned back against the doorway with a sigh of relief, her heart beating so loudly she feared everyone in the house could hear it.

The room was small, maybe fifteen feet by thirty feet across, and it was filled with one huge wooden block that held dozens of gold-plated filing cabinets. Knowing she had no time to waste, Thea flicked on the small flashlight that was attached to her keys and held it up to the closest cabinet, feeling a bit like Nancy Drew. A tiny gold label that read "Swallowtail" blinked back at her. Nope. Thea exhaled through her nostrils. She shut the Swallowtail drawer and opened the next one: Emperor. Nope. She reached for one more, and there it was, on the gold plate, this one shinier and newer than the rest: *Banner.* She quickly pulled out her file.

RECRUIT: *Thea Soloman.*

STRENGTHS: *Speed (state track record holder); quick to adapt; high leadership potential.*

WEAKNESSES: *Lacking in martial arts skills; recent loss will perhaps make unstable.*

ADDRESS: *3415 Canterbury Lane.*

OTHER: *Cousin recently deceased, homicide. Luminary investigation ongoing. See Natalie Fisher file.*

TEAM ASSIGNMENT: *Banner* ~~DENIED~~ *ACCEPTED (Approved by Robin Peterson)*

Thea's hand trembled. She forgot where she was, forgot that she was here to investigate the Porters. She could see only the words floating in front of her. *Cousin recently deceased, homicide. Investigation ongoing. See file.*

See file. She leaped up. Natalie had a file. *Did the Black Coats know something the police didn't?* Thea took a step forward, the flashlight banging loudly on the cabinet.

Calm down, she warned herself. She began opening one cabinet after another, moving as fast as she could. Quickly, she found a filing cabinet marked "Targets." Thea scanned alphabetically until her eyes lit on a black file labeled "Porter, Adam A."

Palpable relief washed through her. This was bad, but at least it wasn't Drew. At least Drew was still *hers*. She grabbed the file and folded it in half. It was risky to take it but even more risky to leave it. She stuffed it into the back of her pants and moved on, her mind only on Natalie now.

There was a loud thud outside the door and Thea froze. She heard a beep—*oh God, someone is opening the door*. She didn't have time to think. She darted forward and tucked herself into the small space between the filing cabinet and the window. The door was opening slowly when she looked across the room in horror. She had left the file cabinet open. Thea stopped breathing as someone stepped into the room and spoke. "I thought I heard something up here." The voice was strident, cold. Julie Westing. Thea's blood froze.

A male voice answered her. Thea stuffed her shirtsleeve into her mouth to keep from making a sound. It was Sahil. "It was probably just the house. The power surge turned everything back on. Everything looks okay up here."

"Mmm-hmm. I just wanted to check." Thea could see their heads now. Julie was looking at the cabinets, but Sahil's eyes were trained past Thea, on the open file cabinet. He stepped forward, blocking Julie's view of it, then blinked and turned back to Julie. "As you can see, everything is fine. May I please return to my room? We have a late night ahead of us."

"Yes, of course, Sahil." Her words were pleasant, though her voice was unkind. "But first, could you check that our problematic little situation went away? I'd like the Black Coats to enter into our new metamorphosis as soon as possible."

Sahil's voice was as smooth as rich chocolate. "Of course, Julie. Can I walk you back to the Haunt? I believe the presidents are waiting there for you."

Julie turned. "Yes, Sahil, that would be lovely."

They stepped toward the door. Sahil's eyes rested once more just above Thea's head before he turned away. Then he said matter-of-factly, "Did you check the latch on the window? I would hate to lose our limbs because we weren't careful."

Julie punched in the code. "I checked it just last week. Oh, and remind me to change the code on this tomorrow. We wouldn't want a certain ex-president to come snooping around."

They walked through the door, shutting it hard on the way out. The room darkened immediately, and Thea let out the breath she'd been holding. There was nothing she wanted more than to get the hell out of this room. Sahil knew she was in there—she was sure of it. Why was he helping her? What did he know?

Thea turned to the beveled window, wavy lines of moonlight falling on her face. What had he said about the latch? On the upper right of the window, there was a long, thin piece of metal that ran down the side of the frame. Thea could see now that if you opened the window, the movement would send a shockwave down the metal piece and straight into . . . Thea pulled back the vintage lace curtains and there it was. *A bomb.* It was a small black box, metal. On the outside was some sort of digital clock—not a countdown clock like in the movies, but rather something that blipped random red-lit numbers—a measure of power perhaps? Dread clawed up Thea's chest as she stared at the cold, unfeeling machine. Two copper pipes ran out of the bottom of the box and underneath the filing cabinet through a drilled hole, cleverly disguised with a decorative flourish. If someone tried to break into this room, the bomb would explode and send plumes of fire directly beneath the filing cabinet. The records of the Black Coats would burn, and the person who tried to steal them would be blown to smithereens.

One thing was certain; she would not be going out the window, which meant that the camera would catch her on her way out the library. She took careful steps away from the window and bent back over the file cabinets, looking desperately for her cousin's name. In the second-to-last filing cabinet, she spotted a drawer labeled, "Ongoing Investigations."

The world seemed to stop turning as she reached for the file marked with her cousin's name in messy Sharpie: "Natalie Fisher." Thea flipped open the file, squinting in the darkness.

The file was empty. "No! Dammit!" Hands shaking

with frustration, she put the file back. She took a deep breath. For now, the file on Mr. Porter had to be enough. If she thought too much about Natalie in this moment, it would derail her.

Thea crept silently to the door and pressed her ear against it, listening for any sounds on the other side. Hearing nothing, she took a deep breath and pulled up her hood. She was hoping for the best but knew that her coiled body was ready for the worst.

Thea slipped through and pulled the door shut behind her, hearing the buzz of the lock. Her hands ran over the bookshelves as she made her way to the stairs. She might not be able to go out the window of the records room, but the windows in the library would still provide an escape. A small port window overlooking the historical section caught her eye, along with the high bookcase beneath it. On the shelf sat biographies of warrior women: Queen Tomyris, Artemisia, and Zenobia were among the names that Thea's thigh brushed as she hoisted herself up into a crouch, her hands slipping in the dust. *Sorry, ladies.* Thea had just reached up when she heard the door to the library open.

She didn't have time to think or even to look behind her. Instead, she reached up, opened the window, and pulled herself out, her hips sliding through the narrow porthole just as the people entered the room. She found herself on the roof of a small balcony, definitely not made to stand on.

It gave a groan under her weight. Iron spikes pressed into her feet as she made her way down the side of the house, the roar of her adrenaline drowning out the sound of the night around her as she pressed against the siding. Below her, a round turret was a swift jump from the ground, and she held her breath as she aimed for it. Her feet hit the tiles with a slam, and then she slithered down into the gardens on the east side of Mademoiselle Corday.

Thea climbed to her feet and sprinted for the cover of the dark forest outside the house, and then aimed herself in the direction of the main road. When she turned back to look, a few lights in Mademoiselle Corday had fluttered on. They knew someone had been there.

Mirabelle's car sat in front of the black iron mailbox at the end of lane. The car door popped open, and Thea slid in, her sides heaving from the sprint. "Did you get it?" Mirabelle asked.

Thea pulled the file out of the back of her pants and exhaled. It felt like the first time she had breathed in an hour. "One file on Adam Porter."

Mirabelle looked at her for a long moment. "Do you want me to read it, maybe tell you what it says? Will that make it easier?"

Thea pulled the file close to her chest. "No. That's kind of you to offer, but I think this is something I need to read by myself." *Or with Drew*, she thought. "What you can do is drive. And fast."

Mirabelle shrugged. "Fine, you can tell me about it

tomorrow, on our way to our Balancing."

Thea's head jerked up. "What?"

Mirabelle held up her phone. "Yeah. I got a phone call from Kennedy when you were inside. We have a Balancing tomorrow evening. Code Evening." She gave a delighted shiver. "I'm already excited."

Thea sat still, the file burning her fingertips. As they sped home, she watched the glowing lights of Mademoiselle Corday flickering like fireflies through the trees. One flutter, two flutters, and then they were gone.

TWENTY-THREE

Mirabelle waved from her car as Thea locked her front door behind her. She would get her car later. She turned at her mom's voice. "Thea. I was just reading in the kitchen. Come have some cookies with me."

Cookies. Something so normal sounded so wonderful and comforting right now. "Thanks, that sounds good. I probably can't sit and chat, though. I have a ton of homework tonight. Finals."

"Hmm." Her mom took a long look at Thea.

"What's wrong?"

Her mom shook her head. "Oh, honey, you forgot, didn't you?"

Thea blinked, combing her mind for something she was supposed to do, some event she had planned with her parents. She shook her head. "I'm drawing a blank."

Her mom put her mug down with a frown. "Thea, tomorrow is Natalie's birthday."

Later, she thought about the strange sensation of your heart failing, the unique pain of forgetting someone who wasn't in the world anymore. *Natalie's birthday.* She gasped as her mother reached for her hand. "Oh my God. How did I . . ." She covered her mouth. "I'm a terrible cousin."

Her mom shook her head. "No, you aren't, honey. You're moving on. Your constant suffering will not bring her back."

Thea entwined her hand with her mother's, noting how similar their hands were. The same long brown fingers, the same round fingernails. She choked back a sob. "I'm still sorry. Her birthday. How could I have forgotten?"

"You've been busy. It's okay. You have permission to live your life, Thea. Grief is the last bit of love we can give to the one we lost. It doesn't always have to feel sad." Her mother stood, kissing her once on the forehead with a sigh. "Take some cookies and do your homework, honey. We can talk about this tomorrow."

Bitter tears blurred Thea's vision as she stood and headed back to the foyer. She clutched the file with one hand before sprinting up the stairs, her heart churning angrily. She was mad at Drew, mad at Nixon, mad at Natalie for being gone. *Why did you have to get yourself killed?*

Maybe it was anger that propelled her to text Drew, or maybe it was the fact that it was Natalie's birthday tomorrow and she needed to tell someone about it. Either way, Thea couldn't pick up her phone fast enough.

Are you up? I need to talk to you about

something. Can you meet me at my house, twenty minutes?

I'll be there.

The coolness of his words stung.

Thea put down the phone and stared at the black file on her bed. She wanted Drew to be with her when she opened it. She wanted to see his face when she did. If his dad was guilty in any way, Drew should know about it. No more secrets. As she glanced in the mirror, her own hazel eyes flashed back with defiance. *Drew's not the one keeping secrets, Thea.* With a grimace she took a closer look at her face, deciding that a quick touch-up wouldn't be the worst idea; her mascara had made dark circles under her eyes, and her hair was in desperate need of moisture. Even if her relationship with Drew was about to shatter, somewhere inside of her she still wanted him to want her. A breeze whispered through her window as she tucked her curls back into a low twist. *You want him, too.*

When he pulled up in front of her house, Thea let him in the front door. "Follow me," she said emotionlessly. They headed straight into the backyard, not a word passing between them. He followed Thea away from the house, toward the corner of her yard where her dad had spent much of the fall. Texas wildflowers had been planted around the bench that he had made with his own hands, a bench carved with Natalie's name. It had been her dad's own form of grieving. How right, she thought, that they would be out here tonight, the night before her cousin should be celebrating her birthday.

Two large oak trees arched overhead, their spindly branches blotting out the moon. Drew sat on the bench and reached his hand out to her. Thea shook her head. "I can't."

"Is this it then, Thea? Because I'll be honest, I can't be with someone who treats me as though I'm her favorite toy one day and then totally disposable the next. In fact, I would say that I can't be with someone who has only a fleeting interest in our relationship." He ran a hand through his hair. "I feel like your heart has borders that I'm not allowed to pass through, like I need some sort of secret passport—"

Thea interrupted him. "What does your dad do?"

Drew leaned back, surprised. "I— What?"

"What does your dad do, Drew? I'm asking you a very simple question. My father is a civil engineer for the city of Austin. What does your father do, exactly?"

A shadow passed over his face. "My dad is a public defender. I told you that."

"So, he's a lawyer?"

Drew fidgeted. "It's more complicated than that. He works in the public sector, defending those who can't—"

Thea pulled out the file folder from its spot beside the bench. Drew sat back. "What is that?"

Thea let the file slap her hand. "This is a file about your dad. See where it has 'Porter, Adam A.' right here? If I open

271

this file, what am I going to find? I'm giving you a chance to come clean before I find out. I am giving you the benefit of the doubt because I care about you, even though you don't believe it."

Something changed in Drew's face. The playful grin that always seemed on the edge of his mouth disappeared. In its place was a grimace on a boy who suddenly looked very much like a man. An angry man. "You're giving me the benefit of the doubt? You? That's laughable." He stood and crossed the distance between them, close enough that she could see the intensity in his eyes and feel the heat of his breath. Drew paused. "Tell me, Thea, did you get that file from the *Black Coats*?"

Time seemed to slow around her, the grass arching slightly in the wind, the stars blurring above. Thea felt like she might faint, the words from his mouth falling around her like heavy stones. *The Black Coats*. He knew. Drew Porter knew about the Black Coats.

He walked toward her and snatched the file folder from her hands. Thea stood frozen. He snapped, "You want to know about my dad? Fine. You don't need to read this to me; I'll just tell you. My dad is—well, was—a detective. Five years ago, he began to see a pattern in Dallas. Men, especially those between the ages of twenty-five and forty-five with prior violent records of hurting women, were disappearing. Most of these men were people no one would miss, so it went unnoticed. But my dad, he helped rehabilitate these kinds of guys. No doubt, most of these men deserve to be in prison forever. But some of them—like our friend Harry and his museum—can change. They can turn their lives around." He paused. "No matter how bizarre that life may turn out to be."

Thea felt a quiet breath of relief escape from her lungs. Whatever Drew knew, whoever his dad was, there was still a piece of the Drew she adored in this person. He continued, oblivious to her shock. "My dad started investigating. It was a year before he ever heard a name. *The Black Coats.* It was given to him by Harry, a man who had been beaten many years ago so badly that it had damaged his brain. When my dad found Harry, he was in a mental ward, staring at a wall and talking about black butterflies. My dad was the only one who heard more than madness in his stories. He helped Harry slowly put his life back together, got him on the right medications."

Thea paused, her mind whirling with the implications of what Drew was saying. "Did you ever think that maybe someone like Harry deserved it? So he would stop hurting others?" she asked defensively.

Drew snarled, "And you reserve the right to decide their punishment? You, Thea Soloman, judge and juror, student of criminal justice in that she beats on people sometimes?"

Thea looked down. "You don't . . ."

Drew continued, the night seeming to curl ominously around him. "There have always been whispers of the

Black Coats in Texas, but most people chalk it up to urban legends, rumors, or just wishful thinking. They've been called many things: the Black Belles, the Cloaks, the Lovely Reapers, but it's always just abstract enough to make it unbelievable." He stopped pacing and shoved a hand into his pocket. "My dad and I have always been really close, what with my mom leaving and all, and I've watched him hunt this group for most of my adolescent years. Sadly, all the most powerful organizations in Texas are filled with Black Coats alumni, including the police force. He couldn't gain ground. Every time he found a lead, it would fall apart days, or even hours, later. My dad lost his job on the Dallas police force because of the Black Coats, because he wouldn't let it go. We are living here on the last of his severance."

Thea stared at him, unable to believe what she was hearing. Drew was pacing around her now, running his hands nervously through his hair. "After he left his job, Dad had a flash of brilliance: he had to go to the place where the Black Coats were rumored to have gone a little rogue, a little overzealous. Austin."

Thea took a step backward. She didn't like where this was going.

"But just like in Dallas, my dad had no luck here. He finally gave up and began doing some private-eye work on the side. Our lives settled down. I thought—for once—maybe we were going to be okay. We like it here. My dad was getting better, leaving his obsession behind and looking to the future for once."

Thea's voice was soft when she spoke. "But . . ."

Drew stopped walking and took a long look at her. "But then came you. I had sworn to myself that I wouldn't date anyone this year. I didn't want a girlfriend; I didn't even want a relationship, but then I saw you climb out of that fountain looking like an absolute goddess, and I fell. I couldn't stop thinking about you, this extraordinary girl with sad eyes but a fire that burned the air where she stood." He gave a dry laugh. "I didn't see you coming, that's for sure."

Thea stepped toward him, the world pressing in on her. "And then?"

Drew looked up at her, and Thea was surprised to see tears in his eyes. "And then I put together that you were a member of the Black Coats. Unfortunately, I didn't put it together quick enough to avoid falling in love with you."

Her heart stopped beating, and she found that she couldn't meet his eyes. "And when was that? When you put it together?"

"I knew for sure that day you left on me on the lawn, but I already had my suspicions. When you said your organization was only for women, it was like it all came together at once. After that, the evidence fell like rain. I don't know how I even missed it at first: the Black Coats recruit girls who have experienced some sort of tragedy, girls who have a reason to hate men. Damaged girls."

His words moved straight through her, leaving her hollow. *Damaged girls.*

Drew continued, "I tried following you, but you are impossible to track now that Mirabelle has started driving you, she also being a Black Coats recruit. Once I knew what you were doing, I started trying to ferret out the details that have escaped my dad for years. It was easier said than done; I was falling for you even as I heard the constant lies coming from your mouth. I wanted to expose you, to separate myself from this, to give my dad what he has hunted for almost my entire life. But I couldn't. So I told my dad the truth. We agreed that I would only try to glean just one essential piece of information from you—the location of the house—but nothing else. My father, believe it or not, cares deeply about my heart."

Thea couldn't breathe. "Your dad knows. About me, and the Black Coats. He knew when I was at your house."

Drew wouldn't meet her gaze. "Yes, but even then he realized that I couldn't separate myself from you, couldn't compartmentalize where our relationship was leading me."

Thea looked up at him as the clouds parted, moonlight not sparing her his strong features. "You pulled me into the moral gray with nothing more than a smile." He reached for her, and she stepped backward, turning away from him ever so slightly. "Can you understand? Thea, you are both the key to the truth and a lock that has closed around me."

When he looked at her, Thea could see that Drew spoke

in acute misery. "I have no idea where we go from here, but I know two things: I'm in love with a member of the Black Coats, and I won't deny my father his life's work. I won't." Drew was close now. He reached out for her, and Thea let his fingers caress her cheek. Her lip trembled. She reached for him. "Let me save you from them," he whispered.

Thea let her hand drop in midair. "I don't need saving from the Black Coats. You don't know anything about them. Drew, they saved *me*. You wouldn't even recognize me if you saw me four months ago. You love confident, strong me, but you didn't know sad little Thea who couldn't even hold it together."

Drew gave a small shake of his head. "I would have fallen in love with you in any state."

"Then don't ask me to compromise mine!" Thea took a step away from him. "I've seen firsthand what the Black Coats do, and I believe it's necessary. We have changed lives, saved lives. You don't understand the evil that these men do. They hurt women, Drew. They use women; they manipulate women. These men deserve justice."

"Justice," snapped Drew, "is not what you are giving. Whatever their crime, men don't deserve to be executed and have their bodies hidden away forever, where not even their mothers can mourn them."

"Bodies? Executed?" Thea threw her hands up into the air. "Drew, the Black Coats don't kill people! I've never killed anyone. I would never!"

Drew stared hard at her, and Thea felt all the air around them crackle with electricity.

"You're right, Thea. The Black Coats don't kill people. But the *Monarchs* do."

Thea blinked. "What did you say?"

The back door slammed open, making both of them jump. Thea's dad called out over the yard. "Thea, is everything okay?"

She put her hands on the sides of her head. Her parents had heard them arguing. *Fantastic.* "I'm fine, Dad. We're just talking."

"Uh-huh. Hi, Drew."

"Hello, Mr. Soloman."

Her dad's voice was stern. "Drew, it's pretty late. I think it's time for Thea to go to bed and for you to head home. I'm sure your father is worried about where you are."

Drew bowed his head and stuffed his hands back in his pockets, slowly drifting back from Thea, the cracks between them widening. "You're right, sir. I'll head out. Good night, Thea." After a long pause her dad went back inside.

Thea watched in silence as Drew turned and walked away from her. She opened her mouth to say something, but the words didn't come. He exited their yard through the side gate, his form blending effortlessly into the darkness. When the gate slammed behind him, Thea plucked up the folder, letting the paper slide into her hands. It was as if everything around her was shifting and spinning. With a deep breath, in the light spilling from the house, she read the words to herself.

TEAM MONARCH, CODE MIDNIGHT

TARGET NAME: *Adam Porter*

DATE OF BALANCING: *May 13, 3:30 a.m.*

OFFENSE: *Former police officer Adam Porter's investigation of the Black Coats has become a problem. He is getting too close. Make sure he is eliminated with a probable explanation and no possible leads. We will meet at the Breviary when you are finished.*

Signed,

Julie Westing

The words twisted through her, but all Thea could focus on was the giant watermark of a black monarch butterfly, stretched over the entire page, beautiful and menacing. It was the same symbol that she had seen on the weather-vane at Mademoiselle Corday. She had seen it on the door to the house, on books and in pictures, and on the pin that Robin Peterson was wearing when Thea had last seen her alive. The symbol of the Monarchs was everywhere, and as the ground spun underneath Thea, she wondered if she had known the truth the whole time.

TWENTY-FOUR

Thea skipped school the next day and spent the morning with her parents going through the motions, knowing that spending time with them was crucial right now. They were both suspicious, and she needed to pour water on that situation before it crackled into a wildfire. They ate breakfast at the Magnolia Café and then caught an afternoon movie that Thea barely paid attention to. As the plot played out on the screen, all she could see was Drew's face from the night before, his words echoing in her mind: *The Black Coats don't kill people. But the* Monarchs *do.* She desperately wanted it to be a lie, and yet as soon as she had heard the name—the Monarchs—so many answers had fallen into place.

That's what Nixon had been doing at Drew's house.

Thea shuddered at the thought. If Nixon hadn't run into her, Drew's father would be dead. And if Drew would have woken up during the assault, would he also be dead? Thea closed her eyes just thinking about it. *I can't lose anyone else. I can't.*

The lights came up, and the three of them headed home. Mirabelle was picking her up for the Balancing at six. After hanging with her parents for another hour or so, Thea politely excused herself to her room to take a nap, something she actually intended to do. Instead, she found herself staring at the black monarch stretched across Adam Porter's Balancing sheet. After a few seconds, she picked up her phone and texted Drew. He didn't know that his dad was a target, but he did know that they had a file on him. Whatever happened between them in the future, she wasn't about to let the Porters be in danger. She bit her lip, wondering what to write, settling on the most basic command.

Drew. I think you and your dad should leave
    town.

He texted back immediately.

My dad is already out of town. He flew to Dallas
    this morning to meet with his old boss. He'll
    be back for graduation.

Thea let out a breath of relief. Adam Porter was safe for now, which meant Drew was as well. Her fingers traced over the keypad. There was so much she wanted to tell him, and yet the common ground for them was rapidly shrinking. Where could they go from here?

Finally, she shook her head. "Buck up, Thea Soloman." She took a deep breath as she typed exactly what she felt.

We have a lot to talk about. I'm not sure where to start.

The message popped back up immediately.

I don't know what to do, either; but I know when I looked at you last night, all I could think about was how much I still want you.

Thea leaned back against her pillows with relief, her apparently unreliable heart pulsing joyfully at his words. She started to type but then deleted it; satisfied to leave it there for now. Mirabelle's horn honked outside her window, and Thea gritted her teeth. Kicking some ass tonight would feel great. Thea hoped that this Balancing would help restore a little of her faith in what she was doing, but more than that, she couldn't let on to the Black Coats that anything had changed. She looked at herself in the mirror as she straightened the collar of her black coat, her eyes reflecting the ugly storm that was raging inside of her. *I'll get this done, and then I'll figure out what to do with Drew.* Thea jogged into the living room and yelled through an open window. "I'm leaving! Mirabelle is here!"

"Okay, honey!" Her parents were in the backyard, pretending that they weren't finishing off a bottle of pinot grigio as her dad gardened and her mom read quietly on the porch swing.

Casey leaned out the window as Thea approached. "Hey, girl!"

Thea had sunk into the leather seats before she noticed someone missing.

"Where's Bea?" she asked.

"Aw, poor Bea. She has the flu," answered Louise.

Thea sat up. "Wait—can we do that? I thought it had to be all five of us or not at all. Nixon was adamant about that."

Casey adjusted the rearview mirror, her voice hard. "Yeah, well, Nixon's not in charge anymore. Besides, this is a chance for us to prove to Kennedy that we are a team worth keeping. Let's rub it in her smug freaking face when she sees how easily we can tackle a Code Evening."

Louise nervously blew out her freckled cheeks. "Okay, but without Bea, it just doesn't seem right. It feels off." She looked at Thea. "That's what I was telling them on the way over."

Three sets of eyes turned and rested on Thea. Her thoughts felt fragmented, torn between the matter at hand and Drew, the Black Coats, and the Monarchs.

"Let's just do it," she finally snapped. "I'm with Casey. Let's show Kennedy what we can do."

At her command, Casey pulled away from Thea's house and made her way out of her tranquil neighborhood. Thea reached forward and grabbed the Balancing sheet.

TEAM BANNER, CODE EVENING

TARGET NAME: *Chris McCray*

DATE OF BALANCING: *May 15, 7:00 p.m.*

OFFENSE: *Chris McCray is an accountant who has been accused of trafficking young women for the sex trade. Please make sure this person is too scared to complete their work.*

Signed,

The Black Coats

Mirabelle held up the file. "We have his work address. He usually works until at least seven. Let's hope he didn't decide to go home early." She grinned. Thea tried to silence Drew's words playing in her mind: *Justice is not what you are giving.*

The wealthy suburbs of Austin receded as the car wound its way just outside of town. Mirabelle's car passed a handful of new hotels on the right, and the road curved left, leading them away from civilization. The road stopped in a circular parking lot, an isolated office building in front of them. It was a new build, and at its base sat a handful of stores, all vacant except for one: McCray Accounting, Inc. Thea's chest was tight with unease as she stepped out of the car. Mirabelle leaned forward and looked through the windshield, slowly unbuckling her seat belt. The parking lot was empty save for a single sedan and a bunch of construction equipment.

Casey got out of the car. "Well, this is definitely creepy."

There was no sound other than plastic sheeting snapping in the wind, and small bits of gravel blowing in circles near their feet.

Thea straightened her coat as a trickle of sweat ran down her forehead. "Let's get this done as quickly as possible. Louise, you lead."

They moved forward as one black mass, Louise taking quick steps to the door, followed by Mirabelle and Thea. Casey took the rear, the keys clutched in her hand. Thea made her way over to the windows and looked inside. The office was empty. The door was unlocked, and they stepped inside, where a pleasant chime announced their arrival. The storefront was barren. Instead of a firm, there was only a single desk at the back of the room, holding a potted plant and a sleek laptop. The room smelled of new carpet.

Someone was moving in the back room; they watched as a shadow passed over the floor. It grew in size as their target moved toward the door. Thea spun and locked the door behind them before motioning to the group. "There might be a rear exit. We need to move!"

Louise gave Thea a quick nod and plunged forward down the hallway with Mirabelle behind her. Thea heard a gasp, and then she was moving behind them, to where her teammates stood frozen, unsure of what to do next.

In front of them, a tiny woman stared back, her eyes

wide in fear behind frameless glasses. She was wearing a crisp white shirt under a black sweater draped over her thin shoulders and a pencil skirt, reminding Thea of a kindly librarian.

Louise turned to her leader, her pert face twisted in confusion.

A witness, thought Thea. This wasn't good. Thea stepped forward, projecting a cool confidence that she did not actually feel at the moment. "We're looking for Chris McCray. Is he here?"

The woman stepped backward. "I'm Chris McCray. How can I help you?" She raised a shaking hand to her chest.

Nixon's words flashed in Thea's mind. *Occasionally, we will have a woman target. There are, unfortunately, women who hurt women out there and they are owed justice just like any man. It's rare, but it has happened.*

"Are you here to hurt me?" The lady stepped backward, her lip quivering.

Thea hesitated for a moment. They couldn't hurt this woman, right? She saw Drew's disappointed face in front of her. *Thea Soloman, judge and jury.* She took a step back. "I'm sorry, I think we must have the wrong . . ."

But by then it was too late; her hesitation had cost them everything. She heard the front door chime, that cheery, ringing sound, even though she had locked the door behind them. *Something's not right,* she thought, before the chilling realization struck. The abandoned building. The car in the parking lot. The empty office. *This is a trap.*

"Go!" she screamed to her team, but it was too late. She heard the sound of heavy footsteps behind her. A gloved black hand grabbed her waist, pinning her arms against her. Thea kicked off the wall, but there was another man, grabbing her legs and twisting them so that her body was wrenched sideways. A cloth was pushed forcefully over her mouth and nose. When she could breathe again, she smelled the chemicals seeping into her lungs, the pungent burn of chloroform. Thea turned her head, her body flailing to no avail.

Casey was already slumped on the floor with a man crouched over her. Her hand was clenching as she reached for the car keys, inches away from her fingers. As Thea watched, a black boot came down on her hand, breaking Casey's fingers. Casey's screams filled the room, the sound tearing apart everything left inside of Thea. Behind her she could hear the sounds of Mirabelle struggling; her normally strong voice was whimpering, pleading.

Thea could see in front of her that Louise was still fighting strong—Team Banner's little teacup of fire. One man was down, and two more were struggling with her. Louise twisted and rammed her elbow into one man's nose; blood splattered the new carpet beneath her as another man lifted her off her feet. *How many are there?* Everything in front of Thea blurred and spun. *Hold on, hold on,* she shouted to herself.

Chris McCray stepped in front of Thea's face with a soft smile. Then she roughly grabbed her cheeks, her long fingernails pressing into Thea's skin. "So you're the girl that Julie is so worried about. You don't look like much." She clicked her tongue. "Naughty, naughty Thea, sleeping with the enemy."

When she stepped back, Thea saw that it wasn't actually a sweater draped over her shoulders. It was a black coat. Louise continued to fight as a fourth man stepped up behind her holding a silver pipe. Chris McCray was yelling now, her voice bouncing off the back of Thea's skull. "Get her down, but don't kill her!"

Louise twirled, her fist flying forward, but it was too late. The pipe slammed across the back of her head, and she collapsed to the ground like a rag doll. Thea screamed as she was pulled down into the swirling black, her thoughts discombobulated and firing randomly as her limbs went limp. *At least Bea isn't here. I didn't tell Drew . . . I'm so sorry, Mom. My team . . .*

Her lungs burned as she breathed in the cloth once more. *I can't die on Natalie's birthday.*

Her vision tunneled before her. There was only the sound of rushing water, and then what she had feared most: a nothingness that swallowed her whole.

TWENTY-FIVE

Thea woke up with her back burning, a painful stabbing sensation tracing from underneath her ribs to her right shoulder. She twisted her neck, trying to remember exactly what had happened. Her thoughts were fuzzy and slow. *Where am I?* She blinked. "Hey!" whispered a voice. "Hey, she's awake." She felt something pressing up against her, shoving her sideways. Why couldn't she use her hands? She slumped forward and felt a wave of nausea rise up inside of her.

"Swallow it." She knew that bossy voice. Everything came flooding back. Chris McCray. The office. The men. The pipe. Bile rose up in her throat.

"Swallow it. If you throw up in here, I swear to God . . ." Mirabelle's perfume enveloped her. She turned, gagging, but the bile didn't come up. After a few dry heaves, Thea took a deep breath in.

"There you go. Breathe." That was Casey's voice.

Thea finally found her own—a strangled sound, foreign. "Where is Louise?"

"She's not awake yet, but she's breathing."

She leaned back, her shoulders pressing up against something hard. After a minute, she felt like she could open her eyes, her lungs greedily pulling at the cool air. They were in an empty storeroom, lit by a single flickering light bulb. Boxes of paper goods and office supplies were stacked all around them. Her hands and shins were bound together with duct tape in front of her, along with a piece that ran across her chest and strapped her to a ventilation pipe that ran through the middle of the room and up into the ceiling. Mirabelle and Casey were seated in front of her, bound in the same way but taped back-to-back. Louise lay curled in the corner, asleep, a lump the size of a plum on the side of her head. Thea could see her chest rising and falling, the most beautiful thing she had ever seen.

"You're okay. You're okay." Mirabelle's voice was soothing now.

Thea let out a strangled cry. "I led us straight into a trap. Oh God, I'm sorry."

Casey nudged her foot against Thea's. "How could you have known?"

"I should have." Her mouth trembled. "Your hand!"

Casey nodded. "I can't tell because of the duct tape, but I'm pretty sure at least three of my fingers are broken.

No piano lessons for me this month." It was a joke, but in Casey's somber delivery, Thea heard a real fear.

"Phones?"

Mirabelle shook her head. "They took them." She twisted around so that she could rest her head against the cool pipe. Thea pulled against her restraints, exerting every sliver of energy she had left, her head still buzzing.

Casey raised her head. "It's not going to work. We've tried for the last thirty minutes. Might as well sit tight, wait for whoever's coming to pack us into a railcar." Her voice turned angry. "Oh, Thea, now that you're awake, there's something I've been wondering about: What the hell does your boyfriend have to do with this?"

Thea looked at Mirabelle, who simply shrugged. "There is something about being tied up, about to be murdered, that makes me not want to keep secrets anymore."

Thea focused on pulling her hands apart, or sliding them backward through the duct tape. Nothing moved. "Arrggh!" She sat back, her chest heaving, her eyes meeting Casey's accusing glare. "I should have told you. I should have told all of you. I'm sorry."

Casey settled back against the wall next to her, wincing as she flexed her hand. "Tell me everything. From the beginning."

Thea closed her eyes and began talking, twisting her hands back and forth, hoping to loosen the duct tape. The longer she talked, the stranger the story became, each thread tangling tighter and tighter: Drew and Adam Porter, his interest in the Black Coats, the empty file on Natalie, what she had overheard from Julie and Sahil, and finally, what Drew had said about the Monarchs.

Casey sat forward, pulling Mirabelle backward. *"Ow!"* she screeched.

Casey didn't notice. "The Monarchs?" She sat back with a shake of her head, her darkly lined eyes widening. "That makes so much sense. For a long time, I've wondered what the Black Coats' real purpose is. I mean, yes, we are serving justice and all that, which is, I have to admit, incredibly intoxicating, but how does that *really* serve the Black Coats? What is their endgame?"

"We wash the floors," mumbled Mirabelle. "We fold cloth napkins."

Thea frowned as she looked around the room for anything that could help them. If only they could move. She leaned her head back against the pipe, her curls drenched with sweat. "No. We are still being recruited."

"For what?" asked Casey.

Thea focused her eyes on the ceiling. "For the Monarchs. They probably select the best of us to become them—but only after we've used our inheritance, because then they'll have something to hold over us for the rest of our lives."

There was a long silence that was broken by Mirabelle stifling a cry. "Thank God I didn't kill Marc. Thank God, thank God."

Thea looked at the doors. There were two doors on either side of the room, both made of reinforced steel and most likely bolted from the outside.

"We tried pressing against them," sighed Casey. "Neither door budged. We already tried everything."

Thea opened her mouth and screamed as loud as she could, but it only reverberated off the thick walls. And besides, who would hear them? They were in an empty building outside of town. By now night had fallen. Team Banner was utterly alone. Thea bit her lip angrily. She had gotten her team into this, and now it was time to get them out of it. She had to think of something. "Can you guys try to get some boxes down?" Thea strained against the pipe.

"It's just paper," moaned Mirabelle.

"It doesn't matter. We have to do something. *Move!*" Thea kicked her bound legs out toward a shelf, colliding with the shelving unit. She kicked at it until a box tumbled to the floor. Slowly, Thea used her legs to draw the box over to her, wincing as her muscles protested. "Mirabelle! Stop crying and get those boxes open."

Her friend took a breath. "Okay." Mirabelle and Casey struggled to their feet, arguing the whole time about who needed to do what.

Thea's bound hands tore at the plastic sealant. The box opened. Paper, just as they had suspected. She kicked it away. "Next."

They froze as a moan came from the corner of the

room. Thea looked over as Louise rolled onto her back. A thin line of blood was crusted across her forehead, with another at the corner of her mouth. Her bloodied hands were bound tight, but her legs were free. Her eyes fluttered open. "Thea?"

Thea bent her head forward, encompassed in the sweet relief that her friend was okay and knowing that the memory of a man hitting her with a pipe would be seared into her mind forever. Louise gagged and then pushed herself to her knees.

"Take deep breaths. There you go." Thea tried to make her words reassuring.

"My head." A piece of Louise's mousy brown hair fell over her eyes as she moaned. "It's exploding." She filled her lungs once more and opened her eyes. "I am seriously considering resigning from the Black Coats."

Thea smiled gently. "That makes four of us."

As Mirabelle and Casey continued to pull down boxes, Thea scoped out the room, looking for something useful. She blinked. Two boxes in the far corner weren't the same size as the others. She leaned forward, the tape pressing hard against her chest. She squinted as she tried to make out the words on the box. *Office World, a unique company for your growing needs.* Underneath it were the words she was looking for. *Office Supplies.* "Mirabelle!" Thea nodded toward the box. "Third row up, two boxes over. Look."

Mirabelle's eyes widened. "Do you think maybe . . ."

They looked at each other. "Scissors," they said in unison. Mirabelle and Casey began moving toward the shelf. Thea felt hope growing in her chest, when she heard voices outside the door.

"Shhhh! Stop! Sit back down where you were. Louise! Pretend you're still out!"

Louise collapsed onto the floor in her original position. Thea stared at the door, wanting to look whoever came through straight in the face. She would not go quietly. The metal door swung open, bringing with it a blast of cool air. She gasped out loud when President McKinley strolled in, flanked by five men. A few were muscular, but three of them were just dangerous-looking—the kind of men Thea would avoid on the street, with wandering eyes and hands. McKinley clicked her tongue. "Ladies. Do you have everything you need?"

Thea leaned forward, praying that her duct tape would snap, feeling helpless and furious all at once, her eyes burning as she stared at McKinley. "You can't kill all of us. Four teenage girls missing all at once would bring the FBI."

McKinley sighed. "You know, Thea, you are right." Then she smiled wickedly. "Fortunately for us, we have so many friends in the FBI that one phone call would clear that problem up completely. But it's not Team Banner we're punishing. *It's you*. And if your teammates speak of what they saw here, we will kill them one by one!" She put her hands on Thea's face and then tapped her fingers against her nose. "As we speak, a letter is being written in which you'll tell your parents that you are running away to Seattle because you can't handle being here, where Natalie died. And you know what happens to runaways. Poof! They disappear all the time."

Thea looked at Casey, who dropped her eyes to the floor, her chest heaving. Her eyes flicked to Louise, who hadn't moved. Thea looked hard at President McKinley. "How can you hurt me? Being a Black Coat is about saving women, protecting them."

"That's exactly what I'm doing," hissed McKinley, her face distorting in anger. "You led the son of a cop straight to our doors. Adam Porter was getting dangerously close before we stepped in with our Dallas branch. Your foolish actions threatened a society that has saved hundreds of lives, and for that . . ." She stood and rubbed a white cloth over a knife that she had pulled from her coat. The men stepped forward. "I'm willing to betray my conscience a little. In fact, you might say that I have a darker side than most. At times, Robin found me a little too harsh for the Monarchs and did her best to tie my hands, but now that Robin is six feet under and Julie is in charge, her standards are a little more, how shall we say . . . flexible. She knows that sometimes you have to get your hands dirty." She leaned forward, her mouth close to Thea's ear. "And that's what I am. Julie's dirty hands. Ever since we were Monarchs together."

She sat back, resting a hand on Thea's shoulder. "I promise, I'll be kind. You'll barely feel anything. I'm not a monster. I don't want you to be in pain." She squeezed Thea's shoulder. The blade was cool against Thea's neck, and she could smell bleach on the president's hands. Mirabelle began crying softly. *This can't be it; this can't be . . .*

The light bulb flickered. McKinley paused. It flickered again. The men shifted uncomfortably. "It's just the power," snapped McKinley. "They haven't finished securing the lines for the office." The light bulb dimmed once before lighting again. McKinley turned back to Thea. "I won't enjoy this, truly I won't. But the Black Coats are more important than one girl's life."

Suddenly, there was a loud pop of electricity and the windowless room was plunged into pitch black. The door rocked open, and there was a shuffling sound. Then Thea heard a shout and something landed with a thud near her feet. The lights flickered again. McKinley stood, her knife held defensively out in front of her. A man's body lay by Thea's feet.

The light bulb flickered again. Darkness. Then light. And then . . . a slash of red lipstick. "You might not enjoy this, but I will. You *bitch*." The lights came on. Nixon flew forward, her fist meeting McKinley's face, sending her flying back out of the room. The man closest to her grabbed a gun from behind his back.

"Get down!" Thea screamed at Mirabelle and Casey. A

bullet ricocheted off the shelves and buried itself deep into a box of paper, shreds exploding from the point of entry. Nixon grabbed the shooter's hand and forced it up to the ceiling, firing several more shots as she rammed her hand up against the flat of his nose. He gasped and staggered backward. Her movements almost too fast to see, Nixon slammed his head down against the metal shelving.

The second man was on her now. He grabbed her from behind, but Nixon arched her body up and away, launched vertically, and flipped her legs toward the ceiling. She landed squarely on his shoulders before she whirled in the air, her black coat flapping around them in a blur. There was a crack as she thumped the butt of a knife up against his temple, and then Nixon rode his unconscious body down to the floor.

Thea struggled against her bindings, screaming at the other girls to do the same. The largest man in the group, his arms covered with graphic tattoos, stepped forward, caught Nixon by the arm, and twisted. She screamed in pain and jammed her foot up against his face, her sharp heel leaving a spurting puncture wound. He yelled and lost his grip momentarily.

"Thea!" The second her arm was free, Nixon slid a knife across the floor to Thea. She grabbed it in between her bound hands and began sawing at the duct tape across her chest. *Just a little more; just a little more.* Nixon was struggling with the largest man now. The tape binding Thea snapped.

She lunged away from the pipe, knowing that she had only seconds to make the right decision.

Only seconds . . . Leaving her own hands still bound, Thea fell forward and cut Louise free, because if her training had taught her anything, it was to trust the best woman for the job. Their little mouse exploded and leaped onto the back of Nixon's attacker, bringing her fists together hard against either side of the man's temple. He slumped to the ground. Another man surged forward and grabbed Louise's hair, but Thea kicked her feet hard across his kneecaps. A loud snap echoed through the room. Thea smiled. *That's right, you prick, these legs are strong.* He dropped to his knees, and Louise delivered a right hook to his face, followed by a hard kick to his throat. His eyes rolled up into his head and he was unconscious.

The huge man stumbled to his feet again. Nixon rushed at him, but he was as quick as she was and threw her sideways, her body hitting the shelves. With a grunt he hauled Mirabelle up against him, his meaty hand curled around her jaw, a thin knife against her throat. A trickle of blood began to stain her collar. Still bound to Mirabelle, Casey was writhing.

"Don't move!" he bellowed. "I'll kill them both!" Nixon froze, her eyes like burning coals. Louise crouched on the floor like a cat, her mouth clenched tight. Thea's chest was bleeding as she sawed through the duct tape around her hands. "Who do you think you are?" the man screamed with Mirabelle's body rigid in his arms. "Women, acting like this!"

At that moment, the duct tape broke. "Sorry we forgot to bake you a pie," spat Thea as she shoved Nixon's knife deep into his upper thigh. The man stumbled, reaching for Mirabelle's neck, but it was too late. There was only a blur of black as Nixon whirled and something silver sliced through the air near Thea, moving too fast to be seen. She turned just in time to see the small metal butterfly bury itself in the man's forehead, leaving only a vertical line of blood as its razor wings cut deep into his skull. As he fell forward, Thea lunged to catch Mirabelle and Casey before they hit the ground. Near the door, another man raised his arms in surrender and tried to kneel. Just before he hit his knees, Louise delivered a roundhouse kick to his head. He slumped against the shelves, unconscious. Nixon took a deep breath.

Thea raised her eyes to her president, her body shaking with adrenaline. "Thank you."

Nixon wiped the blood off her mouth. "Thank you, *ma'am*."

When they turned around, McKinley was long gone.

TWENTY-SIX

An hour later, most of Team Banner was seated in a circle on the floor of the office with Nixon standing in the middle. Casey held an ice pack against Louise's head. Mirabelle was still a bit shaken, and Thea sat behind her, one hand pressed against her spine to steady her. McKinley's henchmen were either piled or tied up in the back room. Only one was dead, the rest unconscious.

Thea's eyes kept lingering on the closed doorway, her stomach churning. *Dead. That man with the razor butterfly in his head was dead.* She felt like she was teetering on a precipice with sanity on one side and a whirling black abyss on the other.

Nixon reached out and put her hand on Thea's cheek, and it brought her back from the brink. "Don't be sorry for him. McKinley made a mistake by climbing in bed with monsters. I know the names of those men; they have killed and raped and planned to do it again. I won't lose a minute's sleep over them, so let me carry it." She sighed. "Don't worry. The live ones I'll leave at the police station. They aren't going to talk about what happened here." Their president took a moment to look at each of their faces. "I'm so proud of you right now."

"Proud?" Casey sputtered. "You just had to save our lives!"

"True," said Nixon. "But that is no fault of your own. It's mine. I should have protected you. I should have been honest with you. I should have known the Black Coats would set a trap to teach Thea a lesson." She turned to Thea. "It was meant to scare you. McKinley wouldn't have really killed you—she just wanted to scare you—but those men might have."

Thea stood up, her head flush with Nixon's. She hadn't realized until now that she was almost taller than her president. "You owe us answers."

Nixon arched a perfect eyebrow. "That's fair." She took a deep breath. "Everything I've taught you about the Black Coats still stands. We are an old organization that cares about justice for women. At first, it was just what you do now—normal Balancings." She paused. "However, over the years, Julie grew restless. She saw that there were some men—murderers—who deserved more than a slap on the wrist or a punch in the face. Julie believed that we were called to bring justice to men who had killed women by giving them the same punishment: death. A Code Midnight."

Thea's blood chilled. *Code Midnight.* The words that she had seen on Adam Porter's sheet.

"Robin and Julie disagreed on this point," Nixon continued, "and eventually a truce was made, though the decision wrenched the Black Coats in two. The Black Coats continued running under Robin as they always had, and Julie—well, Julie broke off to run the Monarchs, which then seeped out into other branches of the Black Coats. Both organizations have grown to work under the Black Coat umbrella."

"So they are real." Mirabelle stared hard at Nixon with bloodshot eyes, her fear morphing into anger. "The Monarchs."

"Yes."

Thea took a threatening step toward Nixon. "You were there that night to kill Drew's dad. A police officer. A man who hasn't killed anyone."

"He was a threat to the organization, and so Julie ordered us to act."

"And so you were going to *kill* him?" Thea was furious now. "So now punishment is not just for men who hurt women, *it's for anyone who gets in the way of the Black Coats.*"

"So it would seem." For the first time ever, Nixon seemed unsure. "I didn't know who your boyfriend's dad was when I went to the Porters' house; I thought he was

303

another dangerous abuser. I had just been told my assignment by a fellow Monarch when we were en route. It was all very odd. I realize now that they didn't want me to know. When I saw you there, Thea, I knew immediately that something was very wrong."

"Yeah. It's wrong to kill innocent people," snapped Thea.

Nixon sighed and looked at the ceiling. "Please understand; though I agree with the need for the Monarchs, I have long dreaded the day when Julie Westing would take over the Black Coats. Robin had a clear head for the distinction between justice and vengeance." Nixon shook her head. "Julie, on the other hand, sees only the Monarchs. She doesn't really care about the Black Coats. She sees Banner, Emperor, and Swallowtail only as a means to supply the Monarchs down the road, whereas Robin loved nurturing these teams of girls who would go on to do great things in the real world. Which I believe you will. Each of you." She smiled.

"Go on," Thea intoned, unmoved by her confession.

"Julie has proposed an amendment to the Black Coats constitution that will change everything. It makes participation in the Monarchs *mandatory*." Nixon fumed.

The girls were silent. Louise quietly sat up before leaning forward. "I'm not killing anyone. *Ever.* That's the opposite of what I've spent my life working toward in martial arts. Not you, though. You kill people, right?"

Nixon squared her shoulders. "Yes, I do. And I had no regrets, at least not until I was sent to kill Adam Porter." There was a thud in the back as one of their prisoners shifted. Nixon's eyes darted to the door. "We can't stay here long. It's not safe." She turned to Thea, their eyes meeting. "Thea, you are the problem, which is why Julie sent McKinley to threaten you. In Julie's eyes, you almost led Adam Porter right to us. You have been unintentionally feeding information about the Black Coats to Drew Porter for months, and Julie felt a price must be paid. Not only that, but Julie wanted *me* to suffer for defecting from the Monarchs after Adam Porter's failed Balancing. The best way to do that was to attack my team. She and McKinley set up this botched mission, with the intention of teaching you all a painful lesson. I found out about the trap through a friend on the inside." Nixon took a deep breath. "That's all I can tell you now."

"That's all you can tell us? Are you serious?" Thea stepped into the circle now, her fists clenched. "We could have died here at the hands of the very organization that we've been asked to serve! Who are the other Monarchs? What about Adam Porter? What is happening to Bea?"

Nixon nodded her head. "Bea is fine, Thea. Believe me, Julie would never do anything to hurt Bea."

"Except when Bea refuses to be a part of the Monarchs. Bea is barely comfortable with what *we* do! She can't be a Monarch." Thea pressed. "Who are they? The Monarchs."

Nixon stared at the ground. "Thea, would you ever sell out your team?"

Thea didn't even blink. "Never."

"Then don't ask me to do the same. The Monarchs are my team." She paused. "Were my team. But that's all done now." She took a step backward, remorse crossing her face. "This is where I leave you, girls. I can't help you anymore from here on out. I put you in danger, and I won't do it again by associating with you. I have some things I need to clean up here in town and then I am moving on."

"Moving where?" asked Louise.

"On." Nixon's eyes were far away.

Casey shook her head. "No! You can't leave us now. What do we do?"

Nixon sighed. "I had a tough conversation with Julie a few minutes ago. We came to a conclusion and a truce was declared. At my urging, she passed a resolution that Team Banner is dissolved and no longer a part of the Black Coats. You are free. None of you should have any trouble returning to your normal lives, as long as you don't speak about anything you've seen. She's afraid of me. As she should be."

Mirabelle put her hands on her hips, and Thea was relieved to see her sassiness returning. "And what about Thea and Drew?"

Nixon's eyes clouded over. "Julie said this morning that she believes the debt is settled and that this scare was enough. It got out of control too quickly and she may have to answer for it." Nixon brushed off the lapel of her coat, now smeared with blood. "Adam Porter has been offered a cushy job in Dallas to get rid of his meddling, and I'm sure Drew will go with him. That is the last I heard." There was a grunt from the back room as one of the men was trying to free himself from Nixon's elaborate knots. "Team Banner, it's time to say goodbye. Each one of you, go home. Take a shower. Live normal lives. Work for justice in your own ways."

"But how can we?" muttered Mirabelle. "Now that we've been through this?"

Nixon leaned her forehead against Mirabelle's. "I don't know the answer to that myself." After a moment, she pulled back and straightened her coat. Team Banner watched as Nixon slowly fastened each button, all the way to her neck. She tightened her bun and checked her reflection in a small compact, her flawless skin catching the moonlight coming through the windows.

Thea's chest tightened when she turned to leave. "Are we going to be okay?"

Nixon shrugged. "Thea, I think you've known for a while that I don't have all the answers." She spun on her stilettos. "Good night, Team Banner. It's been a pleasure. You'll find your phones by the door, and lock it behind you."

Thea watched as Nixon took one long glance at them before disappearing into the back room. Someone began screaming.

＊＊＊

Somehow she still made it home by curfew. When her mother opened the door, Thea fell into her arms, relishing her mother's warm smell.

"You okay, honey?"

Thea nodded, squeezing her tight. "Just glad to see you, that's all."

"Me, too. Your dad and I are heading to bed. He made me watch that new show, where divorced couples are stuck on the boat with each other?"

"That looks terrible." *What I mean is, I love you and I'm sorry.*

"It was." Her mom kissed her forehead. "We'll see you in the morning, yeah? It's Drew's graduation, right? Anyway, there's a plate in the fridge if you want it. Your dad made shrimp tacos." Thea's stomach rumbled. She padded into the kitchen and popped the plate into the microwave, glancing at her phone. Graduation was tomorrow. She had almost forgotten. There was still no word from Drew, so she took a deep breath and texted him everything she wanted to say. After Natalie's loss, she should have known better: the time to say important things was always now.

> I'm sorry for lying to you. You were right—about almost everything. Can we talk after the ceremony tomorrow?

Then without thinking, she typed:

> Drew Porter, I think I might love you, in spite of it all.

Thea sat back in her chair, anxiously awaiting any response as the night grew long around her.

Finally, it popped up:

See you tomorrow afternoon at graduation.

Thea let a small glimmer of hope pass through her. Maybe there was a chance that she wouldn't lose this, too. Still, before heading up to bed she triple-checked the locks and tucked a knife up her sleeve.

TWENTY-SEVEN

It was funny, Thea mused: she hadn't even thought about the last day of school or graduation at all. Wrapped up in the Black Coats drama, entire months of school had passed by in the blink of an eye. She tugged on the hem of her lace dress, admiring the way the creamy white showed off her rounded calves and hazel eyes. Hopefully, Drew would appreciate them as well. As she came down the stairs, her mom clapped. "You look gorgeous, honey!"

"Next year, this afternoon will look very different." Oh no. Her dad had tears in his eyes.

"Oh, Dad . . ." She gave him a hug. "We still have a whole year until that happens."

He took a forceful bite of his apple. "I know. Imagining you in a graduation gown just gets me."

"Bill." Her mother sat down next to him and rubbed his arm lovingly. "We don't have to be sad about that, because we are just going to go to college with Thea. We're going to be roommates. Our girl just doesn't know it yet."

"I'm leaving." Thea couldn't help but be taken in by this happy scene. "I love you guys."

As Thea slammed the screen door her mom called out, "Tell Drew and Adam congratulations!"

If Drew is even talking to me, she thought. She was anxious to see his face, to reassure him that everything would be okay—somehow. As she started her car, a drip of sweat making its way down her forehead, she glimpsed the bag on the front seat. Inside was her Black Coats uniform, and draped over the passenger seat was her black coat. She felt a twinge of sadness but pushed it away. The Monarchs killed people. They had tried to kill Drew's dad. Her time with the Black Coats had to be through. She pulled out of her driveway and turned up the volume on whatever pop song was on the radio, hoping to drown out her thoughts.

Roosevelt High School was packed, so Thea had to park in the farthest reaches of the parking lot. Already late, she slipped off her heeled sandals and ran barefoot on the hot pavement, passing by the Angel of the Waters statue, its eyes blacked out with a new line of graffiti. She was almost past the statue when she stopped abruptly. On the side of the statue, a glaringly precise piece of graffiti stood out among the others.

A black monarch butterfly.

Thea's chest seized. Had it always been there and she never noticed it? It was possible. The entire base of the statue was a haven for graffiti. She turned away from it and began running again, hoping that the rhythm of her legs and the sound of the ground underneath them would push the rising dread out of her chest. Maybe it had always been there, the Black Coats marking their territory. She tried to quiet the panicked voice in her head. *They're not here. Everything is fine.*

As she neared the stadium, memories flashed into her mind of early-morning practices—the sun barely creeping over the horizon, everything a foggy lapis blue. Natalie in her sweats, stretching at the starting line, her eyes fixed before her, determination etched across her strong forehead. Thea in awe of her cousin's strength. *It's a shame,* she thought as she made her way through the turnstiles and into the packed bleachers, *that sometimes even the strongest women are not strong enough to endure the wickedness of average men.*

She found a seat in the last row of bleachers, trying to find Drew on the field. God, she really needed to kiss him already.

The valedictorian was already speaking, but where was Drew? Thea craned her neck, unable to distinguish him in the sea of black-robed graduates. She leafed through the program and found his name, along with his graduation quote:

INJUSTICE ANYWHERE IS A THREAT
TO JUSTICE EVERYWHERE.
—MARTIN LUTHER KING JR.

Thea shivered under the blazing heat of the sun.

Thanks, Drew, she thought, *for the reminder.* A few rows ahead of her she could see the back of Adam Porter's head, his chin lifted in pride as he awaited his son's graduation. Hopefully she could avoid him. The sun beat down on the crowd. The valedictorian wrapped up his speech to a loud cheer, and the graduates began to march one after another in an endless parade. The vice principal reminded everyone to hold their cheers until the very end, but that never worked. Parents would not be silenced when it came to pride in their children. Thea's parents, she knew, would be very loud.

Thea checked her phone as the names were rattled off. "Kela Jacob . . . Mark Jensen . . . Ralphie Jurgen . . ."

She had one missed call from Bea. A picture of her cheery face popped up on Thea's phone. She would get back to her later.

As she looked at her phone she was aware of a slight movement nearby but assumed it was the couple sitting next to her. When she finally looked up, there was no one there, but there was a black envelope sitting beside her. *How in the hell?* Thea whipped her head around and shot to her feet. In front of her was only the enormous crowd, no sign of anything amiss, but she turned around just in time to see a flash of a black coat disappear behind the bleachers. She ripped open the note written on the same paper that had once invited her to the Black Coats: soft yellows and velvet blacks, marked with knives and butterflies. *Please be nothing,* she thought. She stopped breathing when she read the words, written in lilting calligraphy.

Being a traitor has consequences.

Over the speakers, the names of those walking for their diplomas echoed in the background. "Tracy Paul . . . Kevin Pook . . . Craig Pooley . . ."

Oh God. Thea couldn't breathe as she read the words on the page.

*Do you know why we are called Monarchs, Thea?
Monarchs drink poisonous milkweed, and in their
unique system it creates a poison capable of killing any
predator. And those beautiful wings they are known
for? That's where they store their poison. It's their trap.*

"Drew Porter . . ."

Thea's head jerked up toward the stage. No one moved. The principal leaned again into the microphone. "Drew Porter."

Silence. The teachers seated onstage shifted nervously.

Adam Porter stood up and looked around. Thea ducked before he saw her.

"Drew Porter, there is a diploma here with your name on it." Assembled students laughed awkwardly as the principal scanned the crowd. Then he smiled reassuringly. "Happens every year. I'm sure Mr. Porter will come seeking his diploma sooner or later." They chuckled as he went on to the next name. Adam was making his way down the steel bleachers with an expression of panic on his face. Thea looked back down at the note.

We're going to take good care of your handsome little predator, just as long as you bring his daddy here. Otherwise, we'll see if this boy has some wings of his own.

Kisses,
Julie

Her heart sank as the stadium blurred into the background, the noise of the crowd overwhelming as she struggled to gather herself in a smothering cloud of terror.

The Monarchs had Drew. Thea was moving before she was even aware she was moving. Her flying feet carried her out of the stadium, away from the crowds and the cars and the cheery yellow-and-black banners. Her fingers fumbled over the phone as she texted Mirabelle what had happened. She wouldn't put her team in danger again, but she needed

Mirabelle to be her witness in case she never made it home. The car was in sight now. Thea racked her brain.

She couldn't call the police. The Austin police force was deeply infiltrated by the Black Coats. If she brought Adam to the house, they would kill him without hesitation; he was the one they wanted. Drew would lose his father, and Adam Porter's innocent blood would be on Thea's hands. She wouldn't do it. The Black Coats had played enough games with her. She had to be a step ahead of them. *Think. Think. Think.*

Thea slid into her car and spun out of the parking lot, onto the road heading to Mademoiselle Corday. She watched as her speedometer ticked upward. Seventy-five. Eight-five. Ninety. As she drove she ignored the trembling of her hands, unable to see anything but Drew's face, her mind stumbling over a messy plan. *Go to the house. Find Drew. Leave.* As simple as it sounded, Thea knew it was anything but; Mademoiselle Corday was a labyrinth of hallways and hidden rooms. Drew could be anywhere. She would have to search the entire house, which could take hours. Was he hurt, or simply waiting for Thea to come get him? She ground her teeth together, trying to come up with a plan.

The road diverged in front of her: one lane heading east to the grand, gated entrance of Mademoiselle Corday, and one heading west. That same road that ended at the tree, the one she had come down so long ago, with a black envelope in her hand and a heart desperate for something, anything, to take away the pain. The Black Coats had taken that, twisted it, and used it against her. Damn them. Anger flared through her, but its flames weren't enough to cover her much stronger fear.

TWENTY-EIGHT

The pavement became gravel, and after a few minutes Thea stopped her little Honda in front of that same enormous cypress. A plywood board sat across the ravine now, thank goodness. She closed her eyes for a moment. *I can do this. I have to.* When she opened them again, her gaze rested on the black bag on the passenger seat. At least one thing was going to work out in her favor today.

Thea left her lace dress inside the car, the familiar Black Coats uniform snug on her body, her favorite sneakers on her feet. *If I am going to run, it is not going to be in these stupid ballet slippers.* She took a deep breath and raised her head, with her eyes trained on that black iron weathervane, the skeletal butterfly turning slowly in the breeze.

Please be okay, Drew.

She tried to move as quietly as possible as she neared the house, her footsteps light and fast. Around the perimeter of

Mademoiselle Corday, thick brambles of rosebushes, creeping buttercup thickets, and kudzu draped over a wooden fencing cleverly hid a line of barbed wire. *That is the Black Coats,* Thea thought, *a gold Texas rose adorned with razor-sharp thorns.* She made her way to the side of the house, to a small hill where she could view the perimeter. Once she had some adequate cover, she raised her head ever so slightly, her hands curling in the dirt.

Shit. Around the perimeter of the house, every member of both Swallowtail and Emperor stood in a curved line surrounding Mademoiselle Corday. Some of the girls looked bored—as they were, no doubt—but some of them looked hungry and mean, particularly Valentina and her horde of Emperor nasties.

There was no way Thea was getting through them. She looked at the ground for a minute and then back toward the house. *Maybe I don't need to go through them.* Instead of fighting them, perhaps she could enlist them. Maybe, just maybe, she could lead them.

She took a deep breath and stood, losing the ground cover she had worked so hard to achieve. "Hey!"

A dozen heads jerked her direction, looks of shock upon their faces. "It's her!" one of the girls from Swallowtail yelled. "It's Thea!"

Valentina whipped out a switchblade as the whole of the Black Coats surged toward her. "They told us you would come back." She smiled cruelly. "Fancy a dance, traitor?"

Thea swallowed nervously but still stepped toward the house, and the girls. Her boldness took them by surprise. Some of them stopped moving, confused as to why she was coming *toward* them, but Team Emperor was still swiftly making their way across the lawn. Thea whipped her head around, looking for something that would give her a height advantage, and there it was: a picnic table flanked by antique planters. On the count of three Thea darted for it, leaping over the barbed wire and racing for the table. She was much faster than the rest of the girls, and the table put her halfway to the house. The old wood of the table gave a shudder as she landed on it and made quick work of kicking over the mason jar candles that sat in the center.

"Stop!" She held out her hands, her voice strong and confident. "Listen to me! The Black Coats aren't what you think they are!"

Some of the girls from Emperor paused, but Valentina was still moving toward Thea.

She cleared her throat. "I know why you're here. I know each of us has suffered a loss at the hands of bad men. I know that pain." Natalie's smiling face passed through her mind. "These wounds have scarred us forever." She looked behind her at Mademoiselle Corday, a black fortress disguised as a haven for the hurting. "But this place is not the solution. The Black Coats is a Band-Aid, a distraction from the real pain you feel. It doesn't heal; it just hides. Do you know what the real purpose of the Black Coats is?"

"Shut up!" screamed Valentina, moving swiftly toward Thea.

Thea ignored her, one finger pointing at the house. "The Black Coats are assassins." Team Swallowtail stopped moving. "They kill people. The Black Coats, what we do, is nothing more than a training and recruitment organization for the Monarchs. Do you think this house really serves just to entertain teenage girls? To help heal our hearts?" Thea closed her eyes for a moment, remembering the dark thrill of their first Balancings. "I know you don't want to hear it. I didn't, either."

The teams were closer now, almost at the table where she stood. Thea swallowed nervously. "We have done some good, all of us, but we are serving the Monarchs. Even now, you serve the Monarchs." *There was nothing to lose.* If it was the last thing she did, she would drag the Black Coats' dark secrets into the light. "They tried to kill my boyfriend's father. His name is Adam Porter, and he is a good man and a cop, but he was sniffing around the Black Coats. And so the Monarchs came for him. *I was there.* He had done nothing to hurt women, and yet the Monarchs attempted to murder him. Is this the kind of organization that you want to belong to?" Thea lowered her voice a little, her heart pounding hard, every hair on her body rising. "I wanted to believe the lie more than anyone." She raised her eyes to the house. "But this house will tear you apart if you dare question it. And one day, the Monarchs might come for you."

"I'm going to do them a favor then," snarled Valentina, lunging toward Thea with the knife slashing out in front of her. Thea spun around, and the cut narrowly missed her shins. Adrenaline mixed with anger flooded her senses and she delivered a hard kick to Valentina's jaw. The girl staggered backward.

The teams were pressing in on her now, gathering in a circle around the two of them. Team Swallowtail looked confused, distressed. Team Emperor hungrily cheered their leader on as she slashed at her legs, Thea only a second ahead of her. Valentina was ruthless—and skilled. Her knife nicked near Thea's ankle, drawing blood. Thea let out a cry as the blade cut into her. She spun around, her fist catching the side of Valentine's head. The girl stumbled, blinking to recover, the knife held in front of her. "I'm going to kill you for that."

The roar of an engine stopped them both cold. Everyone looked to the west side of the yard, where trees and bushes shook as something gigantic trampled past them. Something with a distinct purr. They all let out a scream as Mirabelle's silver Audi exploded into the yard. The car crashed through the iron gates that Thea had once stared at in wonder, and skidded through the garden, sending dirt and flowers up into the air. Its tires squealed as it shot around the portico on the side of the house before slamming to a violent stop. There was a second of silence before the engine roared angrily and shot forward toward the teams, who scurried out of the way.

Valentina was momentarily distracted, and Thea used it to her advantage; she dropped to the ground and swept a leg out at Valentina's feet, her sneaker colliding with the girl's ankle. Valentina fell with a screech, but as she fell she grabbed an object from the ground and raised her arm again. Thea didn't even have time to move before she saw the knife glinting in the air, seconds from leaving Valentina's hand, but before it could, someone grabbed her arm. Neon coral nails gripped hard, and Thea felt gratitude wash over her. She looked into Mirabelle's furious eyes as the girl squirmed. Valentina might be deadly, but Mirabelle was strong. Inside and out.

"There's only room for one queen bee here," she snapped. "And that spot is already taken."

Valentina snarled and looked at them both. "Some of us are okay with becoming Monarchs." There were gasps of surprise from the rest of her team, and she shrugged. "You think you are the only one who has had to compromise her conscience? These men deserve to die! This is part of the game—the only game that matters. And even if you don't want to kill, the Monarchs could get you at any time. You'll never be safe, your boyfriend and your parents will never be safe, you will—"

A fist flew across her face, and she slumped to the ground with a groan. Thea looked up to see Casey and

Louise standing in front of her. Casey glanced over at Team Emperor. "Don't worry, ladies, I didn't hit her that hard." Her eyes met Thea's, and she shrugged happily. "She was going on and on and I just didn't want to hear her whole damn tirade. Also, she tried to *stab you*."

Mirabelle stepped over Valentina's form and looked out at the remaining cluster of girls. "Thea's right. The Black Coats aren't what you think they are." She paused. "I thought I wanted revenge. I got my inheritance. And I looked in his eyes and I understood: causing him pain wouldn't fix my own." Mirabelle slowly peeled off her black coat. "I will always fight for justice for women. But not here. Not this way."

A quiet girl from Swallowtail pulled off her coat. "I knew it," she whispered to her teammate. "I knew something was weird."

Thea smiled and stepped forward. "Then fight with us. Fight with . . ."

The crack of a gunshot shattered the moment. Stalking out from the house with a gun raised in her hand, President McKinley was walking toward Team Banner, her black coat blowing around her.

"Grab Team Banner!" she screamed at the two other teams, but it was too late. Thea had sown the seeds of doubt, and they had taken root. Chaos erupted, with girls scattering in all different directions. Team Emperor flew at Team Banner. Some members of Swallowtail turned against Emperor to join with Banner. Two smart girls were running for the edges of the property, done with this whole thing. Everything was a blur, everyone fighting.

What have we done? thought Thea, but beneath that thought drummed a single word. *Drew. Drew. Drew.*

Louise spun near her, her rapidly moving fists taking down a member of Team Emperor. "Thea, go! Find him!"

"I can't leave you guys!" shouted Thea, grabbing a girl who reached for Casey and forcing her to the ground.

Mirabelle easily swatted away a girl from Swallowtail. "We'll find you! Go! We're fine!" Someone punched Mirabelle in the chest and she staggered backward.

Thea looked at the house and then back at her team. Casey met her eyes, blood pouring from her nose as she grabbed Thea's shoulder. "Find Drew, but look for Bea, too. I haven't gotten ahold of her for days. I'm pretty sure . . ." She looked at the house. "She's in there."

Thea didn't need to be told twice; before Casey even finished, Thea was sprinting for the house, darting back and forth between the ongoing fights. McKinley saw her and started sprinting after her, her gun out in front of her. "Thea, *stop!*"

But Thea couldn't; she wouldn't. She weaved through the girls, knowing—no, hoping—that McKinley wouldn't risk shooting anyone else. She ducked under punches as she flew toward the house, clearing the fray momentarily. Another gunshot cracked through the air, and the black wood balcony behind Thea exploded into splinters, a hail of black pebbles showering around her as her feet pounded the brick paving stones. Behind her she could hear the sounds of fighting, the sounds of girls crying and shouting. A glass lantern next to her shattered as McKinley's bullet traced over her head. The shots were a warning; McKinley wasn't trying to kill her, she was trying to stop her. At least, she hoped so. Thea covered her ears from the ringing as another lantern exploded, but her feet kept moving, almost to the top of the stairs now. Her hand closed around the iron door knocker, and her momentum pushed it forward. The heavy door swung open easily, much too easily. The door opened, and a boy's face stared down at her. Her body froze. "Sahil?"

"I am sorry, Thea." Then something hard hit her chest and she flew backward, arching in the air before she was tumbling down the stairs, feeling each step knock her body as she hit it. She rolled over twice, her legs and arms hitting the rough wood before she landed hard on the ground below. She blinked. *Get up.* With a painful groan, she crawled to her knees and then her feet, her body begging her for rest. Instead, she pushed herself up, one hand holding her bruised ribs. Sahil was making his way slowly down the steps to her, white linen fluttering in the wind. He was almost to her now, but what could she do?

She heard Natalie's voice in her head.

Run.

Thea shot away from the house, her quick movements catching Sahil off guard. "Thea!" he called, a strange disappointment in his voice. His voice dropped menacingly as she plunged into the woods on the side of the house. "I guess I will have to catch you then."

Branches slapped at her face as she flew through the dense oak trees, her feet pounding frantically. This wasn't the rhythmic running that she loved so well; this was running for her life, Terror, rather than a quest for speed, propelled her. She didn't want to win. *She wanted to live.* She could hear Sahil behind her, twice as fast with swift, determined steps.

Thea was thrashing around, bursting her way through overgrown clumps of kudzu, through bushes and gnarled branches that tangled over the ground, each one threatening to trip her. She veered right, hoping to throw him off, but she could hear him turn behind her, ever closer.

"Thea!" God, he wasn't even winded. The cut on her ankle courtesy of Valentina was bleeding more now, and each step sent a tiny sliver of pain up her shin. Her ribs ached from the fall down the stairs and something wasn't right there, but she kept moving. *Just run,* she thought.

"Thea! Why don't we just stop and talk?" called Sahil from too close behind her.

"You lied to me!" she screamed. *Everything hurts.* She was slowing. The woods flew past her in a blur of brown and mottled green. Thea tripped and stumbled, catching herself on the fall, bursting forward again. With a jagged breath, she reached inside of herself, hoping to find a well of strength, something that would push her forward; but instead she found something unexpected: herself. She had to be enough.

TWENTY-NINE

The tangled woods spanned out in front of her, more difficult to navigate than before. Sahil was behind her now and closing fast. She couldn't beat him. She couldn't lose him. This chase could end when she was winded and outrun, or she could end it here on her own terms. *You have to decide to act*, she heard Nixon say in her mind. *Don't let him hunt you down like some weak animal, because you're not. You have to be enough.* Her steps slowed as she burst out into a shady glen about a half mile from Mademoiselle Corday. How ironic that even now she also heard Sahil's voice in her mind. *Look around. What weapons do you have?* Her eyes darted side to side as her steps fell out of rhythm. Tree trunks, branches, and an overturned, rotted wood bench.

His footsteps were closer now. "Thea, I just want to talk to you. If you would just listen to me!"

Moving deliberately, she tripped over an overturned

root. Her knees hit the ground hard and her body rolled forward and slid, coming to rest covered in mud and rotted leaves. She grabbed at her stomach and gasped loudly, her hand curling around a thick branch and pulling it underneath her. Sahil was nearing her; she heard the snap of twigs underneath his feet, heard his easy breathing. A shadow crossed over her and chilled her entire body. "The fastest girl I've ever known has a very bad habit of not taking in her surroundings. Thea, you've caused a lot of trouble for us with your little boyfriend." He walked slowly around her.

Thea let out a cry, pretending that she couldn't breathe. Her hand clutched her stomach protectively. "You're a Monarch," she gasped.

"Yes. And I have to do this, Thea. I have to."

"Are you going to kill me?"

He tilted his head, confusion passing over his features. "Honestly, I do not know what to do with you. You climbed into bed with the son of the man attempting to bring down the Black Coats! What were you thinking?" He barked out a painful laugh. "As if Adam Porter could ever dream of destroying my mother's organization. I almost feel bad for the man, chasing this bear through the woods, not knowing the whole time that the bear owns the woods and everything else around him. And Drew—such an earnest boy—insists you did not tell him anything. He's begging us to take him instead of you, as if he were of any use to us."

Sahil shook his head. "You could have been so much more than this. I saw you, hiding inside that shell of yourself. I pushed you forward; Nixon pushed you forward. We knew that we were working with hardened clay— something that needed to be broken and reformed, a monster made of jagged pieces. And then, you were everything we hoped you would be: a leader, a Black Coat, a runner. You radiated potential."

Thea whimpered as he pushed her head down against the ground into the wet mud, his face distorted as something battled inside of him. "Thea, I am truly sorry about all this, but I am giving you something Julie will not: mercy." He crouched down next to her in a deceptively friendly position. "Listen to me. We can still back away from all this. You can still be a part of the Black Coats, of the Monarchs. Once we take care of Adam Porter we can all move forward *together*."

"How can you honestly believe that you're still doing good?" Thea sputtered, her body tightening. "Forcing girls like Bea to do what they don't want to do is the opposite of what your mother would have wanted. I know in your grief you're trying to save this thing she built, but, Sahil . . . it's rotten inside. You know it."

"Do not speak about my mother," he hissed, voice thick with pain. "You could not begin to understand what it is like to hold your mother as she dies in your arms, a withered husk of who she once was, a proud survivor of the unthinkable. She found me in an orphanage across the world and made me a fighter. A son. A warrior who stands up for the weak."

He was close now. Close enough. She was going to have one shot at this. "This isn't who you are, Sahil," she whispered. "And your mother is rolling in her very shallow grave."

She flipped over underneath him, her left arm swinging the branch with all her might. It met Sahil's temple with a hard crack that trembled up Thea's arm and into her teeth. He blinked once at her before his eyes rolled up into his head and he collapsed into a heap with his head slumped over Thea's rib cage. She groaned and wriggled out from underneath his dead weight, rolling his body over so that he was facedown on the forest floor. She leaned over and checked his pulse under the hot skin of his neck; he was breathing. For a moment she watched him as the hazy gray light of the wood filtered over his face. This was a boy who had lost his mother, a boy who was in fact lost to himself.

Oh, Sahil. She bent over him and left a light kiss on his cheek, not lingering for long. He was still a killer, after all. And she didn't want to be here when he woke up.

Thea ran back through the woods, using a different route that took her around the rear of the property. The Haunt came into view, its wavy glass winking in the sun as she sprinted past it. Thea kept her head low as she came to the lone wing that jutted awkwardly from the side of the main building. She ran to door thirteen, that funny door that opened up to the outside of the house. Her hand closed around the glass doorknob and pushed it open. She let out a whispered prayer of relief as she stepped into the house.

Mademoiselle Corday had been waiting silently for her. Thea paused in the hallway, her eyes tracing up and down past the endless doors and the tasteful vintage decor. When she stepped forward, she almost leaped back at her own reflection in a large mirror lined with mercury glass. "Slow down," she breathed.

Drew, where are you? She began pushing open door after door, moving as quickly as she could without making a sound. She passed an open window, white lace curtains flapping in the warm breeze. From outside she could hear a few raised voices, but she was unable to make out who was shouting. Hopefully, Team Banner was okay, though when she remembered McKinley and her gun, Thea's gut clenched uncomfortably at the possibilities. She had just pushed open Team Swallowtail's door when she heard a thump upstairs. It was the smallest of sounds, but it was enough. Thea stopped moving, her hand frozen in place over the doorknob. They were in the atrium, that same place where Nixon had once convinced Thea to join the Black Coats with nothing more than a picture of Natalie. Thea shook her head as she ran into the foyer. How easy it had been to say yes. Thea had made it halfway up the staircase when a dark shape rose above her, blocking her way. As the president stepped into the light, Thea groaned.

Kennedy was walking down toward Thea now, the black coat snug around her waist. "Hey, rookie! What are you doing here?" A smile crept over her wide features, her blue eyes hungrily focused on Thea's face. As she walked down the stairs, her knuckles tapped the bannister.

Thea stepped backward, almost stumbling on the staircase. "I've come for the two things that belong to me."

Kennedy snarled. "Bea belongs to Julie now. She'll be the best asset to the Monarchs we've ever had."

"Please," Thea snorted. "Bea is the least likely Monarch that has ever been."

"It's true." Kennedy shrugged. "She's not a natural, but look what she can do. She doesn't have to be perfect to be useful, and we can use her talent for *so many* things. That's the good thing about an organization full of women; we're multitaskers."

Thea braced herself as Kennedy got closer. "Don't forget murdering. You're good at that, too. Innocent people, even."

"You have to break a few eggs to make an omelet." Kennedy's eyes flashed. "It's not like we don't remember the innocent ones we've killed over the years. Their names are etched over the door, for God's sake."

Thea sucked in her breath. *Johnson. Hageman. Zinn. Cleary.* Not the names of brave Black Coats like they had been told, but innocent men whose lives had been taken by the Monarchs. Four men. She closed her eyes. She would not let Drew's name be added to the list. The president came to a stop in front of her.

"Let me pass, Kennedy."

The president smirked. "I don't think so, Thea. Once you . . ." She was talking again, but Thea was in action, trying to catch her off guard. She lunged for Kennedy's leg, but the president's position gave her the upper hand. Using the bannister to gain leverage, Kennedy leaped up and delivered a swift kick across Thea's temple. Light exploded in her vision, and she stumbled backward, the world spinning momentarily. Thea's hands instinctively shot out in front of her, and she caught the railing just in time to stop herself from tumbling down the stairs. Her whole face throbbed.

Kennedy was saying something above her, but she couldn't hear her; every noise had dimmed to a humming sound. *You're here for Drew. Snap out of it.* Thea lunged and grabbed the edge of Kennedy's coat, giving it a hard downward yank with both hands. They were level on the stairs now. Kennedy stretched her neck before flying toward her with a flurry of punches.

Here we go, thought Thea. She deftly blocked the punches with her hands, once and again and then continuously, faster than she would have thought possible. Fighting had once been a complicated equation full of steps and countermoves, but now it flowed through Thea like water. She didn't have to think about it, *she just did it*. She blocked a punch and then another. Kennedy's grin faltered, and Thea felt the momentum shift in her favor. She pushed forward aggressively.

After a minute, Kennedy leaped backward up the stairs, spitting blood and wheezing. "That bitch Nixon trained you well." Kennedy's right hand twisted out, grabbing on to Thea's forearm and twisting it violently to the side. Thea yelped and delivered a hard punch to Kennedy's ribs, slamming them both against the bannister. Then to her horror, Kennedy forced Thea's head backward, bending her body over the bannister—and over the steep drop to the first level of the house. Thea let out a cry and struggled to get her legs underneath her, kicking out until she made hard contact with Kennedy's shin. The older woman screamed, and in that second Thea let her body go limp, crumbling at Kennedy's feet while wrapping both arms around her legs. Kennedy landed brutal punches to the back of Thea's head. That's when Thea lifted. Kennedy began to tip backward over the bannister with a scream, her hands wrapped deep into Thea's hair to save herself. Thea felt hair rip from her scalp and let out a cry of pain, but she didn't let go. However, instead of letting Kennedy fall over the bannister, Thea pivoted quickly so that she fell backward down the stairs instead. She saw the president's mouth open in a silent scream as Thea pulled her hands away, releasing her into nothing.

Kennedy went rolling down the stairs, her body gaining speed as she hit each step, head over legs, turning violently as she went. These old stairs were steep. Thea tried to catch her breath as she watched Kennedy fall, closing her eyes when she hit the bottom of the stairs with a loud crack. Her body came to a rest on the hardwood floor of the foyer. Thea stepped forward, blood dripping down in front of her eye where one of Kennedy's punches had landed. After a second, Kennedy raised her head to look at Thea.

"You . . ." Her eyes fluttered as her skin turned pale. Thea could see from here that the president's leg was bent at an unnatural angle. "You could have been great."

Thea's lips curled. "I'd rather be good."

Kennedy let out a long breath. She was probably going to be okay, but Thea didn't have time to check. She was racing now up the stairs to the third floor. As Thea pushed open the door to the atrium she had a final, terrible thought: there was a high probability that she wasn't getting out of Mademoiselle Corday alive.

THIRTY

The atrium was exactly as she remembered it: the same black ribbons stretched across the circular walls. The same faces of women and girls stared back at her.

Except this time, instead of Natalie's picture clipped to an easel, her boyfriend was tied to a chair with his mouth gagged and hands bound. Behind him stood two women Thea didn't recognize, each holding a gun to his head. They were both wearing butterfly pins. *Monarchs.*

Blood was crusted across Drew's cheek, and his eyes were glossy, but he let out a whimper when he saw her. His mouth twisted in a way that made Thea's heart feel as though it had been squeezed. She stepped toward him, the tether between them pulling at her with nothing less than gravity. She met Drew's eyes. "I love you," she mouthed. He closed his eyes and nodded, his head drooping forward. *Whatever happened, she needed him to know.*

"That's enough, lovebirds." Julie Westing stepped out of an inky section of the room, a black pantsuit wrapped around her frame, a black choker made of lace butterflies wrapped several times around her neck. She was wearing black leather gloves. A shiver ran up Thea's spine.

Thea heard the cock of a gun and saw the barrel aimed at her, held firmly in one of the Monarchs' hands. The luminary grinned menacingly. "I am impressed by you, girl! I look forward to hearing later how you made your way up here." She shook her head, the light from outside giving her gray hair an unearthly glow.

Julie stepped past Thea, toward Drew, and wrapped her long fingers around the hand of one of the women holding a gun. Her gaze steady on Thea, she moved the muzzle up underneath Drew's chin, his face recoiling in fear. "I would hate to ruin this very pretty face." She mimicked a pout before moving the gun to his temple. "Or maybe I should shoot him here. That way we don't lose that jawline."

"Stop!" Thea hastily backed away with her hands up. "Please don't hurt him! Whatever you want from me, take it, just leave him. He didn't do anything."

"He didn't do anything?" Julie dropped the woman's hand and wheeled on Thea. "How often do we hear that refrain? *But he didn't do anything.* It wasn't his fault that he raped her—he was drunk! She was drunk! He beats his family, *but* he provides for them. He may have killed his girlfriend, but he was a gifted athlete! His wife just fell off

339

the cruise ship! Men, protected by their positions and their power, are getting away with murder and abuse and assault. So please, don't let me hear you say it that *he* didn't do anything!" Julie's eyes became cold slits. "This boy passed on crucial information on the Black Coats to his father. That means he did something. And *you* helped him do it."

Thea was listening, but her attention remained on the two women who held Drew captive. She had to be smart; if she didn't pay attention, things could go wrong so fast. Julie kept talking.

"You didn't have to see your friend, bloody and raped, dragging herself through your front door, begging you not to call her father. And the boy who raped her? Trevor? Not even so much as a slap on his wrist." A smile lit up her face. "That is, not until we took matters into our own hands. Robin and I, we had to stand up for ourselves. And I, I loved her, Thea. *I loved her.* That's what the Black Coats is about, Thea. It's about justice. That's what you don't understand."

"I understand perfectly," snapped Thea, her eyes never leaving Drew's terrified face. "I understand that what you think you're doing is noble, but you're wrong. Even if just one person is innocent, your system is broken." She turned to Julie. "How much worse to take an innocent life than to punish hundreds of the guilty?"

The luminary shrugged. "You're wrong. Besides, what is just one more man? Speaking of men—where is this boy's father?" Julie's face crinkled like paper as an ugly smile slithered its way across her lips.

It was like someone pulled away the curtain from over Thea's eyes. She saw instantly what she had innately felt all those times she had looked at Julie, felt that uncomfortable dread crawling through her in her presence. Julie was a psychopath. An elegant, well-spoken, charming Southern lady who also happened to be a psychopath. When Thea spoke again, her voice was unsteady as she lied. "Adam Porter is on his way here, alone. Let Drew go, and I'll stay in his place."

Julie's eyes narrowed to sharp points as she shook her head. "You're lying. I can tell. You didn't bring him. See, this is why I didn't like you, why I told Nixon you weren't right for the group. You're too headstrong."

"Well, you're crazy," Thea snipped in return, her patience worn thin.

"Maybe. But not as crazy as you're about to be." Julie raised her hand and Thea could see now that it clutched a black folder. Her stomach twisted. Julie was holding Natalie's file, and inside it were the missing papers. "Poor Thea Soloman, losing so many people! First her cousin, murdered by . . . oh, I guess you'll never know. And then her boyfriend, shot during a drug deal gone south! Who knew that this high school soccer star was actually a seasoned criminal with a dark past?"

"What do you want, Julie?"

The crone stepped up in front of Thea, who had to clench her fists to keep from punching away the satisfied look on her face. "It's not what I want. It's what is going to happen. Bea is going to make sure that not only does Drew not remember any of this but also that he forgets you forever. Once that's done, we are going to trade Drew's life for his father's. Adam Porter dies either way. It's your choice whether Drew goes with him."

She pointed the gun. Drew's eyes opened wide as he struggled against the ropes. "So you are going to help us." Julie shook her head sadly. "If you want his son to live, you're going to call Adam Porter and tell him to come alone. If you don't, I will have these ladies shoot Drew right here and you will spend your night wiping his brain fluid off the floor." Julie was behind her now, Thea swallowing a wave of nausea as she smelled a bittersweet rose perfume and a hint of bourbon. The luminary's voice dropped to a whisper. "Not only that, but your precious file will burn, and I swear to God, you will never, ever find out who wrapped his hands around Natalie's neck and squeezed. Because it's not who you think it is."

Thea felt the floor drop out from under her as Julie lightly trailed her hands across the base of her neck. The look of wild fear on Drew's face tore at her heart, and she closed her eyes. There was no choice. There was only his life, and that was all that mattered. "Fine."

"That's what I thought. Bea? Why don't we start with you?" Thea's eyes darted to the figure stepping softly out from the back of the room. In the rapidly setting sun, Bea looked so small, her black coat dwarfing her even more than it usually did. Her cheeks were drawn, her eyes were red-rimmed and exhausted. Her normally creamy skin was the color of spoiled milk. The Black Coats were chipping those Thea loved to pieces.

"Bea, oh my God."

Bea raised her head to meet Thea's eyes. "I'm so sorry," she whispered.

Julie smirked.

"What have you done to her?" Thea demanded.

"Recently, we maximized Bea's potential by taking her on a Code Midnight. She was extraordinary. It's amazing what you can get someone to do when you threaten her friends. Trust me: with Bea's talent, we will never have to worry about witnesses, ever again."

Thea's heart ached for what her dear friend had seen, what she had been made to do. She turned to Julie with hatred burning through her like fire. Bea was kneeling now in front of Drew with the two armed Black Coats hovering over them both.

"Are you here, Drew?" Bea whispered. Drew's head rolled forward, his eyes on Bea's face, and Thea knew exactly what he saw: *Safety. Comfort. Gentleness. A steel trap disguised as a soft cloud.*

"Mmmph," he mumbled through the gag.

"Do you trust me?"

Drew's eyes shot to Thea. One of the other Monarchs pushed her gun up underneath his chin, and Thea nodded.

"You can trust her, Drew. It's okay."

Drew reluctantly turned his face to Bea, who beamed up at him like he was the only person in the world. Her voice changed to that rumbling cadence, the voice she had once used to put Thea into a deep sleep in the car, much to the amusement of the rest of Team Banner.

Her teammate leaned forward and began rhythmically ticking her hands out in front of Drew like the pendulum of a clock. Her arms were wider than usual, her gentle sway rocking her back and forth. "You are safe," she said seductively. "You can trust me. I'm going to help you. I am safety, and sleep." He nodded, with his eyes trained only on her face, and Thea could see that she had him in her grasp. To Drew at this moment, there was only Bea and the sweet rest she was promising him.

"You will reach out your hand." Drew began slightly rocking back and forth in time with her movements. "Watch my hands. You are going to reach out and put your hand on mine." His eyes darted momentarily to Thea and then back to Bea. He blinked slowly.

All eyes were on Bea now, watching her take Drew under her current to a place where Bea had full control. Drew's head nodded automatically, almost as if he were a puppet on a string. The wicked look on Julie's face repulsed Thea as she watched, the older woman's eyes lighting up with the potential power she saw in Bea. With a soft hum, Bea opened her palm, and Drew reached out his hand. Bea looked back at Thea, a tear running down her cheek. "I'm so sorry," she whispered. "It will happen fast." Thea felt a physical pain rising in her chest, and she unconsciously clutched at her heart as she prepared to watch the boy she loved forget everything about her. Bea raised both of her palms to meet Drew's.

"Now, press your hand onto mine. Slowly." Drew leaned forward to follow her directions, but it wasn't his hands that Bea met; instead, Bea grinned as the two Monarchs holding Drew captive both reached out their hands for her. In a second, Bea pressed her palms up against theirs and stood, looking straight into their eyes without fear, her powerful voice booming through the atrium. "Press on my hand and close your eyes. Now!" The two Monarchs obeyed as Julie screamed "No!" in the background. Then Bea violently jerked her hands away. The shock, as she had once explained to Thea, was the moment when she hurtled someone into their unconscious. And she did. "*Sleep*, you bitches."

Their hands fell promptly away from Bea, and their bodies followed, collapsing at Drew's feet. In one moment, Bea had one of their guns and was aiming it toward where Thea and Julie were standing. She pulled the trigger.

A gunshot cracked through the air, then another. Behind her Julie let out a shriek as bullets shredded the ceiling and the wall above her. Pieces of photographs began to fall. Bea kept firing, tears streaming down her face as she emptied the chamber into Mademoiselle Corday with a crazed yell. Bullets pierced tiny black holes in the gold dome, in the oak arches, in the walls. Thea began crawling toward her friend on her elbows as Julie sprinted for the door, the black file still clutched in her hand.

Bea kept screaming, until Thea reached her. With one movement she wrapped her hand firmly around Bea's arm and then up to the gun. With a soft "Shhhh," Thea gently took the gun away from her, holding it tight as she curled herself around Bea. Then she pulled her broken friend into her arms. "I've got you," she whispered, and Bea collapsed against her with a sob.

One of the women stirred, and Bea turned to look at her. "You're falling, deeper and deeper," Bea commanded. "Deeper and deeper." The woman went silent, her chest rising and falling gently.

Thea touched Bea's cheek before she leaped up, her hands yearning to caress Drew's face. Everything fell away as she reached his chair. Thea let out an exhausted cry, frustrated by her hands not working fast enough, until she finally was able to pull him free. His arms went around her and she ripped the gag from his mouth. "Drew!"

"Thea." His voice was kind.

She fell against him, her mouth pressing against his bloodied lips. "I'm sorry; I'm so sorry!" she whispered into his mouth, needing him to know everything. She had come so close to losing him, and she wouldn't again. *Never again.*

"Thea . . ." She held her breath as a painful smile appeared on his face. He looked straight into her eyes. "You owe me some waffles."

A sob escaped her lips as her hands traced his face. He was still Drew. He was still hers.

Drew clutched Thea as if she would fly away. Her hands traced over the bruises on his face, the cut on his lip. "Did they hurt you?" she asked.

He shook his head. "Nothing that isn't easily fixed."

"Not to interrupt," Bea piped up from behind them. "But can we get a move on?"

Thea pointed to Drew. "Drew, Bea. Bea, Drew." With the edge of her toe, she softly poked one of the slumbering Monarchs.

"We don't have long," Bea said. "Maybe ten minutes before they wake up."

"Let's go, then." Thea pushed up to her feet.

"Where did that witch go?" Drew glanced up at the ceiling and closed his eyes, probably remembering something horrible.

"Probably the Breviary," said Bea. "That's where we were going to meet your dad. That's where I was going to help her kill him."

Thea turned. "The Breviary. What is that? I feel like I've heard someone mention it before." Then: the memory of her first day in Mademoiselle Corday, when she had heard the phrase as she walked down a hallway lined with antique furniture, her heart pounding with the possibility of revenge. *The water grows shallower each year. I'm just not sure it's a safe place anymore. They are building that gaudy new home not far from there, and it's a pebble's throw away from the Breviary . . .*

Bea looked at the floor for a moment. "The Breviary is a graveyard, Thea. It's where they bury . . ."

Drew finished her sentence. "The men who meet the Monarchs." He bent over and grabbed the gun on the floor, checking the chamber with ease. "It's empty," he sighed. "You made short work of this place, Bea." The dome overhead was letting in tiny pieces of the night sky, pinpricks of stars now visible through the gold.

Thea turned to Bea. "Where is it, the Breviary?"

"South of Mademoiselle Corday. You know that boggy place, where the land dips down?"

Yes, she knew it. Thea had seen it on one of her runs with Sahil—a nondescript murky pond surrounded by overhanging cypress and oak trees. Sahil had described it as a haven for snakes and mosquitoes, ensuring that she stayed away. *Sahil. Where is he?*

Bea continued. "The graveyard is just on the other side of the marsh."

Thea turned Bea to face her. "Drew and I are going to stop Julie. Find the rest of Team Banner and go to the police. Get as far away from the house as you can. Some of the Monarchs are still out there."

Bea's eyes filled with tears. "But I can't leave you."

"And I can't ask you to come. Bea, you've seen enough." Thea watched an internal battle raging in Bea's troubled eyes. "And you've done enough."

Bea surrendered, her shoulders slumping in defeat. "Okay."

She gave her friend a quick hug. "I'll see you on the other side of this."

"Thea!" Drew was growing restless. "We have to go. If we don't stop her, she'll find another way to lure my dad here, I know it."

The three ran out of the atrium and into the hallway, rapidly winding down the stairs. Bea left them behind and headed toward the exit as Thea stopped with Drew where she had last seen Kennedy. The only proof that she had been there was a small drop of blood on the ground. She heard the door slam as Bea left. Otherwise the house was eerily silent.

Drew reached around Thea's waist. "I know we're in a hurry, but I'm worried I will never get this chance again, and I can't . . ." Then he hungrily pressed his mouth against hers, and she could feel him pouring every regret into her, a kiss laced equally with sorrow and desire. His hands wrapped themselves around her and he lifted her off her feet, pulling her into him. When she looked up into the depths of his green eyes, she saw herself reflected for the very first time: Thea, a grieving girl and a Black Coat. In return she saw who he was as well: Drew Porter, a boyfriend and a son trying to do the right thing. "I love all of you," he whispered. "No more secrets."

"Never."

He held her tight. "I'm sorry I thought you needed saving. Apparently, that was me."

Thea pressed her nose against his, free in a way that she had never been. "I'll save you anytime, Drew Porter."

"Isn't this sweet?" Julie spoke out of the darkness above, completely unhinged. She was on the second level, leering over the balcony at them as they stared up at her. "You've found love while ruining the legacy of this house. You kiss that boy while standing on the bones of women who have gone and fought before you." She cackled. "You've almost done me a favor, Thea. This house has become disappointing to me. I've been looking for a sign, and here it is: one of Nixon's recruits standing in the house I built, kissing the son of a police officer who will take us down. Smiling as she destroys the Black Coats of Austin. You've disappointed me, but perhaps this is a much needed sign that it's time to move on."

Thea opened her mouth to scream as Julie raised a glass lantern over her head, but it was too late. With a cry she hurled it down toward them. They leaped backward, narrowly avoiding the plumes of fire and glass that exploded across the floor. Another lantern followed, and then another, the gas in the lanterns fueling the blaze. Thea watched as the stairs—and their only way out—were swallowed up in a hungry rush of scorching flame.

When they looked up again, Julie was gone, and in her place thick black smoke curled up the walls. Drew yanked her back, away from the flames blasting her cheeks. "Thea! Come on!" She wrapped her hand around Drew's, and then they were sprinting away, Thea's head whipping around in time to see Julie toss three more lanterns down, each one releasing a liquid pool of crackling gold that spread across the floor. "Go, go, go!" Drew shouted.

The old wood of Mademoiselle Corday caught fast, and in seconds the flames had jumped from the wall to the ceiling. The black wood started to smoke and crumble as the fire grew. Above them, the grand staircase was catching. *This house*, thought Thea, *is essentially tinder*. Another lantern exploded when the flame reached it, sending shards of burning glass outward. "Run!"

"Where?" screamed Drew. Everything was burning now. The searing heat pushed them back like a physical blast, black smoke billowing around Thea, in her lungs, in her eyes. Julie had expertly trapped them; they were in the hallway of the classrooms, which Thea knew were windowless for secrecy reasons. She covered her mouth and tried not to inhale the hell that encompassed them and felt like it was melting her lungs. Everything was ash and smoke and hot flame; it raced across the ceiling toward them. There was no escape, no windows except . . .

"Follow me!" Thea pulled Drew inside the wide wooden doors and into the library. Blistering flame had already begun crawling its way through the old books on the north wall, the violently whipping fire having made its way across the floor. Pulling Drew behind her, Thea sprinted up the small staircase as the heat started melting the mirrors in the sitting room, the glass becoming pools of mercury running down the walls. They were going up then, away from the fire.

"Thea! This door has a lock on it!"

"I know!" Thea bent forward, typing frantically on the keypad. *481542.* The keypad buzzed, and a red light appeared. Thea entered it again. *481542.* Red again. "They changed it. Oh God, of course they did."

Thea could feel hysteria building in her. *She was going to burn to death because she couldn't get the door open.* The fire began to crackle at the bottom of the staircase, the books on either side of them burning, their pages lifting into the sky. *There was so much smoke.*

"I'm sorry, Drew, I'm so sorry."

Drew dropped her hand and took a few steps back from the door. "Don't start that. Don't start the death speech. I am not going to die—" *Bam!* His muscular legs kicked against the door. "In this—" *Bam!* He backed up again. "FUCKING RIDICULOUS HOUSE!" he screamed finally as he ran at the door. *Bam!* At his impact, the door began to splinter on its frame. Drew took a step back and got a running start, this time his foot landing near the keypad. The door shuddered and flew open. "Sometimes, you just do things the old-fashioned way." He gasped as a flaming book page landed on his arm.

"Shut the door!" Thea yelled.

"It won't buy us much time!" Drew answered, but he obeyed. He whipped off his shirt and stuffed it into the crack under the door.

"Welcome to the records room," uttered Thea, the filing cabinets lined up from end to end. Drew slumped against the door when he saw the thick panes of glass and the cool night sky beyond them, their salvation so close and yet so far. Under their feet the ground was growing hot, insatiable flames engulfing the house crumbling beneath them. Thea threw the curtains aside. "You're not going to like this." There it was. *The bomb.*

Drew blinked as if he couldn't believe what he was seeing: red cords plugged into a blinking gray monitor, bound to the window latch. Lines of copper tubing, wires. "Can we go through them?" He motioned to the thick windows to the left of the bomb. "Break them?"

Thea shook her head. "The glass, it's that thick antique stuff, but we could try." Smoke burned her eyes.

Suddenly, there was a loud crack and the ground beneath their feet shifted, sending them both sprawling to the floor. The body of the filing cabinet began slowly sinking into the floor beneath it as tendrils of flame started licking their way up. The house gave another shudder as Thea crawled toward the window.

"The house is collapsing!" screamed Drew. "Thea!" He reached out for her with a look she knew she would never forget: the hard resignation that they would both be burned alive, that there was no escape for them.

Thea gritted her teeth. "No. We are not dying here today. I owe you a date."

Even here, in this hell, a small smile. "You owe me more than that."

Even as the ground beneath her feet was burning the rubber of her soles, Thea carefully unlocked the large window and stepped back. It was crazy, but it was their only chance. She looked at Drew. "Ready?"

He nodded. "Together."

There was no time. Thea backed up and laced her hand through his, and then they were running for the window. They threw their bodies straight into the panes. The window bounced open and the first thing she felt was cool, clean night air. The next thing she felt was Drew wrap his arms and legs around her as they fell, making a shell with his body to protect her. She hadn't even taken a breath when the bomb exploded with a sound louder than any sound she had ever heard; a sound that pushed her body out of itself.

BOOM!

The vibration shot through her bones, the blast of billowing heat sending them flying forward. As they dropped from the second level, a hellish inferno of fire and smoke and burning wood swirled around them. Disjointed images flashed in her mind as the house fell away from her: Drew's body behind her, the feel of his hand clutched to her chest. A fiery orange flame consuming the night. Plumes of black smoke twisting like demons. And finally a monarch weathervane, spinning as it burned. *This might be the end of everything,* Thea thought as she fell.

I'm coming, Natalie, she whispered into the smoke. *I'm coming.*

THIRTY-ONE

All Thea could hear when she came to was an incessant ringing in her left ear. Pieces of smoldering paper were floating down like snow, dusting her eyelashes, singeing her cheeks. Above her, a raging inferno of black wood and orange flame was billowing out of control. The light from the fire made everything around her as bright as day. She could hear voices in the distance, but something about her hearing was unbalanced.

Thea stretched her legs and gasped as she felt a still body underneath her. "Drew!" She turned over, finding Drew's soot-blackened face. He wasn't breathing. She had just pressed her mouth against his when he coughed violently. Thea sat back with a cry of relief.

"Lost my breath." He took a huge gasp of air, wincing when he exhaled. "Ahhh, God!" He grabbed his leg. "Something's wrong. Thea, I think my ankle might be broken, and . . ." He moaned, pressing against his side. "Possibly my ribs." Her fluttering hands felt their way down to his right ankle and yanked up his jeans cuff. Sure enough, the ankle was distorted. His breathing was unsteady. "Where is Julie?" he moaned. "She can't get to my dad."

Thea took his face in her hands. "I'll find her, I swear it. She'll pay for what she's done." *And she has Natalie's file,* Thea thought to herself.

Drew shook his head. "No. It's done. Walk away. Please."

She looked up with panic as she heard voices coming closer.

"Come on." She hooked her arms underneath Drew's and began pulling him away from the fire, her back screaming with the effort. Finally, she rested him against a trellis covered in yellow roses. They glimmered in the flames. She kissed his forehead once.

"Thea." His eyes were pleading with her, and she could tell he was rapidly losing consciousness, which worried her. "Just stay."

Thea rested her forehead against his. "I love you, but I have to go. I have to finish this." As she ran away from him he screamed her name. She darted past the shadows gathering on the side of the lawn and past the hungry bonfire that was once Mademoiselle Corday. Fire was consuming every inch of the house now; she saw wicker furniture burning on the patios and the Haunt melting in on itself.

Thea flew past it all, barely able to hear her footsteps above the howling wind and the crackle of burning wood.

She ran into the woods behind the house, following a dark gravel trail through overgrown bushes and thickets of green. The entire valley was lit up with a hazy gold from the flames. As she ran, her lungs pushed out the smoke that had taken residence there and her legs pumped faster than she knew possible. Each step took her farther away from the Black Coats, and she shed the house like a skin as she sprinted through the woods. Her feet crunched as she looked down. Ink-black gravel led away from the house. What had Robin said? *There is a long black road between the assault, revenge, and recovery, and unfortunately, you will walk it alone.*

The terrain dipped, and the ground became slick as Thea neared the marsh. It appeared up ahead of her, a large pond of green algae sitting ominously silent. Cattails poked up through the surface and high grasses protected the water from the jagged rocks around it. Beyond the marsh a small light bounced and moved. Something was moving in the shadows there where the trees swallowed the shore of the pond. The light swayed and she saw a cruel face emerge. *Julie.*

Thea paused for a moment and turned her head. Something stopped short right when she did. *Someone was following her.* When she turned back, Julie was gone, vanished into the trees. Thea crossed over the left side of the marsh, leaping over fallen branches and big gnarled roots, this section of the woods like something out of a distorted fairy tale. The night consumed her as she ducked under a lush canopy of kudzu and continued to follow the unmarked trail.

Ahead of her, a light peeked through a small opening as Thea stumbled out into the clearing and fell to her knees. When she looked up, she realized with horror that she had stumbled into a mass grave. Handfuls of bones littered the ground where the recent rains had flooded the area. With a shriek, she lifted her feet, trying to not step on them, but it was too late. Plain gray tombstones rose up from the ground, one after another. There were no names or crosses or flowers, just rocks draped with brown condensation and moss, no more than a foot apart. The bodies couldn't be buried here; there was no room. Thea's eyes rested on the deep marsh beside her. *Oh God.* The bodies were in the water. She took a step closer, only to leap backward: just above the surface, reflecting the flames behind her, were several pairs of watchful eyes. She shivered; there were alligators down there. She backed up from the edge of the water.

She heard a small creak, a breath. Ahead of her, a flashlight was tied to a branch and was swinging back and forth in the wind, the light flickering with the breeze. *Bait.* Thea turned slowly, hoping the light hadn't brought the monsters closer.

Julie stood in front of her, her eyes wide and wild, a gun in her hand pointed right at Thea's head. "Do you know what you're standing on?"

"Julie, listen to me. . . ."

"The rich soil of justice, made fruitful with the bones of evil men," she intoned.

"You're crazy," said Thea as she moved sideways, her eyes on the barrel of the gun.

Julie went on. "And now you can be a part of it, too! Your parents won't even get to bury you next to your cousin."

Thea winced at the words but stayed calm. "It's over, Julie. And if you shoot me now, you still won't win. It will just be a girl's life on your conscience."

Thea kept her eye on the gun, her mind going over every possibility. *Could she lunge and grab the gun? Could Julie hit a moving target?* From the way she held the gun, Thea thought so. She needed to end this. "You have something that belongs to me."

For a moment Julie looked confused, and then a grave smile crossed her face. She started laughing. "You want the file. You sad, desperate girl," she sneered. "Well, go ahead and take it." She reached and pulled a black file out from behind her. "Help yourself." The file slipped open and blank pages spilled onto the ground. Thea grabbed one, her fingers angrily crumpling the paper in her fist. Rage rose up inside of her.

Julie laughed. "If you must know the truth, there were only blank pages in that file when I got to it." She tapped her head. "But I know who it was. It's all in here, Thea, and if I stop breathing, you will never know who killed Natalie. And it's not who you think."

Thea stared at her for a long moment, blinking as uninvited memories flooded her mind.

Natalie, at five, running through the sprinklers. At ten, playing dolls. At thirteen, lying on Thea's floor while she talks on the phone to a boy, her feet tangling in the cord. At eighteen, dancing in a yellow dress at her graduation party, pride beaming from her face.

Logic and desire battled within her. Her hands ached to attack Julie, to force her into telling the truth, to get justice for Natalie so that the wounds inside her would close.

Except that they never would. The realization struck her heart first and then her head.

It is time to let her go.

Thea's eyes filled with tears. *It is time to let Natalie go.* In her desperation for justice she had put one more life in danger: her own. It wasn't only her heart at stake here; it was the hearts of Drew, her parents, her team. Thea stepped back. *My God—what the hell am I doing out here?* Was she ready to kill to get that file? No, she wasn't.

Julie was still talking when Thea looked up. "Did you hear what I said? Were you crying again just like that time I found you in the hallway? What's funny about that, is that the man who killed Natalie will go on to kill others, and more girls will be crying in hallways forevermore, and you're just going to walk away."

Thea jumped as the sound of footsteps crackled in the woods behind them.

Julie threw her head back and laughed. "They're coming for me now. I can hear them. I'm ready to go with them. My time as a luminary is up, one last gift from Robin. I have one more thing to take with me, though, the girl who brought down the Black Coats by falling in love."

Thea heard the click of the gun and threw herself sideways. The shot missed her, but Julie leaped at Thea with an inhuman growl. Thea spun and met her head-on, knocking the gun from her hand. It landed hard in the mud. Julie raked her fingers down Thea's cheeks and tried to get her hands around Thea's throat as Thea punched her in the stomach. Julie paused, and Thea thought maybe it was over, when something thin and sharp cut into the soft spot between her ribs. Thea let out a cry as she instinctively threw Julie off her and curled over to protect her wound. Her hands came away covered with her own warm blood. *She stabbed me. Oh my God, she stabbed me.*

Thea tried to stay on her feet, tried to lunge for the gun, but the pain was too much; she couldn't stand, and she watched as Julie stumbled back to her feet and picked up the gun from the dirt. With a mad look in her eyes, Julie pointed it toward Thea's heart. "*Soulevez-vous, femmes de la vengeance.*"

Thea heard the shot echo through the marsh. Her hand grasped at her chest, waiting to feel the life slowly dripping out of her.

But it didn't.

Instead, Julie toppled over with one hand clutching her left shoulder; the gun fell to the ground. Thea was so stunned she could barely hold herself upright, and the pain in her ribs was making it hard to see straight. Blood splattered her shoes, and all she could do was watch in horror as a dozen women in black coats emerged from the darkness. An older Asian woman appeared at the front, a rifle in her hands. "Monarchs," whispered Thea, her body tightening at the word.

The woman holding the rifle stepped forward and spoke. "We aren't here for you." Her jet-black hair was pulled severely from her angular face. "Are you Miss Soloman?"

"Yes." Thea tried to reach her hand out but couldn't seem to let go of the hole in her side. There was so much blood. At her feet Julie moaned, "I created the Black Coats. I gave you all life!"

The woman ignored her and turned to Thea, coldly professional. "Before she died, Robin brought the problems in the Austin branch to our attention." She gestured to the burning house behind them with a sigh. "We waited too long because of who Julie was, and because of what Mademoiselle Corday meant. Too late we realized that sometimes the creator has to die for her creation to fully live. From here on out we will take care of things." Her eyes fell on the smoldering plume of smoke that had once been Mademoiselle Corday. "It's time for us to evolve."

Thea was growing dizzy quickly, and her brain struggled to process what she was hearing. The Monarch continued. "Thank you, Thea, for helping us with that. You've been a great asset, and we owe you our loyalty."

Julie was being picked up by two other Black Coats now, her body twisting back and forth as she writhed in pain, her screams of madness smothered by the gag they put over her mouth. One of the women injected something into her neck, and her body went slack.

Another woman in a black coat stepped toward Thea. "This is the last you will ever see or hear of us. Feel free to tell the police everything that happened here at Mademoiselle Corday; in fact that is what we desire. On the other hand, you will not ever speak about what just happened here in the Breviary or mention the national organization. We were never here. Is that clear?"

Thea nodded. "I understand."

"I certainly hope so," came the reply.

The woman with the rifle put her hand on Thea's shoulder. "Thank you for your service to the Black Coats." She gestured, and the Monarchs spun in formation. Then, as mysteriously as they had appeared, the Monarchs vanished, taking a catatonic Julie with them, her wide and terrified eyes momentarily locked on Thea's as she was pulled into the dark woods behind the house.

Thea's stab wound was bleeding everywhere as she stumbled out of the marsh and down the trail. In the distance, a dozen police and fire sirens were wailing, their red and blue lights throwing flashes over the landscape. A helicopter pulsed overhead. She closed her eyes, stumbling once and then again.

I'm just going to lie down here, she thought. She was so tired, so very tired, and her body was shutting down, one breath at a time. Thea's knees hit the ground, her hands struggling to keep the blood inside her body. *I'm just going to close my eyes for a minute. . . .*

"Oh no you don't, you lazy girl." It was Mirabelle's voice that cut through the swirling black, Mirabelle Watts who bent over her, picked her up, and cradled her against her chest.

"You're not holding her right! You're not supposed to pick up someone injured. God, Mirabelle, haven't you ever read a book?" Thea heard Casey's voice now.

Louise's sweet, bruised face looked down at her, one eye swollen shut. "You're going to be okay, Thea. The ambulance is here and we're going with you."

Thea's mouth felt like it was full of cotton, but she still managed to croak, "Drew?"

"He's fine." Bea's cheery smile washed over her. "His dad is here and he brought a lot of police officers with him. McKinley and Kennedy were arrested." She grinned. "Louise took them out when they tried to run."

Speaking was so exhausting. "Sahil?" Thea whispered.

"He's gone, Thea. Vanished. Just like Nixon," Casey answered.

The voices of her team faded to a background hum. As she watched, the night sky bravely decided to show its face through the smoking husk of Mademoiselle Corday, and all was lit up, everything in the dark dragged into the light.

Thirty-Two

Five Months Later

After hospitals, physical therapy, lawyers and detectives, juvenile court hearings and post-traumatic stress counseling, they were allowed to go home. Then, after all the interviews, the press, the testimonies and sealed records, regular life was finally allowed to move on. But not until the shocked looks on her parents' faces had faded and after she had a long, awkward walk with Adam Porter, did Thea feel that life had actually resumed. That she could breathe. That she could live.

All this and someone was still chasing her.

Thea tried to make her legs move faster, to fly in the way they once did, but it wasn't working. The faster she moved, the more the ache under her ribs pulled at her. Her muscles pulsed with a sharp pain that she never could quite shake. Her pursuer was closer now, maybe only a foot behind her, and even though she stared straight ahead and pushed herself through the pain, she still wasn't fast enough. The runner flew past her on the right, and Thea watched her competitor's sneakers thud over the chalked lines at the finish, heard the crowds chanting another name. Thea let her body naturally slow down as she turned and jogged back toward the bleachers. Her side radiated heat; her handsome doctor had told her that the wound Julie left her with would never heal completely. It would be a pain she learned to live with. A pain she learned to run with.

Her coach blew the whistle, and Thea waved behind her, calling it a day. She would get there. Someday.

"Yeah, Thea! Second place! It's just like first, only it's not!"

Thea started laughing as she looked up at her own personal cheering section: Mirabelle Watts with her face streaked in yellow and black paint, her hair pulled up in a ridiculously high ponytail; Casey looking bored but still cheering, a single black ribbon in her hands waving slowly back and forth; Bea and Louise hugging each other with excitement and screaming for Thea. She grinned up at them, mouthing, "Calm down!"

Behind them sat her parents. The joy on her father's face was almost embarrassing, but it was not nearly as heart-wrenching as her mother's fresh tears. She nodded at her mother, who smiled and wiped her face with the back of her hand. They had been so shocked at what their darling daughter had been involved in. It would take years to earn back their trust, but lucky for her, their love didn't change. That was the nature of parents, she guessed. They would love even when they shouldn't.

Today was the first track meet of the year, her first without Natalie, and somehow Thea felt okay. In fact, Thea was better than okay on this warm October morning. The smell of the track, the feel of the sun on her skin, the jersey tank with the hornet on it—all of it was making her heart soar.

And that wasn't even taking into consideration the handsome college freshman waiting for her at the bottom of the bleachers.

"Hey, nice run!" Drew leaped up to hug her, and Thea alone noticed the way he slightly favored his right ankle. They leaned against each other, both a little broken, both a little wiser. He kissed her cheek and wrapped her up in his arms, smelling like sunscreen and his pickup truck. His olive eyes looked straight into hers. "I can't even tell you how proud I am of you right now."

"You, too. I saw you finish those hot dogs," Thea teased.

Drew flipped his sunglasses on. "It was a major accomplishment, to be sure. Hey, I wanted to see you run, but now I have to head to that art show for class. Are we on for our date tonight? Six?"

"I'll be waiting."

"I know you will." He playfully tugged on her curls, sending her heart violently tilting. "Oh, and I have something to tell you. I declared my major today."

Thea turned her head, a naughty smile drifting across her face. "Human anatomy?"

He raised his eyebrows at her suggestively behind his glasses. "We can talk more about that later, but I'll give you one more guess."

She squeezed his hand. "Criminal justice?"

"I knew I fell in love with a genius." He planted a long kiss on her sunburned lips. "Hey, it might be cold tonight, so make sure you bring a jacket or something. Maybe a red windbreaker? A yellow parka?" He smiled. "A black coat?"

Thea narrowed her eyes as she lightly punched his arm. "That's getting old."

"Never." He gave her a serious look over his glasses. "Hey, I love you. You looked so great out there. How did it feel?"

She thought for a moment before squeezing his arm. "It felt right. And I love you, too."

With that, she made her way carefully up the bleachers, where her team was still cheering her on. Mirabelle, Casey, Bea, and Louise wrapped themselves around her, their smothering love overwhelming. Even though she hadn't won the race, Thea knew that she had won a thousand others. Whatever the Black Coats had taken from her, she would never be able to repay the debt she owed them for introducing her to these strong women. The Black Coats of Austin may have been completely dissolved, but they had left a heart for justice beating in the chest of five girls who Thea knew would grow to do great, hard things. She was sure that, like herself, they each tried their best not to think of the Black Coat hanging in their closet, doing nothing more than gathering dust. Maybe someday they would pull them down and dust them off. But that was not for today. Today was for sunshine and medals.

Later that afternoon, after making sure the new owners weren't home, Thea wandered across the street and let herself through the back gate of Natalie's old house.

The backyard was so different. Her aunt and uncle had always let things grow a little wild, but these new people were gardeners, and Thea couldn't believe how much it had changed. Where there were once rocks and overgrown weeds, there was now a lush garden of huge white poppies, black-eyed Susans, and long purple heather that waved in the warm air. The garden was filled with butterflies. A fountain bubbled in the corner, and the yard was spotted with the shade of a dozen new saplings.

Thea caught her breath as she scanned the porch, seeing *their spot* from all the way across the yard. She walked toward the back of the yard to a small notch in the fence and knelt before it, the cool dirt kissing her knees. There, carved in the reddish wood in a sloppy middle-school scrawl, were their names:

NATALIE + THEA = FRIENDS FOREVER

Tears gathered in her eyes. She pressed her palm against her lips and then laid it against the words, closing her eyes for just a moment, burying a part of her heart that she would never get back. Then she smiled through her tears and reached into her dress pocket. She carefully tucked the second-place ribbon into the gap in the fence.

"Second place," she whispered. "You beat me again. But I'll catch up with you. Soon enough." Then Thea turned to watch a single monarch butterfly dance over the flowers, a beautiful killer inexplicably drawn to the sweetness within.

EPILOGUE

**Somewhere deep inside
Sam Houston National Forest, Texas**

At the exact moment that Thea crouched on the track to begin her race, Frank Betcher was sitting on his couch. He couldn't believe his luck that this woman had come home with him. He had never seen such a beautiful woman, and here she was, in his cabin. Incredible!

Just hours earlier, at the bar Bitter Sand, she had touched his hand ever so slightly when he had handed her a drink. It was nothing big, but it was enough to get Frank excited thinking about all the possibilities. He flirted, and she flirted back. Together they had tumbled out of the bar and stumbled their way to his car and, finally, up to his cabin. Normally, he wouldn't have taken anyone to that place given what he had hidden there, but when would he have a chance like this again? This gorgeous blond woman, wandering into his trap, ready and willing? It was like a miracle.

Back at the cabin, Frank Betcher grabbed a beer from the fridge, giving her time to change into whatever naughty thing she had in that purse of hers. That made it easy: less evidence to bury later. He flopped onto his plaid couch, an uncontrollable smile breaking across his face. *This is going to be fun.*

She leaned her head out the door, raising her eyebrows with a drunken laugh. "Are you ready?" Then she giggled and blushed, and Frank found himself gripping the drink tightly in his hand. *Oh yes. I'm ready.* Frank Betcher was always ready.

When the woman turned her head ever so slightly, he imagined his hands wrapped up in her long blond hair, his fingers running down her cheeks and then slowly tightening around her neck. Would she be a screamer or like so many others: a silent sufferer, trying to beg him with her eyes? Would she fight? Those were his favorites, the ones where he got to watch them realize that their lives were being slowly snuffed out, the ones who kicked and writhed. The fighters particularly excited him.

Frank took a long sip of his beer, repeating the dead girls' names to himself in order, like a badge of honor. *Hailey. Amy. Sophia. Jenn. Natalie.* And soon there would be six names.

He couldn't believe his good luck the past year. First that girl Natalie, running out of gas just a few miles from this cabin and finding the lights of his home in the dark. It had been so quick: before she had known what was happening he had been on her, his hands around her throat. From the time she had knocked on his door to his running his hands over her dead body had been less than ten minutes. Like pennies from heaven she had fallen right into his lap.

It had been so easy to put gas in her car and drive it far away from the cabin. Sheesh, Natalie had been almost too easy, and as if his karma was feeling generous, they had blamed the murder on that poor sap who lived about five miles from him. Now there was this woman at the bar, so eager to come home with him.

A lucky day for him, maybe. For her, not so much. He choked back a laugh and flexed his big hands.

The woman opened the door. "You ready for what's coming to you?"

"Oh yeah, baby, come on out."

She stepped out, and he sucked in his breath. "What the hell?" Instead of getting undressed, the woman had put on more clothes, covered up by a black coat buttoned to the collar. "What are you playing at, girl?"

She stepped forward, her eyes cold.

"Wait, stop . . ."

The woman wordlessly raised a gun with a silencer in her gloved hands, the muzzle pointed directly at his forehead. "For Natalie, and for the rest." There was a gunshot, and then there was nothing. Frank Betcher's head splattered on the wall behind him, the killer dead before his beer could even finish pouring out onto the cabin floor.

Very calmly, the woman picked up her purse and exited the cabin, but not before marking his basement door with a giant X of black spray paint, where she knew he hid the evidence of his murders. She proceeded to walk the three miles to her car through the mucky forest, dropping her blond wig into the river and covering her tracks as she went. Her car was parked in a shady grove, hidden from view.

Sahil looked up at her from the passenger seat, aviator glasses hiding his brown eyes. "Is it finished?" he asked. Nixon nodded and reapplied her lipstick.

Within minutes they were on the open highway, heading north. The papers stolen from Natalie's file fluttered and leaped in the warm air of the back seat. Sahil picked up a phone and dialed the Austin police line. "Yes, I have an anonymous tip to report on the Natalie Fisher murder. Yes, I'll hold."

The road stretched out before them, the heat simmering across the wide expanse of granite. After a half hour or so, Nixon opened her window. A black coat fluttered out and came to rest on the highway, nothing more than a spot of black on the already desolate landscape.

Acknowledgments

First of all, thank you to my readers. I have the best job in the world, thanks to you. I wouldn't be in this position and able to share this story without the help of some truly incredible people.

Thank you to my two editors for *The Black Coats*, Emilia Rhodes, who first saw the potential in Thea's journey, and Alice Jerman, who saw the project through to the very end. You are both so wise, and I'm so lucky that I got to work with each of you. You deserve special editor coats, with hidden pen pockets and clandestine laptops. You are the type of editors who writers hope to work with.

Thank you to everyone at HarperCollins for your enthusiasm and hard work, for seeing this story of revenge and justice for what it was and believing in it. Thank you to Jon Howard and Clare Vaughn for the copy editing; to Jenna Stempel-Lobell, who has now designed four perfect covers for my books; and to the epic team at Epic Reads, who do the hard work for me.

Thank you to: my agents, Jen Unter, who sold and championed *The Black Coats*, and to Ginger Clark, who now watches my back like a hawk. I'm grateful for you both.

Thank you to Kelley Pichel for her tenacious editing and honest advice.

A passionate embrace and confetti cannon should be aimed at the following individuals for their support and love: Cynthia McCulley, for taking on challenges like the fiercest among us; Tricia McCulley, for always modeling a strong woman and speaking loudly for those who have no voice; and Ron McCulley, whose architect's soul inspired Mademoiselle Corday. Thanks for showing me 19,000 pictures of old Victorians.

Thanks also to Denise McCulley, Butch and Lynette Oakes, Cassandra and Maddie Splittgerber, Nicole London, Kimberly Stein, Elizabeth Wagner, Brianna Shrum, Mason Torall, Angela Turner, Karen Groves, Sarah Glover, Emily Doehling, Erin Armknecht, Patty Jones, and Katie Blumhorst. I'm grateful for your honesty and friendship, for believing in book after book, imaginary conversation by imaginary conversation. Creativity flourishes under the care of those who love the creator. Thanks for loving me.

The presidents in this book were inspired by the girls I lovingly call my coven: Katie Hall, Amanda Sanders, and Erin Burt (Kennedy, Nixon, and McKinley, respectively).

Thanks for beta reading the first draft—your feedback helped sculpt this book into what it is. In addition, you three reminded me, at just the right time, of how beautiful and life-changing female friendships can be, something that is the core of this story. Also, let's try not to get separated in a swamp again, okay?

Thank you to all the librarians, teachers, bookstores, book bloggers, bookstagrammars, writers, and readers who have raised their voices to help foster literacy. You are more important than you know. Keep reading, keep dreaming, keep writing.

Thanks to the city of Austin, which, in two days, won me over and claimed the city for this story as its own. I can't wait to go back.

Thanks above all to Ryan and Maine, who remind me every day of how much I have been given. Thanks for all the hugs, picked garden flowers, and coffee runs. You give me something to fight for.

A Note from the Author

The Black Coats was the book that wrote itself. Born out of the still-burning ashes of a (failed) book, the story of a grieving teen and her quest to find peace through vengeance rose up like an angry demon, screaming for her story to be told.

It was both the easiest and the hardest book I have ever written.

The inspiration came from a handful of different places, each a thousand miles from each other.

A black peacoat lying abandoned on a road in Nebraska.

The unexpected loss of a young friend, whose death left our lives spinning.

My perpetual fascination with vigilante justice. (I would be Batman if I had the wealth and physical prowess. I am sadly lacking in both these areas.)

And finally, my growing anger at the mind-blowing

statistics of violence against women and the ever-present question in my mind: Why wasn't anyone talking about this?

I finished this book in the middle of 2016, long before the #Metoo movement had started, and long before we had a president who boasted of sexually assaulting women. Violence against women felt like a taboo topic, even though *so much* aggression was being hurled at women in their homes, in their workplaces, and out in the world. It was just all unspoken. Now, with my book in edits, I watched with amazement as the things I had written about became the national conversation. Women stepped out of the shadows and left us in awe. I write about heroines who conquer worlds and yet I have never seen such real-life bravery in the face of enormous consequences as these women exhibited.

I rejoice in the fact that these things are being discussed on a global scale, that women are finding more safe places to speak up. That as a group we can say, *Enough.* That we can say, *Me too, but not anymore.* We can say, *We're with you, you are not alone.* We are all saying *No more.*

There is still so much work to do.

I hope *The Black Coats* encourages you to lend your voice to the fight. While Thea learns in the book that vigilante justice is itself morally gray, there are ways to fight for women that don't involve shadowy organizations: Volunteer. Support charity organizations that help women and children who are victims of domestic abuse. And vote for those who would speak for them. Rise, women of vengeance.

Thank you for reading *The Black Coats*.

Colleen Oakes

RESOURCES

FOR SEXUAL ASSAULT: RAINN National Sexual Assault Helpline: 1-800-656-HOPE (4673)

FOR DOMESTIC VIOLENCE: The National Domestic Violence Hotline: 1-800-799-SAFE (7233).

FOR CHILD ABUSE: Childhelp National Abuse Hotline: 1-800-4-A-CHILD (224453)

ML   2/2019